THE SPIRAL GARDEN

THE SPIRAL GARDEN

a novel

Anne Hines

McArthur & Company
Toronto

First published in Canada in 2005 by
McArthur & Company
322 King St. West, Suite 402
Toronto, Ontario
M5V 1J2
www.mcarthur-co.com

Library and Archives Canada Cataloguing in Publication

Hines, Anne, 1958-
The spiral garden : a novel / Anne Hines.

ISBN 1-55278-488-6

I. Title.

PS8565.I63S64 2005   C813'.54   C2005-900607-2

Design + Composition: *Mad Dog Design Inc.*
Printed in Canada by *Friesens*

The publisher would like to acknowledge the financial support of the
Government of Canada through the Book Publishing Industry Development
Program, The Canada Council for the Arts, and the Ontario Arts Council
for our publishing activities. We also acknowledge the Government of
Ontario through the Ontario Media Development Corporation Ontario
Book Initiative.

10 9 8 7 6 5 4 3 2 1

For Liz,
Keltie,
and Judith.

Lights on the way.

Vision begins to happen in such a life
as if a woman quietly walked away
from the argument and jargon in a room
and sitting down in the kitchen, began turning in her lap
bits of yarn, calico and velvet scraps,
laying them out absently on the scrubbed boards
in the lamplight, with small rainbow-colored shells . . .
Such a composition has nothing to do with eternity,
the striving for greatness, brilliance—
only with the musing of a mind
one with her body, experienced fingers quietly pushing
dark against bright, silk against roughness,
pulling the tenets of a life together
with no mere will to mastery,
only care . . .

Adrienne Rich, "Transcendental Etude"

The author wishes to thank her editor,
Beth Follett. Always.

Also, Bernice Hines, for her generous assistance
with proofreading.

PROLOGUE

There is an old story about a holy man who sequestered himself in a remote mountain cave and spent his days and nights in solitude, praying, far away from the rest of humankind. Many years he spent there, living on a meagre diet of nuts and berries, praying day and night to God. At last, worn out by time, or the privation of the body, or simply by the burden of his solitude, the hermit realized that he was near death. As he sat staring into his fire on what he knew to be his last night alive, God spoke to the holy man, not in whispers as would often happen in prayer, or as the man foraged for sustenance or scoured the mountaintop for firewood, but in a clear, audible voice. God said that he was pleased; that the man had fulfilled God's wishes for him in this life, and, in return, God wished to give him a gift before he died. Whatever the man might ask for. The holy man immediately said, "Tell me the truth about this existence. Why we must struggle and be alone, even in a crowd or with those we love most. Tell me why we must weep and why we must die." So, God told him the answer.

Immediately, the holy man began to search for a way to record God's words. He charred a stick in the fire and began writing carefully on large flat stones, line after line pouring forth from his memory and soul, until the night had passed and the sun began to rise. At that moment, the holy man's energy was spent. He was about to die. He looked at the stones on which he had written the Truth of God, the greatest gift humankind could receive. Then, with his last waning ounce of strength, the hermit dragged the stones to the fire and pushed them in so that the heat of the coals erased the writing.

What the hermit realized was that the Truth, once written down, would be read by people with different experiences and expectations, who brought to the words their own desires, ambitions and fears. Every one of them would understand the truth differently. The result would be only dissension and pain.

Someone once told me that Truth is like mercury. It takes a different shape according to its vessel. If we try to hold onto it, it slips through our fingers. And yet who among us, if God offered us any gift, would not ask for that very thing?

I think, in the end, I would rather have courage than certainty.

Book One

ONE

November 30, 2003

It's fall again. Damp, bright leaves sticking to the kitchen window like suncatchers, though there's rarely sun these days. Enough water on the lawn between the house and the church to float an ark. I have thought about washing the floor, but when I do, someone always rings the bell and I have to climb over the counter, swing around the wall to the bottom stair and then hopscotch across the few islands of dry tile to get to the door. I know there's a way to wash the floor without cleaning myself into a corner, but I can never remember what it is. You start at the end, I think. Other than that, I am a very good floor cleaner. I take some pride in this since I had to teach myself to do it. None of this hands-off, stand-at-the-end-of-the-mop stuff for me, I can tell you. Down on my hands and knees. Sleeves rolled up, hands plunging lobster red into scalding liquid, sloshing oceans onto the ceramic tile and drawing water back into the cloth like the moon draws the tide. Someone else cleaned our floors when I was growing up. Someone else ironed our clothes, wiped our counters, scoured our toilets. When I married, my mother sent someone to clean my house. It was like living in a hotel. Now, I touch my life with my fingers. I make the bed, letting the soft white cotton sheets billow into the air like clouds, take out the garbage, sniffing the sour scent of life and decay. I lay my hands on the dust and dross of my own life. I sample my food as if it's exotic offerings, tasting carefully, chewing curiously, aware that each texture and flavour is as individual as a snowflake.

And to think I almost missed this.

Looking back over almost sixty years of living, I can honestly say that the only thing I am absolutely sure of is that life is a complete mystery. And that linear existence, of course, is a myth. A myth that we cannot seem to let go of no matter how often, in reality, we witness life not moving in a straight line at all. It twists and turns, spirals and bends, bringing us back to the beginning over and over, even to the end.

Nothing is straightforward. Not time, not memory, not love and certainly not the demands of our souls. I cannot count the times a man or a woman has come to me, tearful, bewildered, though they have a good job, supportive spouse, beautiful children, lamenting, "I cannot find peace." And I have to tell them that they're simply working with the wrong list.

What we find, we must lose. What we grasp, we must let go of. What we are so very sure we know leads us only, if we are brave and lucky (and on some days, I can't help but believe, slightly cursed), to a place of not knowing at all. One of our tent-city dwellers says that the French call this *l'inconnu constant*—the constant unknown. But if we are brave and lucky and perhaps not cursed at all, that *l'inconnu constant* is what makes life worth living. What makes it fun.

Well, not all fun. Not all. The Divorce was not fun. Thinking back on that time now, I still feel, "no, that was not a good time." No unexpected upside. No silver lining. I loved Kyle, love him still and what we made together. I would come back lightly to that love again and again in those days, in moments as I went about my tasks, picking up the kids, buying groceries, arranging a school bake sale, planning to have friends over for dinner. Kyle and I standing hand in hand, watching our children grow into themselves, our lives flowing together in a single river of contentment.

The Divorce (which I still see in capital letters, much like WWII or the Great Wall of China or anything else that changes the landscape of the world forever) was Kyle's idea. The whole thing was Kyle's idea. All of it. Possibly. Maybe not quite all. I think it was Kyle's. My Aunt Lydia, however, said to me at the time that a man does not leave a woman without her permission. My aunt can be, as they say, a cross to bear. I've thought of that a million times since then. Real truth is like flypaper. It sticks to you no matter how hard you try to shake it off. I would wonder at night, in those dark still hours when the last thing you should do is contemplate your existence yet it's the only thing you can do: "Did I give Kyle permission to go?" I'd be pulled up short while walking to the bank or driving to get the kids: Was it possible that somewhere, one day, in a moment I cannot imagine or recall, I acquiesced to Kyle leaving me? I will tell you one thing I know for certain. I sure as heck never acquiesced to his leaving me for his dental hygienist.

What I remember most about the Divorce was inching my way through my days. Snailing along. Afraid if I went at my usual speed I would run smack into something. A wall. Fear. Or maybe realizing that it was somehow all my fault. I did run into things anyway. Snail, snail and smack into despair. Snail, snail and smack into loneliness, or panic: Would I have to ask my mother for help to pay the gas bill? Was I too old at forty-three to attract again and I would be alone forever? Raging in my distress that life is twists and turns, spirals and sudden bends and not straightforward at all. I had been promised straightforward. I had been *promised*. I had been thoroughly and lovingly lied to, for all the best reasons. Perhaps this is the moment when we finally grow up. Realizing we've been lied to and then finding in time and to our immense surprise that we can bear it. And then later, for some of us, it eventually dawns on us that knowing the lies produces a kind of miraculous freedom. When nothing is certain, everything is possible.

At the beginning, though, the most I could see was that I must manage to bear it. For my children first, for Kelly and David. Then for those around me who thought they had to step in and love me with lies again. "He'll come back." "You're too good for him." "You'll love again, honey, you know you will." Even Aunt Lydia: "The important thing, Ruth, is that you have the children." Everyone lied except Kit. It's been said that the most faithful friend is one who will tell you the truth. They are certainly the most annoying. Kit had one of her rare, precious moments when she speaks with the wisdom of an angel and not about herself: "Change is a gift not a punishment, my beautiful Cassandra. If the universe is sending you a curve, you must be ready to embrace it." It was on the tip of my tongue to say that she'd embraced more than her share of curves in her time. I think all I did was tell her to stop calling me Cassandra. She did that because of all those years when I vowed I was blissful and complete in my wifely-duty sun-brushed life and she swore equally that she couldn't believe me.

Did I acquiesce to Kyle leaving me? About the same time, my friend Rina Lawrey's husband left her as well. He left her for an older woman. The woman was, well, maybe the age I am now. It's funny, if I think of her at all, I picture her as Mrs. Clark, my piano teacher, permanently about eighty-two, certainly having outlived any indecent sensuality. Rina Lawrey's husband, in his forties, left Rina for a woman twenty years older. And it was, well, wonderful, really. I mean, Rina was devastated, of course. Well, she was ticked off. She was concerned. I would definitely say that Rina was concerned. But somehow, in the midst of all that, even she knew that it was wonderful. Steve Lawrey had fallen in love. Love of the kind you imagine between people like D.H. Lawrence and his German teacher's wife, or Gertrude Stein and Alice B. Toklas, or Hemingway and well, just about every woman. Harold Pinter and Antonia Fraser, a successful woman writer with so many children you can't believe she had time to use the bathroom let alone turn out one-thousand-page, meticulously researched tomes on Mary Queen of Scots, yet she still somehow finds time to leave her husband for Harold Pinter. I could hardly manage to get the kids' school forms in on time. It was that kind of love that Steve Lawrey found. Love that knows nothing of time or security or needing to behave well. Love beyond choice or reason. Love that scoffs at convention and recognizes only itself. Steve Lawrey fell in love with a woman twenty years older than himself. Rina Lawrey had been chosen once by a man capable of that kind of feeling. We all knew it was wonderful. Kyle left me for his dental hygienist who was most certainly not older than me. At the time, there didn't seem to be anything wonderful about it at all.

December 1, 2003

I have three degrees. When I was a child, my father sent me off to school each day with these words: "Knowledge is power. Go out and do good." I don't know if I believe that knowledge is power. I do know that it's expensive and time-consuming. Which is fine, because I've had both money and time at my disposal for most of my life. I have sucked in and spit out a lot of information over the years. I am the proud possessor of many, many facts. Most of them were stored in boxes in my Aunt Lydia's basement after my move from Dawlish Cresent. Aunt Lydia will never die, so they're safe there.

Frankly, every woman my age who had both time and money should have at least three degrees. Many of us do. No longer the Ladies Who Lunch, we are now student-union-card-carrying members of the Ladies Who Learn, most of us in carefully casual sweaters and smart pants, the more suburban in colourful sweatshirts festooned with flowers, or birds, saccharine as greeting cards. Self-conscious, briefcased, fretting about mid-terms in the student lounge, dashing between class and tutorials with looks of wide-eyed concern. Picking our way through the computerized card catalogue in the shadowy, echo-filled library, panelled with time, aged in anticipation of life beyond those walls. I have great respect for people my age in university classes. Those mouldering halls of learning are ironically very much the domain of the young. There were students in my classes who weren't born when I got my first degree. My friend Father Mark Duggan, who I met in my first year as a Master of Divinity, joked that when he came back to school he realized there would be people in his classes younger than him, he just never expected it would be the teachers. In spite of this, Mark bonded with our professor right from his first written reflection paper titled "Exegesis of Paul's theology of the Lord's Parousia." I couldn't even find "parousia" in the dictionary. Never underestimate the advantage of an antiquated religious education.

I have a general BA from my years before marriage, a BFA in art history from when the children were small and I found Kindergym insufficient to meet all of my intellectual needs, and a Master of Divinity from the years when Kelly and David preferred to stay at school over the lunch hour to play soccer or practise with the choir. People find three degrees impressive in a woman of my age and class who dresses well. Mostly, though, it is just putting in time. At its best, it is searching for something that can't usually even be named. Something that doesn't seem to exist in Kindergym, or tennis clubs or shopping, even in raising children or having a man to care for. Something that makes many women of my kind, in a moment of reassessment say, "I think I'll go back to school." Determined that the answers can be found outside ourselves.

By venerable stone casement windows in little library enclaves, I plodded through long afternoons of study, struggling to maintain a barricade of decency against the erotic assault of Georgia O'Keeffe, or applying Christian patience and reverence to the pompous whining of Augustine. Now and then I would glance out the window and be drawn away from a consideration of "stamen and the masculine," or a treatise on Just War, by the crimson leaves staining the stone walk outside, sun triumphing on new snow, or spring rain christening the ancient temples of learning that neighboured my own. In those moments I would sense that there did exist something that does not come from books or tennis clubs or even raising children, but which is more real and more vital. That the sun-drenched moments of belonging I'd felt in my days as a wife and young mother might have nothing to do with the house, or Kyle, or Kelly and David coming home from school soon.

The way I think about that time now is that it was like living in one of those elaborate, winding shrubbery mazes they show in books of English gardens. You follow the designated pathways, laid out in a precise pattern, all looking the same. Most of the time, you see only the leaf walls, the prescribed route before you. Until one day, maybe in "Critical Theory and Hermeneutics," when someone reads from Dylan Thomas to demonstrate the power of words, or maybe it's in Old Testament class where a professor as aged as his subject shares the roots of a Psalm, more ancient than scripture, more pagan and earth-worshipping than Eve, with a passion never shown to his wife, never while watching the Sunday afternoon football game, and it's as if you've come upon an opening in the leaf wall and caught a glimpse of a world beyond. Morning shadows tilt across a fall of trees. Bright light sparkles on a far-off lake. A place you never dreamed existed and yet instantly you know you belong. Then the shrub walls rise up again. The path before you narrows. You wonder if there ever had been an opening. Sometime later, maybe a long time later, a bird flies over your leaf confine, or butterflies sail by on breezes that have come from beyond. And then you have a choice. You have *the* choice. Seeing or not seeing. Remaining on that green pathway that leads to familiarity and the tender lie of security, or searching with diligence, with your soul's every breath, for what's beyond the wall. It's the same in school, or life. I don't know what makes some of us choose to insist on what we've seen; to look and long for another glimpse into that wide, unknown space, above all else. I know that is what I chose. On one of those endless library afternoons, in one of the rare moments of insight in class, or maybe long before that, in a sun-drenched moment that was not about my connection with Kyle or my children, in a moment I can no longer recall, I sensed the beyond, I saw that place I did not know but already belonged to, and I committed my soul to search for something that does not come from books, or relationships, or any of the things I had come to depend on for what I wanted. In the end, Aunt Lydia was wrong to suggest that I had given Kyle permission to leave me. I think the fact of the matter is, I had left him long before.

The Divorce came at the end of my second year as a Master of Divinity. I missed classes. Failed "Advances in the Status of the Feminine in Postmodern Thought." Failed it. From an A average. I had to go back the next year to take it over. Fortunately, nothing in the status of the feminine had, as far as the school was concerned, changed. I breezed through and got distinction.

Mrs. Kyle Broggan
110 Dawlish Crescent
Toronto, ON, M5L 3N2

March 4, 1985

Admissions Committee
Emmanuel College
University of Toronto
75 Queen's Park Crescent East
Toronto, ON, M5S 1K7

Dear Sirs and Madams,

First, I would like to introduce myself. My name is Ruth Broggan. I am a homemaker living here in Toronto. I have two children, Kelly (age thirteen) and David (age ten) and have been happily married for twenty-four years.

As part of the entrance requirements for the Master of Divinity program, you have asked for a few words about why I wish to enrol at Emmanuel College. This is an excellent question, which I am sure you realize, or you wouldn't be asking it of prospective students. I have to say, up front, that I haven't had to write anything more insightful than a grocery list for about ten years. I have written about Georgia O'Keeffe, but there's really nothing in that even vaguely suitable for application of this kind. I did go to the library and look at *Emily Post's Guide to Correct Correspondence*, but honestly, unless you wish me to write a letter of personal recommendation for a valued servant, or a thank you for throwing me a trousseau tea, it wasn't a lot of help. No section at all for "getting a middle-aged woman with no applicable experience into theological seminary." This is too bad because I would like to have known the right way to go about this. I have spent a lot of time thinking about why it is exactly that I do want to study theology, so I will just try to say it in a way that makes sense.

The reason I wish to enter Emmanuel College to study theology is so I don't have to get plastic surgery.

You see, a woman reaches a point in her life when she has to think about who she is. Not because she wants to. We don't want to. No one ever wants to. What we want to do is to stay twenty-eight forever, because being twenty-eight seems a good enough reason for existing, all on its own. I've been twenty-eight and since then had many years to reflect on not being twenty-eight and can tell you that this is absolutely the case.

I think the way life works is that when you are young, meaning comes very easily. More easily. Or maybe you just have less time to think about it. There is "couplehood" to secure, children to have and raise, sometimes a career to pursue. Houses and cars and lifestyles to buy and then buy better ones. And the world supports you in that. You are youthful, you are building, you are productive and . . . you are youthful. That in itself can be enough to make you feel of value.

You can't look at a magazine, or a television show, or a billboard without being assured of how important youth is, particularly to women. When I hear someone comment that an older movie actress looks wonderful for her age, I know what they are saying is that she doesn't look her age at all. For myself, I remember the years when I would look in the mirror and sigh thankfully, "I'm twenty-five, I will be lovely for ten more years at least," or "I'm thirty-five, I will be lovely for five or six more years." But then it becomes more difficult. I am forty-one and a certain kind of loveliness is past. I dress well, of course. But I am not youthful. My skin does not glow as it did. My eyes rarely sparkle, I think. It would be silly if they did. It has become harder, I must tell you, to know what of me to value now.

Perhaps this is all tied to some primal instinct of reproduction. Women attract in their youth for their ability to bear. Men attract at any age for their ability to provide. Perhaps that's why middle-aged men, finding that their house and car and wife and children do not fulfill them entirely, simply assume they have the wrong house and car and wife and children and set out to do it all over again. I have seen this among my friends, and the irony to me is that women reach our most wise, our most potent and glorious, our most able to bring something rich to the world, or to companionship, just at the point when we are most disregarded. Discarded by our mates. Abandoned and invisible in popular culture. Given the worst tables in restaurants. Understandably, it makes many of us bitter and disappointed. It also makes some of us get facelifts. I can't do that. I don't want to. Some days I think I want to. I have a very bad reaction to anesthetic. But more than that, I don't want to just play the same tape again, pursue the same set of things that were supposed to complete me as a human being and didn't the first time. I want to define my worth by something that does not fall away. Because, thankfully, I am wiser than I was at twenty-eight.

An elderly woman once commented to me that the more her eyelids drooped, the better she could see. What I see now is that I am going to need something in my life beyond being my children's mother, my husband's companion, something in my relationship to myself rather than to other people that gives me a new way to define and value the rest of my life. Maybe I won't find this in a Master of Divinity program, but surely it makes sense that enrolment in theological school involve a leap of faith.

Please let me into Emmanuel College. Or I will be forced to get a tummy tuck.

Yours truly,
Ruth Broggan

December 5, 2003

The evening after Kyle left, I took Kelly and David skating at the outdoor rink at the community centre. The air was still and so cold our toes and noses ached. The emptiness of the arena, and the spotlights flooding the rink from high overhead, made us feel as if we were all alone on a tiny, frozen island of light. The kids knew something was up because we never went skating. They had both taken lessons, of course. Everyone's kids took lessons. But no one ever just went skating. I've read about women in another age being considered "accomplished" if they could speak French, or play the piano, or net little screens of some sort. I never quite understood what the screen netting was all about. I'm convinced though that it was at least as worthy an "accomplishment" as any essay on Systematic Theology, which I had contributed to the world. In my day, women were accomplished if their children learned to speak French, or play the piano, or make papier mâché Haida masks. I'm not sure what this says about life in my time, or in the time of the net-ters-of-little-screens, either. Perhaps women today are no longer allowed even the selfishness of acquiring marginally useful skills for themselves, they have to make sure their children acquire them. It's not enough to be judged for who we are, we must be judged for who our children are; something over which I am convinced we have really only the slightest influence. I have a feeling I would fail "Advances in the Status of the Feminine in Postmodern Thought" if I took it again now. I remember one poor woman, the mother of one of Kelly's grade school class-mates, who was at her wits' end because her child refused to go to art class, or join the Mini Monks yoga group at the commu-nity centre. All he wanted was to go to the park after school and play. We all sympathized: How on earth was his mother sup-posed to provide him with a quality childhood? Now, I can see the wisdom. No more skating lessons without the freedom to skate on a wild, snow-streaked lake where blades glide over rip-ples of ice frozen in a winter gale, and pines in the distance waltz with wind in their branches. Not just around the pre-scribed, contained pathways of an artificial ice rink.

Kelly, David and I never skated together. Certainly not since the kids were toddlers and not on a frigid February evening, cold enough to keep everyone else indoors. David swung around the oval rink like an animal released from its pen. Kelly practised prim foot lifts and spins remembered from her ice dance tests, calling to me to intervene as David hurtled by, too close and laughing. I hadn't skated in years. My blades were rusty, sticking to the ice and threatening to topple me. Kelly and David finally left off their solo performances and came to thrust their hands under my arms for warmth or to keep me upright.

"Mom, why are we skating?"

"Because . . . I have something to tell you. Your father . . . your father is not going to be living with us anymore."

Why did I think skating was a sensible activity to be doing as I told my children that their world was changing forever? We should have been doing something safer. Certainly something warmer. Definitely something where I wasn't in danger of falling over and cracking my head open at any moment. Kelly and David froze beside me and I wobbled on my ice shoes.

"What do you mean, Dad's not living with us anymore?"

"Your father . . . your father has met someone else. A woman. Who he wants to be with. And he loves you, too. He loves both of you more than anything. But he wants to be with her now. He's fallen in love. Like sometimes happens when you're an adult. Even a married adult. It's not planned, it just . . . happens."

Greater love hath no parent, that she will lay down her own anger and disappointment for her children's sake. I tried to move my feet forward as if skating and breathing and Kyle leaving were all things that were possible. Kelly pulled at my arm. "I don't believe you!" Of course she didn't. I had not believed it either for the first twenty-four hours.

"Why didn't he tell us himself?"

"I don't know. Your father loves you. I think he couldn't bear to see how much this might hurt you."

"How is that love?"

Looking back, those are the things that stand out. Life not

growing in a straight line, and being the one to share the hurt of change with my children on that cold, barren patch of ice, and the fact that I left Kyle first. It was not until a long time afterwards that I put it all together.

TWO

September 9, 2002
Memo to: Margaret Ketchie
Re: Greetings and thoughts on the recycling of Sunday morning Orders of Service.

Dear Margaret,

It was a pleasure to meet you on Sunday morning and to know that I have such a willing and capable volunteer to assist me as I get to know my new church.

Just to let you know that your idea for reusing the Orders of Service is an excellent one, but I think we should continue with the current practice of depositing used bulletins into the recycling box, not place them back in the pews to be used again the following Sunday. While you may be correct that there is no need to print new bulletins each week simply to indicate the sermon title because, "Anyone can just listen, if they're interested," I think it is still worth a small compromise of our conservationist ideals to allow congregants the convenience of knowing what the hymns are.

Many thanks for your suggestion. And thank you again for welcoming me to Glenview.

Rev. Ruth Broggan

Father Mark Duggan
c/o St. Anthony House
Vatican City
Rome, Italy

September 10, 2002

Dear Mark,

Thank you for your letter! It's exciting to get something in an envelope with the Vatican seal on it, even if it did scare our church secretary half to death. I had to remind her that, being a Protestant church, there's not really much the Pope can do to us. Naturally, when I saw it, I assumed His Grace was finally writing to get my personal thoughts on Vatican II. I was not at all disappointed to find a letter from you, which is very welcome, possibly more so in fact, since I'm certain anything intelligent I might have to say about Vatican II would degenerate pretty quickly into out and out raving. That's the problem with theology. It's all about the heart really, but if you start to get emotional you're considered irrational. Explain that to me sometime, OK?

But I thought you were to have no contact with the secular world for the time being? Does my status as "Reverend" make it acceptable to write to me? Or have they been unable to quash that rebellious streak I love, and you've "snuck out under cover of night," or however they put it in those old Nancy Drew novels, to mail this? In any case, I'm thrilled to hear from you!

I do think you're taking this recall very well. Honestly, Mark, I feel like I'm talking about faulty tires or tainted potato salad when I say "recall." You are not faulty or tainted. You have a mind of your own and you haven't been afraid to use it. Is that faulty or tainted for a priest? Being clergy is like belonging to a political party. You suck up your own opinions and vote the party line or you "cross the floor." Anytime you feel compelled to "cross the floor" (first you would have to cross the ocean!) and join the Unified Church of Canada, there is a warm welcome waiting for you here, my friend. Of course then you'll have to preach our party line instead but ours is often so vague it leaves a great deal of room for personal interpretation, as you've had the pleasure of pointing out to me over more coffees than I can remember. What is it you say that always annoys me because it's perfectly true . . . "those who wish to ensure that their words offend no one, will usually end up saying nothing at all." It's one thing I will say for your faith group: They are rarely vague. Arrogant and narrow-minded at times, but rarely vague. Believe me, there are days when even I find that appealing. But why on earth do they think God gave priests brains if He didn't want you to use them? I don't understand it, Mark. Those nuns we met in our "Introduction to Existentialism" class were bright, forward thinking, ready to take on the world, the Pope, or God if they felt justice was not being done and none of them were hauled back to Rome for debriefing. Do you think if you promised not to wear that shirt that says "I think therefore I'm dangerous" to meetings anymore, they'd let you come home?

In answer to your question, yes I will have time to keep in touch while you're there, in spite of the fact that

I've only been at Glenview Unified for a week. It's 11 a.m. and there's been one lone person through my office door all morning. That was our church janitor who wanted to lay out in detail why, even if the building is on fire or I have reason to believe that the second coming of Christ is occurring in the church basement, I must never, ever accidentally leave my car in the wrong parking space in the church lot, lest the aerobics people who pay to rent the gym each morning not be able to get into the front spaces and have to walk an extra twenty feet to the church door. Now, our janitor isn't dealing with some jittery, fresh-from-the-seminary, neophyte, first-charge minister here. I know as well as he does that the lines of authority between a minister and the church janitor need to be clarified from the get-go. My plan is to leave the car at home and walk across the lawn to the church so I don't get it wrong.

Other than the traditional power struggle with the support staff, I have to say that if I had been looking for a parish different from my one in Markham, this is it. The phone doesn't ring here. People don't line up outside my door to consult me about the food-bank drive, or the Sunday School curriculum, or six weddings booked for the same Saturday time slot. I met one quite elderly congregant this morning who positively growled, "You're the new minister? Don't be expecting to be burying me any time soon." Not really a great opening for an exchange of pleasantries let alone spiritual connection. Our church secretary, Valerie, informed me that there are no shut-ins asking to be visited at the moment. She seemed delighted to share the fact that two or three had called specifically to ask not to be visited. Some of the older generation still harbour doubts about women ministers. We have many, many of the older generation here. There are no calls to return from people wanting a child baptized or a funeral conducted. Valerie says, "People don't usually bother us with that kind of thing." I suppose they like the bigger churches with impressive ministers.

I have to admit, Mark, being let go from Markham has shaken me even more than I'd realized. I've even had thoughts that I've been sent to Glenview as some kind of punishment. For what, I don't know. For speaking the truth? Well, it is uncharitable to think of any congregation as a punishment. I'm sure the problem is simply that I don't have enough to do with my time here yet.

You know, I remember reading in one of those books about Buddhism that I got when Kelly said she was leaving for Halifax to live at the centre, that life is a constant round of falling apart and rebuilding. I think that's quite wise, in fact. And it's not only in our personal lives. I think the church in general could learn from that. We're so horrified when we're not in a building phase, or when splinter groups appear after a particularly difficult disagreement, but maybe that's a necessary part of the cycle somehow, building up and falling away, building up and falling away. Perhaps each time a new structure on an existing foundation. The falling away simply being a return to who you are. Or who you are now. I think that you and I are at one of those stages in our lives, Mark. I'm just not entirely sure which! I guess you're rebuilding your commitment to the church and its doctrines, though not the scary ones I hope.

I am rebuilding . . . I'm not really sure what. Not my confidence so far, that seems certain. And surely after seven years of ministry I'm not expected to somehow go back to the beginning. But if this is not a beginning, does that mean that there is still more to fall apart? All I can say is that if this is what rebuilding a life or a ministry or myself is like, it feels as if there's been a labour strike. Anyway, who said Buddhists have all the answers? They just look smug enough for that to be the case. Much like the Catholics. Oh Mark, I should not criticize anyone else's faith path. It's not as if mine is serving me very well at the moment, whereas I have to say that Kelly always sounds entirely healthy and happy, and you sound, well, a little more chipper than before you went to be retreaded.

Must go now and . . . frankly, I have no idea what I need to do. Nothing I guess. I am finding out a very strange thing: Having time on your hands to sit and contemplate life is far less appealing than you'd think. Having spent the last seven years in Markham tearing around between meetings and ministry groups, never a spare moment to think about anything, you'd think I'd be savouring just leaning back in my reasonably comfy office chair, staring out at the leaves dribbling down, pondering the universe and our place in it. Instead, I would give anything for a congregant with a pastoral crisis. And that is not good.

Write to me again soon. And how wonderful to have an e-mail address for you as well! The Vatican rejects modern life-saving innovations such as condoms which could help control an epidemic threatening to wipe out entire nations, but has no trouble embracing the Net. All right, I will *not* run down the Catholics anymore. Frankly, I have no right to complain about anyone or anything at the moment and that's all I've done for pages. I just got back from a perfect month on the island with Kit, I'm at a brand new church with every possibility in front of me. People will need me. I have good messages to spread. George Bernard Shaw said, "This is the true joy in life, the being used for a purpose recognized by yourself as a mighty one, the being thoroughly worn out before you are thrown onto the scrap heap; the being a force of Nature instead of a feverish selfish little clod of ailments and grievances complaining that the world will not devote itself to making you happy." I will not be that selfish little clod, Mark. I will stop my whining and start looking for the good I can do here!

Take care of yourself, my dear friend, and don't let anyone convince you that you're less than perfect just the way you are.

Ruth

PS~ Will you do me a favour? Next time you write, if you could inscribe "from the office of Jean Paul" somewhere on the envelope? I'd at least have the excitement of seeing Valerie pass out. Oh dear, this is not good at all.

R

To: buddhagrl@nsrcentre.com
From: rbroggan@ucc.ca
Subject: They finally connected my Internet!
September 20, 2002

Dear Kelly,

I am sorry, but e-mailing your mother does not mean you don't have to call now and then. I miss the sound of your voice, honey, and I cannot make out what "btw" and "lol" mean. It calls to mind a verse from Proverbs 30:19: "Three things are too wonderful for me, four I do not understand: the way of an eagle in the sky, the way of a serpent on a rock, the way of a ship on the high seas and the way of a man with a maiden." You know, it's a little unclear to me which three of those four things are too wonderful. Grammatically, I suppose it wouldn't be the sex, which has never been too wonderful as far as I'm concerned, but the whole thing seems awfully open to interpretation, don't you think? I have no doubt that the writing of the scriptures was inspired by God; I just wish He'd been more evident in the editing. But don't tell me those Old Testament types didn't have it good. I could add a thousand items to the list of things I don't understand and it gets longer every year. Now the list includes, "the way of my daughter when she writes an e-mail." I should not have to use a dictionary of "words whose origins can be traced back to about ten minutes ago" to figure out what my children are saying to me. Not after you're twenty or so, anyway.

I do think it's wonderful that Buddhists have e-mail. That is probably the wrong thing to say. I know you're not mired in the middle ages or anything like that, and I've seen ads for credit cards, or no, I guess it was more likely computers, that showed Tibetan monks high up in the Himalayas sending faxes. Who would they be sending faxes to, do you think? I guess other monks with computers. Or Richard Gere. Or Madonna. But no, she's the Kabbalist one, isn't she? All right, I admit I know nothing about what it is to be a Buddhist, but Kelly, that is not for want of trying and if you'd e-mail me something other than "TTYL" and :-), whatever that is, perhaps I would understand a little more. I've read Buddhism for Dummies cover to cover, but it was not a lot of use. I've spent a lifetime getting to the point of being able to listen to my own emotions, so I'm just not ready to transcend them yet. Although I'd be happy to get past a few of the things I've felt since I got here. Can one transcend boredom? I'm sorry, sweetie, I don't mean to sound disrespectful of anyone's faith path (except of course Mark's, but that's usually just to get to see the astonishing shade of red his ears turn when he's apoplectic), but the more I read about your spiritual beliefs the more I feel this is just one more thing that will separate you and me. However, I am determined not to be such a "mother" about this. Nothing separates us except my fear of separation. I will keep reading and trying to understand and trying to let go. In the meantime, I am grateful for the Zen-like patience you show as I learn to be adult about having adult children.

I can't really say that I'm feeling settled here at Glenview, although, after all, it's early days yet. To begin with, the manse I'm now living in is far too big for a single person. The whole house smells of stale air and pine cleaner, in spite of the fact that I've sprayed so much April Breezes room freshener around that I should have hired a crop-duster. The few rooms I actually use still feel empty and foreign, though I've put up my own pictures, and the furniture I've owned for thirty years is arranged around them. Old smells and ancient emptiness. A tomb for people who never really lived. Did I tell you that the first day I arrived I actually sat down on the hall stairway and wondered if I could live here? And, after all, what minister lives in a manse anymore? Give me a housing allowance any day of the week. I feel like I'm in someone else's house. That any minute they'll come up the walk; I'll hear a key turning in the latch and a voice will call out, "Is somebody here?" This place is, well, just very different from my snug little apartment in Markham. There's a study on the main floor here that I can't even go into. There's nothing dangerous about it. I mean, it's not where they found the body of the minister before me, or anything like that. So far as I know. This all sounds awful. There is nothing wrong with this house. It's just this out-and-out loneliness I've been struggling with since I arrived here.

To tell the truth, I don't think I'm adjusting well. Every day I get up saying, "Today, I will see only other people's concerns. I will not be bogged down by my own. Today I will be a light to the people I have contact with. A channel of hope." And I do try. It doesn't help that it's rained almost every day for three weeks. Not Maritime rain. Where you are, it rains like it means it and then it's over. Toronto rain whimpers and spits for an hour, then the clouds let loose and water thunders down like the end of the world for fifteen minutes, then it recollects itself and returns to thin, passionless grousing in small spatters for the rest of the day. OK, this is terrible. I am even complaining about how it rains. Surely it rained exactly the same way in Markham. I was just too busy to notice. Here I have long hours at my disposal to become intimately familiar with how rivulets of water trickle criss-cross patterns on my office window, how puddles collect like tidal pools outside on the lawn. My new definition of having nothing to do is knowing what's going on in nature. I'm not used to it. Weather is supposed to be window dressing; something you notice as a happy accident, an aside to whatever else is going on, or God's little gift to those of us who have trouble thinking up an opening for a conversation. A person is not supposed to spend a whole day watching rain fall. Well, maybe I haven't spent a whole day. It feels like a whole day. I can feel my morning resolution to be a light in the world being washed away with each new raindrop.

The ridiculous thing is that when I was being run off my feet for seven years in Markham, never a moment, let alone an afternoon to myself, having leisure to watch the rain would have sounded like heaven. Now I have realized something about who I was at that time. I was an idiot. I mean, I thought if I wasn't running to refuge-support meetings and Bible study seminars and new mothers' teas, I would have time for all those other things I really wanted to do, such as contemplating life, the universe and the meaning thereof, and it would all be wonderful. But now the last thing I want is to be left alone to contemplate, well, anything at all. There is no peace or possibility in this space, there is just . . . nothing.

We have four church groups who meet regularly each month. Out of those four, there is no point in my going to one of them and two others have told me point-blank not to attend. The choirmaster very graciously and kindly explained to me that they do not welcome new voices, because the same five people have been singing together since the Roman Empire and new members might have disruptive ideas; like wanting to pin down what key they're supposed to be singing in. Fortunately, the musical limitations and exclusionary nature of my church choir is something I can let go of, quite happily. I am also not allowed to attend the Christian Men's Breakfast Circle, which makes sense, although I am dying to know what on earth they do there. However, proving again that I am not a lost cause, I take a page from one of those books you sent me: "We would have much peace of mind if we would not busy ourselves with the sayings and doings of others." I can let go of the mysteries of the Men's Breakfast Circle.

Then there's the planning committee for the annual International Dinner fundraising event. Again, I try to put aside uncharitable thoughts as I contemplate that it takes one entire committee one entire year to organize one simple dinner. And it's a potluck. By "international," they apparently mean roast beef and Yorkshire pudding. I offered to contribute a vegetarian curry this year, and you would have thought I'd proposed performing the Dance of the Seven Veils on the church communion table. Kelly, our church is smack dab in the centre of an area with more cultural diversity than a group photo at the United Nations. Towers of synagogues rise around us, there's a mosque ten blocks away and a Hare Krishna temple just beyond that. This reality doesn't seem to have penetrated the walls of Glenview Unified. I think the "international" component of this annual dinner is that the horseradish comes from Ireland. I have the sensation of being on a remote island with the last small band of Christians in existence.

What's hardest to understand is that the people here seem to work hard not to see that there's a world outside our tiny patch of church and manse and yard. When I brought up the idea of starting a yearly pastor-swapping program with our Jewish or Muslim neighbours, the head of the Church and Spirit (because, apparently, those are two different things) Committee gently reminded me that the centre of a church is called the sanctuary: a place of retreat into what is comforting and familiar. He was sure I didn't want the congregation's Sunday morning peace disturbed by having to think about other people.

Church and Spirit is the one meeting I do attend. Technically, it should be called the Church, Spirit, Stewardship, Pastoral Relations, and Who the Heck Do We Call To Fix the Boiler Committee; there are simply so few people to serve that they've had to combine several groups into one. The committee met last night but there were only two items on the agenda: Grouting the eaves-troughs and my salary. I didn't feel I had a lot to contribute on the grouting issue. And of course I can't be present for discussions about my salary. Anyway, if this is anything like my last church, every one of the committee members will make a point of telling me every detail of the discussion during coffee hour after the service on Sunday. I can picture them all raising eyebrows in gentle bemusement, wondering what it is I do exactly that makes me worth the princely salary of $10,000 less than a first-year elementary school teacher. The fact that I have a Master's degree and responsibility for baptizing and burying them, not to mention providing whatever spiritual guidance is required in between, does not seem to make me worth it. To tell the truth, since I've been here I've begun to wonder if they aren't right about that. Then there's the book allowance figure. If I had a nickel for every Pastoral committee member who has looked significantly over their bifocals during a contract review and said, "Of course, you also have the book allowance," they wouldn't need to pay me a salary anymore. A member in Markham suggested they withhold the hundred dollars a year until I could assure them I'd read all the books I already have. When I came to interview at Glenview, a woman on the selection committee asked why I needed to buy more books every year. I said, "To keep up on the new ideas," and she leaned over, patted my knee reassuringly and said, "Oh that's all right, dear, we're fine with the old ones." It's a wonder more ministers don't go the route of my predecessor here and submerge themselves in The Gospel According to Johnny Walker. Some days, it seems the only way to keep from going insane. Or to keep from knowing you're going insane. No honey, I am not going to become another drunken clergyperson. A glass of wine puts me to sleep. I think that's what the last minister died of. I don't mean being asleep . . . unless, I suppose, it's metaphorical. I think he might have died from drink, though I've heard everything from cancer to "a bad cold." I have a feeling, though, that he was wide awake at the time.

So, I don't go to meetings. I keep telling myself that this is a relief. I remember in Markham we once spent three full hours in a committee meeting deciding how to label the coffee canisters in the church kitchen. You would not think canister labelling would be such a big issue. Not like, say, that one classic central conflict that has tested the esprit de corps of every Christian congregation since the stone was rolled from the tomb—deciding who gets a key to the church kitchen. I have no doubt that when scholars finally translate the last fragments of the Dead Sea scrolls they'll reveal Paul writing to the Corinthians, telling them to stop in-fighting for God's sake and just give the key to Audrey Dickens, the only person from my home church who was ever allowed to have a key to the kitchen and who I am quite sure is as old as that. Or perhaps there is a whole, hidden "Share the Key" gospel contained in the last bits of scroll and that's why the Vatican is refusing to release them. They know bedlam would reign in the church as we know it.

The coffee-canister-labelling problem came about because a different grade of coffee was used for every type of function that went on at Markham Unified. We had coffee reserved for staff use only, which, frankly, was a fairly inferior brand as the three of us had each been known to guzzle down as many as two or three cups a day, and really, who could expect the church to pay for that kind of perk? We had regular decaf for the nursing mothers in the Wednesday "Bibles and Babies" group and the Swiss Water decaffeinated for the Tuesday and Thursday morning exercise class. Then there were more decent blends, by which I mean they actually tasted like coffee and not dishwater, used for Sunday service coffee hour and committee meetings. Finally, we had coffee that was regularly donated to us by Fowlers Kosher Deli for reasons no one could remember anymore, but which was far superior to anything we bought ourselves and kept strictly for weddings, funerals and the occasional ceremonial visit of the powers that be from Church House. Now, you can't just label coffee "staff grade" or "after-church coffee" or "too good for you" or whatever because . . . I don't remember why, but I do remember that it was very clear in our discussions about it. You must keep in mind, of course, that all of this was much more hotly discussed than any of my sermons. And why not? Coffee is more interesting than theology. You can see the effect it has on your life. I'm beginning to think this is what organized religion is all about, Kelly. Getting your labels right. They don't teach you at seminary what you really need to know.

No, I know that the church is more than that. But sometimes it doesn't feel that way. More and more I feel that organized religion is just a way of being able to assure yourself that you're doing things right. Which of course means anyone else is doing things wrong. I remember another absolutely rabid discussion during a Church and Spirit meeting in Markham. It was not a discussion. It was a verbal brawl. A theological rumble. There was name calling. Members stomped off in a huff. What had set everyone off was the suggestion from one of the more religiously avant-garde in the group that we begin our meetings by lighting a candle. Well, this was either a superb, symbolic gesture of invitation, summoning the Holy Spirit to our midst and work or a heretical throwback to "high church," or witchcraft, or both. Depending on who you polled. Within days, factions had formed in the congregation. Hushed, clandestine meetings, both pro-candle and anti-candle, took place to discuss strategy. The dispute was picked up by our church newsletter. It spilled into outbursts during coffee hour. The choirmaster, a man with both feet planted firmly in the pro-candle camp, programmed hymns for the service such as "This Little Light of Mine" and "Jesus Bids Us Shine," and the entire anti-candle contingent in the choir threatened to walk.

Finally, Nancy Livingstone, one of the most respected (you may read "overbearing") members of the congregation, a woman whose family had paid for the refurbishing of the narthex as well as most of the gymnasium, stood up during morning announcements and declared that if we were going to start indulging in pagan or (I think this was worse) Papist "doings" before our church committee meetings, she, for one, was going to "cross the street." This confused us all for a bit because the water filtration plant was across the street. The Presbyterian Church was kind of kitty-corner to us but, honestly, we could imagine Nancy worshipping at the water filtration plant sooner than fraternizing with the Presbyterians. Anyway, that was that. There wasn't another word said on the subject.

During the very next meeting of "Church and Spirit," which, I might add, was particularly well attended in case any other sensational topics arose, suddenly all the lights went out. Hydro was working in the subdivision behind the church and a power line got cut. There we sat in total darkness. There was a long silence. No one said a word. Then Nancy piped up, "Well, I hope some damn fool has brought a candle."

Coffee and candles. What I struggle with is not just that we have an idea that God cares about things being done in some kind of proper order, but also that we believe there is an order for God to care about. That seems less and less clear to me. In the long afternoons here, when I sit watching those drops trickle random patterns down my window, I can't believe there is any order at all to this. To why life changed so much for all of us. To why I got fired from Markham after years of what I thought was very faithful service. Certainly not to why I was sent to this place where I am allowed to do so little. Maybe my problem is just that it's Tuesday and I've already written my Sunday sermon. Maybe it's just that I am so used to being busy and not used to being bored.

Kelly, I'm finding it very hard not to feel as empty as my days here. The mornings are fine. The mornings take care of themselves pretty well. I have a few visits to make, or a call or two to answer, and I can feel like I am useful in some small way in my little corner of the world. I have letters or the sermon to write. But by 3 or 3:30 in the afternoon, I start to feel, well, at a loss, I guess you'd say. Too late to start anything new. Too early to begin evening things. It's a long, slow stretch of the day. I watch the leaves or the raindrops filter down. I listen to the wind if there is any. I watch the squirrels. There are always squirrels. And time does pass. But such an emptiness comes with the passing. Not at all what I imagined time to myself, time to think, would be like. I need more to do and at 3:30 p.m. there just isn't anything to do. It's almost 3 p.m. now.

Anyway, you must not worry about me. I'm sure that in a few more days I will settle in much better and find lots to make me feel productive and be rushed off my feet and will complain about that, as usual. A month from now it will be me who doesn't have time to make a phone call to you. I hope not!

I don't know if I've told you often enough, honey, but I am proud of you for pursuing the things that speak to your heart. In fact, when I picture orange-robed monks cross-legged on a Tibetan mountaintop, chanting their ancient Buddhist mysteries, I feel they may indeed have discovered the secret to coalescence within a faith path: no kitchens.

You must let me know if you're coming for Thanksgiving. I know David is going to your father and Heidi's place and if you want to go too, you know that's fine with me. Sometime though, I would like to show you this house so you'll know what I'm wittering on about. You could help me venture into the study at last. Who knows what evil lurks?

Call me when you have a chance, or even sooner.

Sending you so much love, or "over and out," or whatever it is we're supposed to say by e-mail.

Mom

PS~ Kelly, do you have any pictures of lobsters? Not being a seafaring lot here in Toronto, photos of aquatic life seem hard to come by. When I'm watching the rain trickle in the afternoon, I have a reoccurring image of a lobster, or at least a shell creature of some kind. I don't know why. Anyway, if you can find a postcard or something with a photo, I'd be happy to have it. A crab won't do, I don't think, just so you know.

PPS~ Honey, I am always eager to learn more about your chosen faith path, but please do not keep re-sending that same e-mail that explains how God is not an entity but an "energy flow." Sweetie, I don't understand how to be loved by an energy flow. Of course I do realize the problems inherent in limiting God to a separate entity. You start to think God might care about coffee, or candles, or my personal boredom, for instance. I guess the truth is that metaphors are helpful in illuminating truth until we start believing they are the truth they're meant to illuminate. You can add that to the list of things I don't really understand.

Love,
Mom

Excerpt from the Sunday service, Markham Unified Church of Canada, April 8, 2002
Sermon: "The Wisdom of Kings"

The lectionary text for this morning is from Exodus, Chapters 12 and 13, in which God slays the first-born of the Egyptians to gain freedom for the Israelites, His chosen people. Given that we are now in the season of Easter, the most important stretch of the Christian calendar, the lectionary suggests that the theme for this Sunday should be something suitably grand and hopeful: "Peace for All Nations." It has been our practice, here at Markham Unified, never to stray from the prescribed path of the lectionary, but the fact is that I, for one, am unable to connect a passage in which God kills children with a message of "Peace for All Nations." In fact, I don't even want to try. I'd feel party to the worst kind of theological rationalizing. Although there's pretty stiff competition for what's the worst.

My feeling is, if my freedom can only be purchased at the cost of someone else's anguish, God has something to answer for. The anguish of Christ dismays me. What kind of all-powerful, all-loving God allows, no, chooses, for their child to suffer like that? I know all the theories, of course. Atonement for our sin. God joining more closely with us by experiencing human suffering for Himself. "It's a mystery." The great American playwright, Arthur Miller, said, "Life is God's greatest gift and no principle, however glorious, can justify the taking of it." Perhaps God doesn't read Arthur Miller. Anyway, no one can argue that the committee who gave us the lectionary didn't think we were up to a challenge. Instead, however, I've decided to talk about Proverbs, Chapter 24.

On first reading, one might think the Book of Proverbs somewhat mundane and repetitive. If you stick with it, you will find it is *very* mundane and repetitive. Proverbs is a book of advice. There is caution against having "haughty eyes and a proud heart," suggestions about keeping quiet and out of trouble; reading this book can make one feel like you're fourteen again, being lectured to by your mother. Generally, we don't like this. We don't want to be told how to behave. We don't think we need it. Not like other people. They really need it. But if you can get over your predisposition to adolescent anxiety, hear this as homey suggestions from someone who loves you to pieces and only wants the best for you, your grandmother, say, as she passed you a plate of warm cookies and a glass of good milk, then this can be very useful, reassuring stuff. "Sweetheart, don't visit your neighbour too often, you'll wear out your welcome." Grandma pats your hand and you know you're the most beautiful, miraculous being in existence. "Honey, remember, the beginning of an argument is like letting out water, so stop a quarrel while you can."

What I find intriguing about the Proverbs is they were supposedly written by King Solomon, the greatest, grandest of the

Biblical monarchs. Greater than King David, even, because it was Solomon who God chose to build His temple. Solomon was regal, wise, revered and, if we forgive him one youthful indiscretion, behaved himself with the ladies. This is all the more impressive when you consider that the man was a poet. And yet, this deep thinking, impressive king is credited with writing a book that rivals a newspaper advice column in its concern for the minute details of his subjects' lives. Some of the advice given is quite generous; Chapter 24:21–22: "If your enemy is hungry, give him food. If he is thirsty, give him something to drink." Fine sentiments. It would have been even better if he hadn't followed these with, "This will make him ashamed of himself and God will reward you." OK, the man was no Mother Teresa. It makes him more human.

Some guidance is quite amusing. "It is better to live in a corner of an attic than in a beautiful mansion with a cranky, quarrelsome woman." Makes you wonder what was going on in the palace that day. Solomon even goes to pains to warn his people not to eat too much honey because it will make them sick. It makes me think that if Queen Elizabeth would use her annual Christmas television address to counsel us with something like, "My husband and I wish you not to eat too much honey," we'd all be the better for it. It's too bad Her Majesty doesn't, because we are all inclined to eat too much honey of one kind or another as a woman with her kind of family difficulties well knows.

"Discipline your children as fairly as you can, but discipline them. It is a sign of love." I wish I'd read that twenty years ago. "It is an honour to stay out of a fight. Only a fool insists on quarrelling." Now there's a text for a sermon on "Peace for All

Nations." That one verse alone would cut the length of our board meetings in half, even if I were the only one to adhere to it. "Don't repay evil for evil. Wait for God to handle it." My daughter would call that a lesson in karma. And patience. It means that when someone has taken my stapler again, I must not retaliate by hiding the extra photocopying paper. I'm not here to teach other people how to live. I'm here to learn for myself.

All good advice. So why don't we take it?

The truth is, hiding the copy paper feels good. And I certainly want to be free to eat as much honey as I like even if it does give me a sick stomach in the end. I even think I'd like to live in a mansion with a troublesome woman. I grew up that way and it wasn't so bad. Frankly, walk-in closets make up for a lot.

Of course, the mansion Solomon is referring to isn't bricks and mortar and a hot tub. The ancients knew that we learn by comparing what is new to what we already know. The Bible is metaphor. It's funny how some people become alarmed at that. "Do you mean to say it isn't true?" Of course it's true. And of course it's metaphor. Metaphor only works when it's true.

The mansion Solomon is talking about is the beautiful world that God has provided, the opportunity we have to live in peace, harmony and love. The troublesome woman is the fretfulness, anger and ingratitude we often show. Some other wise person once said, "Neither God nor the devil can do anything to us that touches the pain we cause ourselves with our own decisions and behaviour." We eat so much of the honey of self-righteousness, fear or anger, that our stomachs become used to the pain. We disturb the harmony of our perfect world with bickering and arrogance. We sully the peace that should exist, perhaps especially in the context of a Christian family, with pettiness. Sometimes, over a candle.

Every religion in the world has rules, advice, suggestions on how to move through life in the wisest, most caring manner. A lot of this advice is personal. Not about how armies should function, or governments lead, though there is some of that too. But mostly, it's about how each of us should try to live in relationship to ourselves and to each other. I don't know how to bring "Peace for All Nations," but I do know that what is contained in the words of Solomon may help me bring peace to my own heart and my own little corner of the world. Maybe that's the only place to start with peace among nations anyway. So, if whoever took my stapler will put it back again, I will return the . . . no, I will return the copy paper regardless.

Let us pray.

Note: Records show that following an emergency board meeting two days later, Reverend Broggan's contract was terminated.

Excerpt from the Sunday service, Glenview Unified Church of Canada, September 2, 2002

Good morning. It is with a glad and grateful heart that I take up my ministry with you here at Glenview Unified. I am happy to be here. A member of our congregation asked if the flowers in the sanctuary this morning, which are so very beautiful, were ordered in celebration of my first Sunday as your pastor. In fact, they were left over from a wedding that took place here in the sanctuary yesterday. Looking at these glorious clusters of burgundy roses reminds us of how many details go into planning a wedding and that it is one of those occasions when only the best will do. The union of two people in the responsibilities and joy of life companionship is considered an event worthy of great care, often great expense, always great detail and concern.

It seems fitting that the flowers in our sanctuary today should be wedding flowers. Because this morning we are marking the beginning of another significant relationship. This morning I am joining your church family. In calling me as your minister, you have invited me to join with you in the challenges, responsibilities and mutual support we share as individuals and as a congregation. Together, we can expect to wrestle with the basic issues of life, issues of morality, which many of us wonder about, and issues of mortality which all of us wonder about. Together, we will celebrate weddings and baptisms with joy and hope. Together, we will confront illness and loss, make visits to sick beds, offer comfort at funerals, sharing the heartaches that life will most certainly bring. And together we will share the most sacred of our church rituals, our monthly observance of communion which reaffirms our commitment to Christ and to each other.

We enter into relationship today, that of pastor and congregation, individuals seeking and striving together, with the same optimism and reverence as the beginning of a marriage . . . and, if we are more wise than most people at the beginning of marriage, also with concern and caution. There will be times when we fall short of who we wish to be. But there will also be times when we amaze ourselves and each other by being more together than we ever imagined.

The rules for this relationship are also like those of marriage; that we practice kindness, offer each other patience and acceptance in our journeys, be prepared to forgive each other over and over for being human and always, always remember that the best way for us to be in relationship together is for each of us to be most truly and fully ourselves.

So, it is indeed with a glad heart that I join your church family today; with optimism, with reverence, with concern, with caution. I embrace with my whole heart the opportunity to join with you in whatever joys and challenges the future holds. The petals and the thorns, we might say. I am happy to be here.

Please rise and join in singing Hymn number 580, "Faith of Our Fathers."

September 3
For Kit, from the store

Message from Ruth: Says first service was "satisfactory." Or possibly "in a factory." Have to get a new tape for the message machine. Also says, "avoided most hackneyed references with exception of roses and thorns. Did choose archaic, patriarchal hymn, now deeply regretted. Mother was wrong for advising ditching ministry to become floral arranger." She might have said "coral ranger." That sounds more interesting, don't you think?

Your New Yorker *arrived. Also, more phone messages in box. You're allowed in for two minutes to get them.*

McNelly

Kit Sheppard
Bolin Island
BC, Canada
V1E 1E0
September 21, 2002

Dear Kit,

Please do not leave me any more telephone messages asking why I haven't called to tell you how wonderful your new book is. First of all, how am I supposed to call someone who doesn't have a telephone? I know McNelly will take messages, but I also know that you've been barred from the store so often, it could be days before you get them. Add to the fact that I only just managed to get a copy of the book, because you will not let me buy it at the nice, convenient, inexpensive mega-bookstore that had them a week ago. The little independent store, which is a twenty-minute drive from here (a drive during which, I might add, I contributed to polluting our environment) finally got it in yesterday and I went immediately to buy a copy for myself, one for Kelly and for David and one to send to my friend, Mark Duggan, who is in Rome just now taking a course on how to be less flexible. That was the store's entire stock. And not a cappuccino in sight, of course. I understand why you want me to buy from an independent (and you would approve of this one entirely—incredibly well-informed staff and nary the taint of a Rosemary Rodgers or any other book that might fall under the heading of "just an enjoyable read"), and I am actually happy to do so, but do not suggest that my having to wait seven days to get the book, which other devoted followers have already finished and passed on to someone else as brand new by now, indicates a lack of support for your work. I was simply following orders.

Also, I did not appreciate the comment about "blind religious navvys who think poetry ended with the 'King Brainless James Goddamned Version.'" I am not familiar with that translation, Kit. If you think the *Unified Church of Canada Review* is written by a pack of puritanical illiterates, tell your publicist to stop sending them review copies. And if you swear on my voice mail one more time, I will refuse to answer your messages at all.

Now, having said that, I've read most of the poems in the book and can say wholeheartedly that the *Unified Church of Canada Review* must be blind, deaf and dumb and does not know anything about poetry (something, I might add, upheld by every other and much more significant review, so why are you on about this one, anyway?) because your poems are wonderful as always. Just when I am sure I love your short stories or social commentaries the best, you give us poems like this and I change my mind entirely. Until the next collection of stories or commentaries comes out, of course! You deserve every one of those impressive reviews. I like the *Globe* critic's description particularly, "Kit Sheppard's lush and enigmatic language draws us into a whirlpool of sensuality and bemusement." Even your reviews are sexier than Rosemary Rodgers.

So far, my favourite piece is the one about the native woman making her way through the forest wearing high-heeled suede boots. "In darkest night/what beats in her heart like a drum." So beautiful, Kit. It made me stop and wonder what beats in my own heart like a drum. Which has got to be what a poem is meant to do, right? I was not sure about that other line, "armour of a bleeding hide." I suppose those are the enigmatic parts. I also didn't quite get all of the poem called "Playing Girls with Milo." Was Milo the girl or . . . not the girl? At one point I thought Milo was the fish that came in at the end, but then . . . well, the rest of it wouldn't really make sense, would it? Although maybe I just don't want to think too hard about that. I really think I might look into taking a university course to learn to understand your poems a little better. I don't care what you say, I can't believe every professor totally misses the point of your work. Anyway, all I know now is that it is indeed "lush and enigmatic" and asks me to think, though sometimes it's just uncomfortable questions about what's really possible with a fish, and that's a gift you give us, for sure. You may now sit and quietly contemplate your beautiful slice of ocean and wait for the awards and honours to start piling up again.

OK, I'm going to talk about my stuff now, just so you know and now may want to leave off reading. There might be something else nice about your book at the end (but of course I might just be saying that to entice you to read the whole thing!). It sounds to me as if you aren't writing something new at the moment (please do start soon, Kit, you know it's hard on everyone on the island when you don't have enough to do), so maybe reading this letter will give you something to occupy your mind. It's possible I sound a little bitter, but really, dearest Kit, it's just because

I get tired of you saying I don't tell you anything about my life when the truth is that you just don't listen.

The new church is fine, though I'm not sure that fall is the best time to start at any new place. I realize it's when we do start over, to school and getting back into the routine of life, and in a hearty, bright, glorious autumn, that would be fine. This one has been a thin, grey trickle of a fall. Leaves dripping off trees, puddles swelling to floods that seep through basement windows here in the manse and which form oceans across the lawn I have to traverse on my walk to the church. There is a slow, steady, ceaseless drip—a Chinese water torture from the cellar ceiling onto the concrete floor just now. I keep the basement door closed so it doesn't drive me mad at night when the house is still. I should talk to the church janitor about coming to fix it, but that would involve doing the one thing I just cannot do—talk to the church janitor. I'm not afraid of the man, I just understand that if I tie up his time with frivolous activities like making sure I'm not flooded out of my house, he will not have time to attend to important church business such as sitting with his feet up on the desk and chatting with the church secretary over coffee. And, I will be punished for this by suddenly having my office designated the only suitable place for storing . . . well, everything. I tell you, Kit, if the Catholic powers-that-be want my friend Mark to bone up on doctrinal orthodoxy, they should send him here. The Vatican has nothing on the support staff of a Protestant church for emphasizing the clear relationship between action and consequence. I'd rather suffer the drip.

ANNE HINES

The weather leaves me longing for the sunshine of last August on your island. I miss lingering over coffee out on your front step, watching the morning sun slant through the trees and onto the rocks in front of the cabin. Listening to the waves lap onto the shoreline. Wandering over to Gerrard's to talk marvels and gardens, or down to McNelly's store as the first yellow light picks its way through the pine needles overhead. That lightness that comes from knowing nothing is required of you except to exist and be glad. Freedom that refreshes your soul like cool water. Here in Toronto, the "nothing to do" just leaves me taut and nervous. I have this strange sensation that I'm sitting outside my own life. I find myself falling prey to contemplation of the dark corners of my being, those we really should never, ever contemplate. Things you should not look at. Places I thought would stop bleeding if I simply said they weren't there. Did I make a mistake in not trying to get Kyle back when he left? Did I really let him go? All right, you're probably the last person on earth to ask. Did I make mistakes with Kelly and David? Of course I made mistakes. That's the only guarantee that comes with being a parent—that you're going to make mistakes. But do you think that parents whose children live in other cities have done something to make them not want to be near? You know Kelly and David almost as well as I do. Do you think they don't want to be with me?

Then, I move on to: Did I become a minister because I had no idea what else to do with my life? Or, because if I'm not serving someone else's needs I don't exist? Women who get divorced become ministers. That's a fact. Our sem-

50

inary was full of them. I used to feel really sorry for them, these women alone. Then I became a woman alone, and felt more sorry for them.

When I've finished tying myself in knots about whether or not I made unhealthy personal, parenting and career choices, it all deteriorates into one big, "Have I learned nothing at all?" By then I've usually worked myself into such a state of despair that all I can do is get undressed and go to bed. I would love to eat ice cream, but I will not contribute to that stupid stereotype that women who are unhappy eat ice cream. So I end up even more miserable because I would really like to eat ice cream. Or an entire box of Ho Hos. And no, they don't come in "organic."

In the midst of all this, Kit, I keep having this image of a lobster come to mind. I think it's a lobster. Possibly, it's some kind of crab. No, a lobster. But, I mean, you'd think being in the depth of despair would be enough, right? But no, I am also visited by inexplicable crustacean images. Remember when we were down at the wharf last summer, waiting for the ferry the day I left, and you saw that lobster down in the water, pushing itself under a stone? You said that when a lobster outgrows its shell it sloughs it off and crawls under a rock for a while to wait for a new one to form. For that time, the lobster is entirely vulnerable until the new shell hardens and protects it from harm. I keep seeing that lobster, or something like that lobster, deep down under a wash of rainbow-coloured sea, crouching, waiting, not knowing what ill might befall it. Hoping . . . OK, you will tell me that a lobster can't hope, but I think one in that condition jolly well might. Maybe it's the grey-green watery pools outside my window that are turning my mind to this image. Nothing more.

I think I've written enough for today. Since you're not working right now, maybe you could write me a letter? I need to hear all the news out there. Has Gerrard put away the gnomes for winter? Did his fall delphiniums bloom? What's the talk about down at McNelly's store? Has Deirdre managed yet to find enough pink paint for her shack?

I miss it all so much, Kit. The island, the wind against my cheek, the tang of salt on my tongue wherever I went. The year is dying in tears and trembling, not in the wondrous blaze of fire and defiance you have. Except, I remember a poem from your last book, I think it was called "Season of Cloud" where the fog was so thick in September that the woman in the poem started to believe she was some kind of other world spirit and walked into the ocean and drowned, without even acknowledging the water. Gives me shivers to think about it. So maybe it's not as clear and radiant out there as I imagine, or need to imagine that it is somewhere, on this dreary first day of fall.

Sending you so much love, and wishes of brilliant sunshine on scarlet boughs.

Yours,
Ruth.

PS~ Your book is wonderful. There, I promised you something at the end!

R.

To: mduggan@jesuit.com
From: rbroggan@ucc.ca
Subject: Are you nuts?
October 1, 2002

Dear Mark,

Let me get this straight: they are sending you to the countryside
to take part in a religious retreat? Why on earth would Catholics
need to retreat? You haven't advanced at all in 600 years. Come
home immediately.

> Love you,
> Ruth

> PS~ I am sending you a copy of Kit Sheppard's new book of
poems, a talisman against those who have designs on your soul.
> R

To: buddhagrl@nsrcentre.com
From: rbroggan@ucc.ca
Subject: A shaved head is a whole new ball game, honey
October 2, 2002

Dear Kelly,

Do you have a copy of that e-mail you sent me on "Compassion
for All Beings?" I have a difficult letter to write to the woman in
our congregation who prepares the communion sacraments,
and I need some help figuring out exactly how to word it.
Margaret is a lovely person and a wonderful volunteer; she just

has too much time on her hands. Like me. Anyway, Henry James said, "Three things in human life are important. The first is to be kind. The second is to be kind. The third is to be kind." The fourth is not to tick off people you depend on to help get the communion elements together. If you have that forward handy, I'd be happy to see it again.

Sending you so much love, honey. Also, I heard you're possibly expecting an early snow out there. Please message that you're being sure to wear your hat when you go outside. There is no transcending a head cold, sweetie; ask any of your gurus.

Mom

Mrs. Margaret Ketchie
258 Glengrove Avenue
Toronto, ON M6N 2P5

October 4, 2002

Dear Margaret,

Just a note to tell you how very much the work you put into preparing the bread and wine for communion is appreciated by all of our church family. Without dedicated volunteers like yourself, this central ritual of our faith might not be possible. Your service is greatly valued by us all.

I did want to mention that we might give some further thought to the choice of wine we use in the sacrament. I fully support your decision to change to a commercial product rather than continuing to used the homemade vintage that Calvin Wenty has so very kindly provided all these years. Many congregants have commented that our observance has a new air of solemnity and peace now that taking the wine is not followed by considerable gagging and coughing. For me, it is a welcome change to be able to offer the sacrament to the few children in our number without them bursting into tears. Your suggestion that we invite Mr. Wenty to donate his wine for sale at the annual church rummage sale is an excellent one. Should we manage to sort out the legalities of such a venture, I have no doubt this will prove a highly profitable suggestion. In any case, I recognize that dealing with the traditions and feelings of people, particularly those giving from their heart, can be a minefield and I applaud the courage and sensitivity you have shown.

I do wonder, however, if we have hit quite the right final selection in the wine we began using this past Sunday. I think you would agree that *the* symbolic gesture, *the* tangible image that demonstrates Christ's sacrifice for us, is the moment when the minister holds aloft the pitcher and releases a cascade of red wine into the chalice below. "My blood, poured out for you." Each time I raise that pitcher and pour the wine, I hear my "Introduction to Worship" professor, William Kervin, cautioning us, cajoling us, insisting to us that this is a very, very big moment. In fact for many of us, this makes the whole thing and we are not ever, ever to succumb to covert and unseemly "ritualistic minimalism" wherein we let out a thin trickle into the cup or worry about staining the altar cloth and just tip the pitcher to the edge of the chalice. Raise the pitcher high and let wine fall like a spring shower. It's better than the bread moment, for sure. Far more elegant and evocative, particularly since most Protestant congregations now use a whole, Italian-style loaf, which we think looks tremendously authentic and picturesque but which rips apart about as easily as rubber.

What I am feeling is that, just maybe, the absolutely most perfect vintage to assist us in achieving an impression of equal parts mystery and majesty at this most critical moment, may not be Baby Duck. The effect of wine hitting the chalice, erupting into a volcano of pink foam, gushing over the sides of the goblet, washing across the communion table and onto my shoes was certainly striking and I'm sure everyone was suitably transfixed by the ceremony and not, for once, checking their watches or playing word games on the Order of Service, but somehow I don't think it's quite what is wanted. Several congregants mentioned that, when they sipped, the bubbles tickled their noses, which I think accounts for the giggles and snorts (certainly nothing immediately springs to mind from the liturgy at that particular point that might have had that effect) and, while a vast improvement on coughing and hacking, this was still not exactly conducive to an atmosphere of reverence and awe. Also, while I believe that having the children laugh rather than sob is more theologically appropriate to the occasion, having little Ryan Jenkins come up asking for seconds is not.

In the interests of hitting the desired note, I wonder if we could perhaps choose a less lively selection for our next communion service. Maybe a nice, quiet, passive Cabernet.

Thank you again, Margaret. Your dedicated work and generous gift of your time and talent is a blessing to us all.

Yours in Christ,
Reverend Ruth Broggan

October 6
Message to: Valerie
From: Reverend Broggan

Dear Valerie,

Thought I'd let you know that, if anyone calls, my schedule is wide open this week and next and I'm happy to make myself available for any little thing that is needed. The week after is good too. Just so you know.
RB

To: mduggan@jesuit.com
From: rbroggan@ucc.ca
Subject: Professional opinion requested
October 14, 2002

Mark,

I finally had a congregant ask to be visited. Thank God for Mrs. Zeran. I've been to see her three times. In six days. The last time I went there was no answer, but I'm sure I saw her hiding behind the lace curtains. I need to know if there's a fine line between pastoral care and stalking. Funny what they never cover in school.
Ruth

To: mduggan@jesuit.com
From: rbroggan@ucc.ca
Subject: Kill me now
October 20, 2002

Dear Mark,

Don't you think trying to be more like Jesus, who spent most of his time (all right, when he wasn't healing lepers or walking on water or participating in other Messiah-like activities) railing against the religious elite, means we should, with one voice, rise up in defiance of any authority that seeks today to regulate our spiritual lives? I suppose asking this question of someone who seems to have decided to live in the Vatican for the rest of his life is like asking Kit, "Don't you think all women should stop sleeping with men and just sleep with you?" A good many of them do, anyway.

I cannot complain about your religious restrictions, because I'm having to jump through the hoops of my own faith group today. We're all slaves to the regulations after all, aren't we? Oh well, without them, we'd probably have anarchy and possibly original relationship to the divine, which I believe is pretty much the same thing.

I have to write a report on my ministry here so far for our Unified Church of Canada Church House. Frankly, I'd rather be dragged before Pilate.

Oh Mark, the people in our governing body are just doing their job and I am just scared. I have to make things work here, and, at the moment, it feels like it's all slipping away from me somehow. The best I can hope for is that there is so little for me to do here that there's little for anyone to complain about my doing poorly. That's not true. The best I can hope for is that they had so much trouble rounding up the requisite number of members for a selection committee when they hired me, that by the time they decide I'm unsuited to the post, more congregants will have passed on and a full compliment will be out of the question. You know, call me crazy (Please don't! I'm starting to wonder if it's possible!), but hoping that enough church members will die off so that there won't be enough of them to have me fired, does not strike me as entirely pastoral.

Where has gone the gung-ho, no-holds-barred, gloriously, foolishly confident woman-on-a-ministerial-mission you knew and loved in school, Mark? I have got to get a grip here. I could tell Church House about the excellent idea I had for starting a drop-in centre in the church for all the nannies who live in the area. I just won't tell them that Valerie already tipped off our janitor who is refusing to co-operate with any plan that will require him to perform "additional significant and onerous custodial duties." Such as sweeping the Sunday School room once a week after the group has finished. There's a way to get him onside, of course; I just don't know what it is.

All right, time to gird my loins and wade into the fray. And really, there's always a bright side, isn't there? Being terrified is a change from being bored.

Sending you love,

Ruth

PS~ It is done and I enclose a copy of what I sent.
Love,
R

Dear Colleagues,

I am delighted to be writing to Church House to provide a brief report of my first few weeks as minister at Glenview Unified Church.

As you know, ours is a small congregation, comprised of some fifty families, most single people in their later years. In spite of a significant change in the religious demographic of our area and an absence in the last few years of any other Christian congregation, the people of Glenview Unified soldier on, a small but determined representation of Christ's presence in this part of the city.

Most of our church events are well attended, with the possible exception of Sunday services. Nonetheless, I have been gratified by the response to my sermons and to small innovations I have been pleased to introduce to our common life. A slight alteration to the service of communion, for example, seems to have increased the comfort level of all. I am happy to report also that I have established relationships with our church secretary and sexton and find them eager to share their ideas about all aspects of my work here.

I wish to thank Church House once more for the support and confidence shown in helping me secure this pastoral charge. I have no doubt that, after the unfortunate events in Markham, Glenview Unified is exactly what I need to clarify and affirm my calling to ministry.

I hope to see many of you worshipping with us in the future, as time and your other many commitments allow. I do suggest you call ahead before you come. It will allow us to prepare a proper welcome for you.

With blessings in Christ,
Reverend Ruth Broggan

Mark,

Notice that I did not mention that "a proper welcome" would include trying to get more than twenty bodies in the pews on a Sunday morning. I must not be losing it after all.

Love you,

R

Sermon from the Sunday service, Glenview Unified Church of Canada, September 23, 2002

In our scripture passage today, Jesus teaches his disciples in words that have become familiar to us all: "Seek and ye shall find, knock and the door shall be opened, ask and it shall be given." Luke 11:9 has been used as the lyrics in sacred song, has been inscribed on bookmarks, stitched on banners, has inspired painters and comforted believers for almost two thousand years. For good reason. Just as the rainbow stretching across the heavens is a continual reminder that God will never again flood the earth, these words of Jesus are among the most tangible and reassuring of God's promise to us, that divine grace and guidance are available at all times. This is what we call one of the "feel good" verses.

But there is more here than meets the eye. Of course there is, or those of us who make it our business to illuminate scripture would be out of a job.

I had occasion this past week to pick up my copy of *Confessions* by Saint Augustine. I don't remember why I picked it up. Possibly I needed something to rest my coffee cup on. My own confession is that this is not a book I read except when under duress. *Confessions* is a fifth-century autobiographical account of one man's journey through the stages of life to adulthood, moving from a secular world and worldview to life as a priest, with a deep commitment to the Christian church. It contains many lengthy passages that go something like this: "Oh Lord, I was so lost and miserable before I embraced the orthodox church and learned all these Biblical quotes that I can now recite until it makes readers batty." If you don't believe me, I am happy to lend my copy to anyone who wishes to check. Keep it as long as you like. Suffice it to say, this is not the kind of "feel good" book you pick up on a dreary afternoon when you're hankering for a little light inspirational reading. It's not something normally read by even the most devout Christian, unless forced by some Machiavellian seminary professor who believes with Philip Melanchthon that, "Human life without knowledge of history is nothing other than perpetual childhood, nay, a permanent obscurity and darkness." I must say that, for many of us students, reading Augustine did more to engender obscurity and darkness than dispel it.

Nonetheless, *Confessions* and other works by Augustine are seminal books to our faith. It's from the mind and views of Augustine that many of the foundational doctrines of our church developed. In a sense, we believe what we believe because Augustine believed it first. An example of this is our concept of justified war. Before the fourth century, Christians were pacifists, refusing to bear arms or to join the army, for which they endured extraordinary censure and suffering at the hands of the ruling Romans. Augustine created his doctrine of a "just war" to enable Christians to engage in combat with the "barbarians at the gate," and in every age since, armies have marched into battle, certain that God supports any war fought in the name of Christianity.

The central theme of Augustine's *Confessions* is the ability of God to rescue humankind from sin. And, make no mistake, Augustine is keen to assure us of what sinners we are. To be fair, he is keen to assure us of what a sinner he himself is. But, his assertion that crying as a baby for his mother's milk proved he was inherently greedy and manipulative, or that, as a young boy, nicking an occasional pear from a neighbouring farmer's orchard showed him an almost irredeemable delinquent, makes it impossible not to understand his examples of evil behaviour in himself as suggestions of a similar tendency in us all. Which, of course, is his point. In fact, no Southern Baptist preacher at a pro-choice rally could be more damning or despairing of the virtue of the human race.

Nowadays, it's easy to dismiss Augustine's railings as unfashionable. In spite of this, in our heart of hearts, I think we believe he's right. I, for one, read in the paper about someone accused of corporate fraud, or governmental corruption, and I automatically think, "I'm sure they did it." Never mind that the basis of our judicial system ensures "innocence before proven guilty." Or if someone is rude to me, or offends me in some way,

I am convinced they can have no redeeming characteristics whatsoever. As your friend and minister, I'll give you a little personal advice here. One of the really unfair things about life is that you're never allowed to hate anyone. The second you peg someone as "too annoying or just outright bad to have anything to do with," they will turn around and do something wonderful. Another of God's ways of reminding us that there are many sides to any story. But Augustine would have us believe that we are all hopeless sinners and that the only possible hope for redemption for humankind comes through the orthodox church's intercession with God. Today, in that same heart of hearts, many of us believe that those who sit here in church each Sunday morning, even if we go out and declare war on our neighbours tomorrow, are more acceptable in God's eyes than those who choose not to.

During Augustine's lifetime, the thorn in his theological side was a monk named Palagius, who hailed from the Celtic regions, which we now call Scotland. Palagius believed that humankind was born inherently good and Christ's mission was not to confront a corrupt world but rather to liberate the essential good in each individual heart from its bondage to various kinds of suffering and evil. Palagius championed the idea of an "in-dwelling God," a divine spirit, active and alive in each of us, and equally in each of us. He believed that a deeply personal, intuitive relationship with God was possible and desirable, and that our hearts already know how to forge that connection, without direction from religious institutions. He encouraged followers to search out the secret places in their own souls and be attentive to the "inner teaching" that God had placed there. Palagius enraged Augustine and the pundits by arguing against the church as the arbiter of divine will to the people. He insisted that dictates and doctrines were inventions of the human mind, nothing to do with divine command. What mattered was how you respond to the divine spark in your own heart, through your own effort and actions. At a significant council meeting, Palagius's beliefs were struck down as heretical and Augustine's creeds were upheld. Humankind was pronounced sinful, and the doctrines and teaching of the church declared the essential and only link between people and God. In retrospect, one cannot but wonder how many "holy wars" and personal heartaches might have been avoided if that final vote had been different.

"Seek and ye shall find, knock and the door shall be opened, ask and it shall be given." Augustine and Palagius were both men of passionate faith. Both seekers of truth. Both knocking at the door of doubt and questioning, convinced in their hearts that scripture and the will of God Himself had led them to the truths they presented to the world. And yet, they arrived at entirely different places. How is this possible?

Years ago, I was privileged to take a course on "Interpreting the Hebrew Scriptures," what we call our Old Testament, with Rabbi Sydney Englander, a man of great faith and great passion, two traits that are the hallmark of an exceptional teacher and make for a wonderful experience for a student. Rabbi Englander introduced us to the Mishna, a voluminous collection of commentary on the Jewish scriptures by rabbis from ancient times up to about AD 200, wherein scholars interpret Biblical passages, decipher rules and expound on the requirements of faith and ritual. They don't all agree. Not by a long shot. Rather, what you find is a myriad of interpretations and opinions to consider. Rabbi Englander joked, "Ask three Jews for an interpretation of a scripture passage and you'll get six answers," suggesting that Jewish scripture interpretation has a tradition, not of simply asking, "What is the scripture saying?" but also, "How many different things is the scripture saying?" How many messages are contained here that might help us to understand not the certainties of life, but its varieties?

The material in our New Testament canon was chosen by Gentiles, but the structure is based on the Old Testament, and much of the material, we believe, was written by Jews. I have wondered if it's this tradition of seeking many answers that lies behind the many different depictions of Jesus in the books of the New Testament. Mark portrays Jesus as a volatile and very human rebel, who was careful to hide his identity as Messiah from the masses. Matthew gives us a Jesus who is publicly recognized and worshipped as God's chosen, with a mission to preach both the approaching end of time and the importance of upholding traditional Jewish law. Luke's depiction is of a stoic martyr on a specific mission to the Gentiles. Finally, John presents an ethereal saint with one foot already in heaven. Four very different, sometimes even contradictory, impressions of the same life; these books do not speak with a single voice, or offer one clear answer, but rather engage us in a dialogue of the many shades, sides and suggestions of who Christ might have been.

To my mind, this "dialogue" is more exciting than one single, cohesive statement of fact. Certainly it is more challenging. To me, scripture is the ultimate testament of God's respect for our free will. It allows us to decide for ourselves what we believe and how we will live in the world. It is perfectly designed to encourage us to love as much as we are able or to hate as much as we choose. The absolutism that has been encouraged in scriptural interpretation, the belief that there is one, clearly designed and eternal meaning to be drawn from what is really a very subtle, even flexible text, can keep us from seeing what a miraculous book this Bible really is.

What I draw from the lives of Augustine and Palagius, each so deeply devoted to Christianity and the Christian community, to God and God's word, and what I draw also from Rabbi Englander's insightful and inspiring teaching brings me back to "Seek and ye shall find, knock and the door shall be opened." This verse does not say, "Let someone seek for you." One cannot depend on the writings of Augustine, the opinions of Palagius, the views of an inspired teacher, or even the dictates and creeds of our own Unified Church of Canada, or what I offer to you each Sunday from this pulpit, to provide you with your answers. This is a personal quest and while I believe that we may all end our journeys in the same place, I also believe that the road we take to get there will look different for every one of us.

God calls on each of us to enter into a personal search for what is meaningful in our lives. Assumptions and expectations should be put aside. Pride laid down. Courage and faith must replace certainty and self-righteousness. Courage and faith are the only currency of truth.

Then, when we come to a decision, or find a place that feels right to us, we must put down that assumption as well, move beyond that choice into the unknown once more. Pound on the door of heaven and demand a new answer, a deeper understanding. Journey again.

The only truth that someone else can provide you with is

the assurances of those who have journeyed before. Some of those assurances are chronicled in our ancient writings; that if we have the courage and faith to seek, God has promised answers. That is a big thing. If we knock, the door to possibility will open. If we ask, we will be answered. If we seek, we may not find truth that looks like everyone else's, but we will certainly find ourselves.

A rainbow of promise is contained in those words. But first, we must have the inner fortitude to ask. We must search for our meaning. And then search again.

Our closing hymn today is "Bless Now, O God the Journey."

Oh, I have been asked to announce that anyone wishing to contribute to the poinsettia fund for our Advent season should see Margaret Ketchie after the service. Margaret wishes me to assure everyone that all the poinsettias will be red again this year, as some found the pink-and-white striped ones last year a little sensational. Please rise to sing.

To: mduggan@jesuit.com
From: rbroggan@ucc.ca
Subject: Grateful for small mercies . . . and a chance to serve!

Dear Mark,

I helped someone! A woman called from Toronto General Hospital at around 2 a.m., her mother was dying and could I please come down and pray with them. I raced downtown, found the room and sat with the woman during her last few moments. The family wept. I wept. Is it bad that I wept partly because I was so happy to finally have someone need me? Such an incredible relief after the last few weeks of feeling entirely useless and more and more empty. As I was leaving, I asked the daughter of the woman who died how she'd thought to call me. They certainly aren't members of our congregation. She told me that her family has belonged for years to one of the very large, very high-toned churches in the city. I wondered then, why hadn't she asked her own minister to be with their mother. The woman said, "Oh mother would never want us to bother Reverend Dunfield at this time of night!"

Still, this counts as my being needed, don't you think? Probably Reverend Dunfield gets needed all the time. It won't hurt him to give me this one.

Mark, maybe this means something is starting to turn around!

All prayers to this effect will be gratefully appreciated!

With love,
Ruth

To: mduggan@jesuit.com
From: rbroggan@ucc.ca
Subject: Have you lost your mind?

Dear Mark,

What the hell do you mean by telling me that if I'd just stayed in my marriage like God intended, I would have a family to look after now and I wouldn't be so hard up to find meaning in my life? Do they put something in the water over there, or are you just hitting the sacramental wine too hard? I write to you saying I might be having a spiritual crisis and your answer is to start channelling my mother? Or, what's more scary, buying into some antiquated crock of religious doctrinal bullying designed to bolster the church's control over people's personal choices? Seeing that the Vatican has now embraced modern thought to the point of putting its sixth-century attitudes on the Internet. I suggest you do a search, plugging in the keywords "dental hygienist/straying husband" and see if even your database doesn't immediately pop up, "Get outta there, sister." Leaving aside the fact that Kyle left me, I happen to think that God supports choices that free our souls. I even think God wants our happiness above a church's, any church's licence to tell us what that happiness should look like. So you can keep your smugness and your power and your billions of dollars in real estate and art and I don't know what else that the church clings so hard to and that you could be using to spread a little freedom and happiness around the world that needs it, and most of all you can keep your Goddamned certainty that you have any idea of what God or I think is best for me, because what you think now, frankly, has nothing to do with real life or real people in the real world.

Mark, listen, I really need you right now. I will stop ranting at you at once (though frankly, you really deserve it) if you will just be the Mark I've known and loved since that first moment we met in the student lounge at Emmanuel College and shared our mutual loathing for that Systematic Theology professor. I need you to be the Mark who is capable of thinking outside the box, or the confessional booth, or whatever. The Mark who once told me that the only possible purpose of church doctrine is to give us a place to start asking questions. The Mark who got into trouble for being brave and wonderful enough to stand up in a pulpit on a Sunday morning and preach that the failure of the church to support Jews in the Holocaust and your failure to protect innocent children from sexual abuse by the clergy are equal travesties of morality. I need you to forget that you're a Catholic priest in a deprogramming tank at the Vatican for a moment. Because there is something you have to do for me that is really important. Mark, dearest Mark, my dear friend, I'm starting to think I'm really in trouble.

What I need you to do for me is this: tell me if you think all the stuff in the Bible is true. What I need to know is, do you really, in your heart of hearts, in the deepest, most private places of your being, think that any of this is right or trustworthy or credible? Please, Mark, I need you. It's not fair to dump these fears on my daughter and anyway she'd just go into some long rant about perception and "bardos" and how nothing is real anyway, and that never makes any sense to me. Whatever I am feeling, it's real enough to wake me up in a cold sweat in the middle of the night. And I can't call Kit because she'll just tell me that this is proof that she's been right about everything since the universe began.

What I need you to tell me, Mark, is whether or not God exists. It's late afternoon here and I am less and less sure.

Ruth

PS~ I am very glad you've been put on a committee that you're excited about. I just hope "Bring Rome Home" isn't what it sounds like.

PPS~ I am also excited for you that you're going to be meeting the Pope, but please remember what my Aunt Lydia says:

"When someone sets themselves up as infallible, they've already made their first mistake." Of course, she's generally referring to her bridge partners, but I think it's something to consider.

I want you to get on a train to Florence, go to the church of Santa Croce and look at the beautiful monuments honouring Dante and Galileo. Proof that your faith tradition does value those who bypass the party line and think for themselves. Granted, not until after said bypassers are long dead and the rest of the world has been honouring them for years, but it does happen. Message me a.s.a.p. to confirm that you have done this.

R

Kit Sheppard
Bolin Island
BC, Canada. V1E 1E0

October 23, 2002

Dear Kit,

Last time I wrote to you about dampness and grey. Today, I am writing about light.

Finally, we've had a bit of sunshine here. Almost every afternoon for the past week, a few rays have snaked through a crack in the cloud cover and for an hour or so Toronto has been bathed in a rich flood of deep yellow light. This seems to happen around three-thirty in the afternoon on the days it does happen. I'm usually home in the manse at that time, since no one calls at the church in the afternoon. It's the time for our congregants' naps, or bridge groups, or possibly they watch *Days of Our Lives*. I know Valerie, the church secretary, does. On a tiny black-and-white television tucked under her desk. I can't decide if that's an OK thing to be doing in a church office, but there's no point trying to figure it out, really, because if it's been done for more than a few years it'll take a visitation of Moses, tablets in hand, saying, "Thou shalt not watch soft porn in the church office" to change it. And he'd need the backing of Christ himself at that.

Anyway, the point of me telling you about the rare hours of sunlight is this:

When you come in the front door of the manse, there's a dining room on the left and what they used to call a parlour on the right. It feels like a parlour still, very stiff and silent, not what you'd consider a "living room" at all. The dining room has a solemn, disapproving air. I feel as if I've offended the house spirits with my antique pine furniture, which seems just as unacceptably casual here as it was overly grand for my place in Markham. Sometimes, in the afternoon, I do sit in the parlour and watch leaves fall into puddles on the front lawn, when I have nothing else to do. Mostly, I take my meals in the kitchen at the back, read the paper or watch television in my bedroom upstairs and avoid being in the other rooms altogether.

There is one more room off the main floor hallway, just before you go down the passage to the kitchen, or up the stairs to the bedrooms. I'm guessing that years ago this was probably the minister's study. I've never used it myself. It's just as easy to walk across the lawn to the church office to make calls or write my sermons and there's the advantage of having been seen doing my job. I glanced into the study the first day here, wondered why someone had painted the walls of the room a hideous grey whereas the rest of the house is a hideous beige, shut the door and planned never to go in it again. Frankly, it gave me the shivers.

Well, one day last week I was sitting at the front window, thinking maybe I'd fill fifteen minutes of time by making myself a cup of tea. I walked down the passage to the kitchen just as the sun must have broken out of the clouds, because suddenly, from under the closed door of that study room, one brilliant splash of blood-red colour rolled at my feet. I pushed open the door, sure that the room must be on fire . . . and it was, fire like I'd never seen before, Kit. Bright burgundy and fuchsia flames, salmon and rose tongues of colour, blazing corals, writhing, undulating, like ocean waves on fire at sunset. The walls, Kit. The walls were blazing wildfires and sunset waves. Flames blazing without burning.

I couldn't move. Maybe for an hour. Or a few minutes. Long enough for the fire, if it had been real fire, to have gobbled this aging wooden house and me and everything in it entirely. I kept telling myself over and over, "it isn't real." This scorching, opalescent charge of flames and fuchsia can't be real except in an evening sky that foretells heaven, or a painting that portends hell.

Finally, I pulled myself together enough to be able to see what was making this happen. It was the walls. The entire surface of those walls, right up to the moulding and over the outlets is actually layered, inch by inch, every crevice and crack, lacquered over with tiny, perfect snail shells.

The shells are arranged together in spiral patterns.

Forty shells placed in perfect order in every spiral. I know, Kit, because I counted at least twenty of them. Circle after circle, spiral wheel after spiral wheel, positioned tightly, precisely together. Over and over and over. Each snail back a tiny spiral in itself. There are even shells on the light switches, Kit, and over the baseboards and window frame. When the sun manages to push through the clouds in the afternoon—it is just at the right angle at about three-thirty or four to tilt through the window of this room—the shells wash with the colour of fire and sunset, seawater and opal, blood and wine. Just like the sun used to pour through the front windows of my grandmother's house in the late afternoon, infusing the cranberry glass dishes on her low table with deep red light, staining the living room carpet with crimson.

The fire lasted about two hours, I think. The sunlight faded, shadows crept across the walls, leaving them slate grey and barren. Empty carcasses glued to a wall. I switched on the electric light. It was horrible, like illuminating a morgue. I turned to retreat back to the hallway. That's when I noticed a patch of wall near the door frame, completely bare. Maybe a square foot of empty space, maybe less than that. No shells. Whoever did this, whoever glued spirals onto a wall to be set on fire, hadn't finished.

Kit, maybe you could go down to McNelly's store and phone me. I wish you'd get a phone yourself. You don't even have to answer it when you don't want to. I need you to tell me something, anything. Better still, come here and tell me; give me something to hold onto. It's not just the boredom of this place that's getting to me, Kit. I'm starting to feel that something else is not quite right.

Sending you more love than "lips may speak or tongue can tell,"

Ruth

PS~ "In our sleep, pain which cannot forget falls drop by drop upon the heart, until in our despair, against our will, comes wisdom through the awful grace of God." I think it's from "Song of the Sirens." Who wrote that? I'm sure you'll remember. I was thinking about it this afternoon as I sat in the shell room.

R

To: mduggan@jesuit.com
From: rbroggan@ucc.ca
Subject: All is forgiven
October 27, 2002

Dear Mark,

Thank you for calling me! You sounded like Mark! I appreciate both of those things more than I can tell. Makes me feel that all may still be right.

Now, tell me what you think of this.

I had a visit today from the local rabbi. I know I make it sound as if here in Toronto we have a rabbi on every street corner, but really, in this area, we practically do. The demographic of the neighbourhood has changed significantly since these houses were built just after the Second World War. Our little patch of park with church and manse is hemmed in on all sides by synagogues and Jewish day schools, a little bastion of dogged, determined Christianity in the midst of swirling, swelling Sephardic and Ashkenazi life.

To get to Beth Aitz Chayyin synagogue from where I'm sitting in my office right now, you go down the steps to the side hallway, out the door, across the parking lot and up their side steps. It's a couple of hundred yards at most. I was sitting in my office this morning, pondering some theological profundity like what to do with the $23.32 we collected in offerings from the children last year, not to mention who on earth gave us 32¢ . . . or 2¢. It turns out not to be mine to decide about anyway. Our most fervent volunteer, Margaret Ketchie, arrived at my office, breathless, having been alerted by Valerie to the fact that I'd gotten my hands on the children's offering and she explained that these funds are always used to buy disinfecting products for the nursery. How much disinfecting can be required since there is a baby in church about once a quarter? But then I suppose $23.32 doesn't go far for cleaning products. And I should be grateful for having this weighty theological problem solved for me so neatly. How often does that happen? Anyway, Margaret left after receiving assurances that I would never, ever do anything again of any kind (which seems possible)—and I was sitting at my desk, casting around for anything else to apply brain power to, when the side door banged open and a tall, bearded man in a very beautiful blue suit burst through the door and said, "Reverend Broggan, yes? Pinsker. Rabbi Joseph Pinsker. From across the way. I'm here to discuss interfaith parking."

Mark, you could have knocked me over with a feather . . . or a bagel . . . or something. I realize that a man in a nice suit walking into my office might not be front-page news, but let me tell you, around here he couldn't have done something more unexpected if he'd had to part the Red Sea to get here. Beth Aitz Chayyin was built thirty years ago, and I'm sure most of my congregation have still not acknowledged its presence. I suggested an interfaith gathering when I first arrived here and everyone assumed I meant getting together with the Anglicans. They weren't even keen on that. I don't think there's any real prejudice against our Jewish neighbours. It's more like we simply don't see each other. Parallel universes. Distant planets. So "other" we don't enter each other's consciousness. At least that's how it seems from this side. Clearly their side is at least aware of the fact that there's a parking lot over here.

Rabbi Pinsker, who is a very impressive man—lively, articulate, handsome, a man who has "clergyperson's clergyperson" stamped all over him, if you ask me, leaps into explaining that from Friday evening to Saturday evening the parking lot of their synagogue is full to overflowing. He and the other rabbis (there are five rabbis there, Mark, five clergy in one church . . . I mean, synagogue . . . or maybe "shul," he called it "shul"; five would make a respectable Sunday morning congregation on a rainy October day in this church) encourage their congregants to observe the law of the Sabbath that says they should walk to shul. But they have members who live faraway or are physically impaired, and so the parking lot is jam-packed even an hour before services begin. I admit, the street on a Saturday morning does look like the evacuation route of a Florida suburb during hurricane season. This is technically a "no parking" street, and as Rabbi Pinsker pointed out, it's hard during the service to surrender your soul to God when you're worried about your Lexus being towed.

Rabbi Pinsker asked if, perhaps, our congregation might be willing to share our parking lot on Friday and Saturday. He very kindly did not add, "Since it's empty most of the time anyway." He also very kindly offered to let us use their lot on Sunday mornings. I said I would talk to our Property Liaison person (I was not putting on a show, I'm sure we must have one . . . right?) but I thought it was an excellent idea. Maybe we could put up a sign saying, "We share a God, please share our parking," but Rabbi Pinsker thought they could just make a simple announcement about it at their service.

As the rabbi got up to leave, he said, "Well, if there's any way I can return the favour, just let me know." And I said, "Actually, there is a way. You can tell me how we know there really is a God."

I'm willing to admit that it might not be the most common question in the world for a minister to ask a rabbi, particularly one she just met ten minutes before. But it occurred to me, who better to ask? Here was someone unfettered by anything that happened after someone wrote Malachi. Wouldn't he have a fresh perspective? Or, I guess, an older one? But a different perspective nonetheless and that's exactly what I needed, perhaps, because the usual stuff wasn't working well for me at the moment.

So, I said it. And I didn't even feel embarrassed. Just hopeful that there might be an answer. And that I might believe it if there were. Rabbi Pinsker sat down on the chair across from my desk. He started to talk. He talked for upwards of an hour, I think. About Jewish dietary laws.

Actually, he started by detailing how priests in Jerusalem, before AD 70 when the temple was the centre of Jewish religious life, used to go about performing ritual slaughter. Rabbi Pinsker explained that the animals brought for sacrifice were precious, the best that people had to give, and that there was a very strict procedure both for the killing and for making a proper offering after. The way he described the process made it sound like one of those ancient, intricate Japanese ceremonies, which are almost like performance art, except that this was with a cow instead of tea. He went through all the steps, where to apply the blade, how to drain the blood, how leftover meat from the sacrifices was shared among the poor. Suddenly he stopped and asked, "So, you see why I'm telling you this?" And I said, "Because I feel like a slaughtered sheep?" This was not really making me feel any better. Rabbi Pinsker heaved a tremendous sigh and asked, "Why do you feel there might not be a God?" I said, "Because I've been fired from one job and am now left in a place where all I do is write one sermon a week that nobody listens to, visit a few people who don't want to be visited and plan ways to spend money that someone else takes away to buy disinfectant."

Rabbi Pinsker nodded as if he understood this. Then he launched into an explanation of how the laws of preparing kosher meats today follow similar rules to those of the temple sacrifices. Finally, I said, "Rabbi, thank you, this is all very interesting, but Christians don't have dietary restrictions. We can eat Kentucky Fried Chicken on Easter Sunday, for all we think God cares."

And he said, "Reverend Broggan, what I am trying to get at is that when the temple was destroyed, the people stopped making animal sacrifices. But we still, to this day, through love and labour, continue to commit acts that honour our relationship to the divine. Some of these acts have to do with how we receive what God gives to us, for instance, the mindfulness we show in the preparation and eating of food. Sometimes they have to do with what we ourselves offer—our time, money or talents. Still giving to God whatever is most precious to us. The best of what we have. Reverend Broggan, what is most precious to you?"

Right now? At this moment? Mark, I knew the answer to that. I knew it right away. "My sanity." Rabbi Pinsker shrugged and stood up, "Well, I've heard of stranger sacrifices than that."

And he walked out the door without answering my question. Mark, what do you think about that?

Ruth

Kit Sheppard
Bolin Island, BC
Canada. V1E 1E0

October 28, 2002

Dear Kit,

What would you do if everything you had based your life on turned out not to be true? You're going to have to suspend your belief that you don't have beliefs, I mean, in anything but your own genius. Oh Kit, I don't want to be criticizing you right now. I'm not. I never have. OK, maybe I have a few times like when you were being so absolutely rotten to Rachel. But in spite of that I have always, always recognized and been amazed by the fact that of everyone I have ever met on the face of the earth, you alone, entirely, one hundred percent, in every cell of your being, insist on being who you are. Even though who you are *is* sometimes very annoying to other people and you *were* rotten to Rachel. We all, every one of us, want to be who we are. Most of us have no idea who that is. I know who I am as the minister of Glenview Unified, who I am as Kelly and David's mother, as a daughter, a friend, even as an ex-wife. I just don't know who I am as Ruth. Kit, I'm over fifty years old: I've studied theology for a decade. Not only do I not seem to know a thing about what God wants us to do, I don't even know what I want to do for myself. Isn't this where I was ten years ago when Kyle left me? I seem to begin and then I have to begin again and then again. But somewhere at the bottom of the beginning again, isn't there something that stays still? A truth? I don't mean a truth dependent on facts. If you learn nothing else in theology school, you learn that facts have as many faces as there are mouths to spout them. I said that badly. What I mean is, even the Bible, the book on which we base our way of being in the world, or at least *some* of us do, presents the god as loving parent, God as ruthless tyrant, God as egalitarian, or preferring one group over another. I've always believed that how a person sees their god is how they see their world. If I can't know my god, what hope do I have of ever knowing myself?

There is a story in the New Testament about a woman who has suffered hemorrhage for many years. We asked, in theology school, what hemorrhage meant in this case, and our professor thought perhaps it was something like having leukemia. But I don't think so. I think her life's blood, her soul, was leaking out of her and had been for a long time and she knew it. One day the woman heard that a kind of mystic healer was in the neighbourhood, and she managed to get herself to where Jesus was preaching and healing, telling herself that if she could just get close enough to touch the edge of his robe, she would be healed too. Perhaps she felt her own increasing emptiness enough to know a full soul when she saw one. The woman pushed her bruised, exhausted body through a crush of people packed close around Jesus. She stretched out her fingertips and touched the hem of his garment. Instantly, the woman felt well and whole. Jesus could not have physically felt that touch, but he sensed her presence or maybe the energy being pulled through him, and he asked, "Who touched me?" The woman admitted what she had done. Jesus said to her, "Your faith has made you whole." There are sages and prophets, ancient and modern learned believers, who say that God looks down one day and says, "You, now," and the grace of being a whole soul, or at least of having the awareness that such a state is possible, is yours. There are others who say that what we ourselves bring to that moment is what's truly important. That faith is a partnership in which God and we believe in each other equally . . . in each other's potential for revealing our wholeness.

I'm not whole, Kit. I'm more empty or fragmented now, even than I was in the first days after Kyle left. It seems I've devoted almost half a lifetime to service of one kind or another and, as I sit through another empty afternoon, it occurs to me that I really have no idea what God wants me to do. Maybe it's time to call on this concept of partnership. What do you think that would look like? I am feeling it's time to take action in some way. Knock and the door shall be opened. Ask and it shall be given. But first we have to ask. We have to ask. Ask. The Bible says that woman's faith made her whole. But Kit, maybe it was her courage.

I mean, don't you think that when you need to know something, it just makes sense to ask?

Ruth

To: buddhagrl@nsrcentre.com
From: rbroggan@ucc.ca
Subject: More things I wish I'd told you sooner
November 1, 2002

Dear Kelly,

Years ago I was in Notre Dame Cathedral in Montreal on a very hot summer afternoon. Light streaming through the windows turned the gold leaf that layers, well, just about everything, into a river of molten lava. It was so beautiful it made me ache in my stomach. This was the first time I can recall reacting physically, connecting with my body to something beautiful. In the afternoon I sit in a room where the walls flow like crimson waves. I have an image of Jesus walking across water, fire-coloured under an evening sky after a storm, which is also beautiful. Someone told us in seminary that the scriptures, accurately translated, say Jesus walked on the shoreline not actually over the waves, but I think it's a nicer picture, don't you? It doesn't make me ache. I find it quite peaceful.

Love from your mother

Transcript of sermon by Reverend Ruth Broggan from the Sunday service: Glenview Unified Church, November 3, 2002. Recorded by Margaret Ketchie, volunteer recorder for "Sermons for Shut-ins."

The sermon title listed in your Order of Service is "The Greatest Gift," a fitting topic to kick off this season of Advent. However, I've pretty much lost interest in our church calendar at the moment, so I've decided instead to preach on "What I Did on My Summer Vacation." I know there will be a number of you here today who won't know the difference.

I spent the month of August with my friend Kit Sheppard, who, as many of you know, is one of Canada's most celebrated authors of poetry, short fiction and social commentary. Kit lives on a tiny island very far north of Vancouver. Bolin Island could be used as the dictionary definition of "the middle of nowhere." There are no cars, no electricity, no ferries during the winter months. From December to March, supplies and mail come by private boats or snowmobile, when someone gets around to bringing them. They do have telephones, though not everyone has one. Most houses have generators and they all have, not indoor plumbing exactly, but an environmentally sensitive alternative that means no frigid races to and from the outhouse in January.

As you can imagine, Bolin Island is not easy to get to. From Vancouver Island, it takes three ferries and two car or bus trips in between. From the international airport, it takes a good two or three days, depending on the ferry schedules. Along the way, I stayed in motels. These motels were like any little roadside overnighters anywhere. They all have one thing in common.

Can you tell me what it is? No, not a vibrating bed. I wish there were, I'd take a vibrating bed over a mini-bar any day of the week. The thing that every motel room possibly in the world has in common is that in every room, in every bedside table, there is a Bible.

We all know that. The Gideon Society is famous for their placement of Bibles in hotel rooms. Sometimes the Gideons don't provide the whole Bible anymore, just the Psalms and New Testament. In any case, the idea is that when people are away from home, if they are feeling lonely, vulnerable, uncertain and afraid, they can turn to the Bible for words of comfort.

I think this is stupid.

It is my opinion, having studied the New Testament up the whazoo in theological school, I'd place it second only to one other book on the list of "Things you really don't want to read when you're down," and that's the Old Testament. They're both full of stories of people leading arduous, unfulfilling lives. Adam and Eve get kicked out of Eden. Moses never gets to see the promised land. David, the author of the most beautiful, treasured sacred poetry in history, isn't worthy to build the temple. And don't even get me started on Job. In the New Testament, John the Baptist, a man of such conviction and charisma that there's more written about him in his day than there is about Jesus, dies horribly in prison. Paul, our greatest, most fervent disciple, also ends up jailed, probably beaten, certainly shunned by most of the Christian community. Mary, the human being who most readily and willingly enters into partnership with the divine to carry out God's great plan, lives the rest of her life branded as a whore, rejected by the son she did it all for before watching him die slowly in agony before her eyes. When Mary herself dies, she is raised to sainthood and adulation by being stripped of everything that made her human or real. Now those of us who turn to the Bible to show us how to live have to ask, is this really what we're hoping for ourselves? All these people were devoted followers of God. All of them trusted, sacrificed, were prepared to follow where God led them. None of them were granted happy lives. Even Jesus, God's chosen, lives without the comfort of home or family, is denounced as a criminal, tortured to death and dies in apparent obscurity. There is not a single historic reference to Jesus written during his lifetime. His teachings inspired an exclusivist religion that not only negates much of what he suffered to preach, but which causes more harm and cruelty in the world than any faith tradition in modern memory. Not a very great legacy for so committed a life.

Of course, people get very angry when you take this view of the Bible. Ministers are not supposed to talk this way. I haven't read the good minister handbook lately, but I'm pretty sure "don't trash the Bible" is still in it. "Don't trash the Bible from the pulpit" is probably a chapter heading.

In seminary, we were taught a lot of fascinating stuff about the Bible and then cautioned not to share any of it with you. Apparently, you're not ready to hear the truth. It will make you skittish and uncertain. I say, what is the truth for, after all? As a minister, what I am supposed to do is mete out the truth in small doses, or dumb it down, or both, so as not to alarm you. Truths such as, the New Testament to which we turn for the last word of God and which is contradictory and hopelessly patriarchal doesn't preach love at all, or at least not equal love. It's anti-Semitic, except for the teachings of Jesus, who puts down the Gentiles. It is homophobic and often misogynistic. It has no problem with the ownership of slaves. Many of the letters of Paul were likely written by other people. Many of the books of the New Testament as a whole were written at least fifty years after Jesus' death, after the fall of the temple in Jerusalem, when the world Jesus knew had disappeared forever. What we have in these books are not eyewitness accounts, but copies of copies of copies of stories that may have circulated orally long before they were written down. All we know about the final authorship is that whoever's name is on them is probably not the person who wrote it. The books in the canon are only a very few of the many, many texts that were available to the church leaders, who, in AD 428, finally decided which ones would be held up as the true Word of God and which did not quite support their idea of what people ought to be taught to believe. Their choices have determined social structure and dominant worldview for the last fifteen hundred years.

These are all things I'm not supposed to tell you. It's like *Planet of the Apes* when Doctor Zayer struggles to hide the truth that humans can talk in order to protect the peace of mind of the ape population. Someone said, "Human beings cannot bear too much truth." Truth leads to somewhere other than peace, I guess. Ye shall know the truth and the truth shall alarm you. It will set you on your ear.

But, these are all facts about the Bible and the people of the Bible that we know. Or think we know. I myself came to feel that our seminary history courses should be retitled "Biblical Scholars Sit Around and Guess at Stuff." Mostly we just think we know.

And what we think we know most assuredly is that the Bible is a record of God's love. The Bible is supposed to be inspiring, uplifting. We've been told it is. We've been *promised*. It's designed to show God's love for us, after all. And this is what I want to talk about. I say, show me where that is.

I'm not going to get into how God doesn't love you if you're not an Israelite in the Old Testament, or a follower of Jesus in the New Testament. I'm going to choose one story from the book of Mark, which, I believe, says it all.

I want to say upfront that Mark is a book I like. I like its rugged, sparse description. I like that the Jesus it presents us with is a very human, raging, contradictory, defiant. Not the ethereal, too-good-for-this-world saint we find in Luke or John. This is the kind of Jesus who you could picture engaging a crowd with his passion and fervour. He makes the Jesus of the other books seem as alive as blown leaves.

Mark 1:12. Jesus, a man with nothing in his past worth recording as far as Mark is concerned, walks out of obscurity and down to the River Jordan where he is baptized by his cousin John. Suddenly, the clouds part, a dove descends, landing somewhere on Jesus, theological consensus being generally "in the head region," and a voice booms from the heavens, "You are my son, the Beloved, with whom I am well pleased." It's a big moment, for sure. What I am concerned with here is what happens after that big moment. Immediately after. God, having expressed his great love for and pleasure in his son, has "the spirit" drive Jesus out into the wilderness to live among wild beasts and be tormented by the devil. Granted, we are assured that God sent angels to minister to Jesus. Maybe they brought him sandwiches and cold beer from time to time. But the painters of every age certainly portray Jesus lying exhausted, damaged, even bleeding as the angels attempt to bind his wounds. Of course we're told over and over that Jesus needed to be tested. Toughened-up maybe. So he'd be worthy of his illustrious mission: preaching unpopular truth before being cruelly murdered.

You know, if one ever wanted conclusive proof that God is male, I'd have to say you have it here. I know, God as father is supposed to be a metaphor, but it's funny how metaphor works over time. "God is like a father," bleeds into "God is a father," which segues neatly and forever into "Fathers are God." Metaphor is powerful stuff. No wonder they used it to write scripture.

Anyway, there's an argument to be made that we know God is male based on this insistence that readiness to enter the fray must be proceeded by some kind of spiritual boot camp. "Forty days of survival training in the desert, son. Make a man out of you . . . if you can take it." And that is how we still learn many of the big life lessons, through pain, through hardship, through being cast into wilderness of one kind or another. I suppose my contention would be then, that if God were a woman we'd learn the really important lessons by taking long baths and eating chocolate. If God were a gay man, we'd be required to match the colour values in our living room. If God were lesbian, we'd be cast alone into Home Depot. God as a gay man or a lesbian . . . shocking, eh? The power of metaphor.

The point is, this is the test that Jesus was subjected to and surely any test tells us as much about the teacher as the student. If that's how God treats the person he calls "my beloved," the child he is most pleased with, I am a little concerned for the rest of us.

In spite of this proof of the true nature of God, southern Baptist preachers, though they are not alone by any means, continue to assure us that if we believe in Jesus, everything will work out. We'll be comfortable. Taken care of. The way will be smoothed before us.

Where does the Bible say that? Where did belief bring anything but suffering and pain? Which follower of the Bible got comfort? Even David, who was showered with riches and honours, was denied the one great desire of his soul, to build a temple for the God he loved.

The truth, the way I see it, is that this is not a book about comfort. This is a book about real life. And the real-life God, if there is one, is not promising us comfort, or a life free from pain. If anything, the Bible is suggesting the opposite. Believe and be damned. An aware life is a curse.

Personally, I think God has something to answer for.

Because the truth is also, I am in pain. I believed and have been led into confusion. I committed my life to His service and I am in despair. I changed my world in all sorts of horribly difficult ways, ways that hurt people I love, and I have been led into a wilderness of emptiness. I listened. Hard. And I hear nothing. Except the wild beasts that howl in my own soul.

There's one good thing the Bible does give us. People standing up to God. Moses bargains and complains. Sarah scoffs. Even Jesus cries out from the cross, calling God on his promises in no uncertain terms, "Why have you forsaken me?" Where are you, loving God? How could you walk with Adam in the garden and leave us to this? To confusion? To emptiness?

I believe that at some time, every human being, maybe in one single moment, or in every moment of the day, makes a bargain with God. Maybe that's why Jesus went into the wilderness. The testing was not about whether Jesus was worthy to live for God. It was about whether God was worthy of the life Jesus was about to undertake. I picture the young man, standing solitary on a dusty, barren stretch of scrub land, crying to the heavens, "If you want this, show me you exist." Beating his chest, tearing his hair, fighting the demons that infest our minds, our hearts, causing us self-doubt and fear. It takes angels to save us from those, for sure. "If you want this, reveal yourself. Tell me it's not for nothing. Tell me that if I do this, it will all matter in the end." Bargaining with his life.

Why not bargain with God? After all, He needs us as much as we need Him. The gods of the Romans, the Norse, the pagans, all slipped away. Vanished into the mists when people did not believe. I want something to believe in. Something that will matter in the end. Our Christian theology tells me that there is something God wants me to do: worship Him. But whatever I think about God at this moment, I can't believe He's so fragile He needs worship. Just a little too human at that point, if you ask me.

I am prepared to meet God more than halfway. I will offer up what matters the most to me, if He will give me back something that matters more. That's the deal. The bargain. I will go, if you tell me clearly, promise me entirely, that it will count for something. That is one promise I am prepared to believe. Because one thing makes me believe that such a bargain is possible.

I don't have any other choice.

Amen.

November 3, 2002
1:30 p.m.

Dear Kit,

I have just preached the worst sermon of my life. I mean, really. I said things I actually mean. I mean, I've said things I've actually meant before, but this time I said them from the pulpit. I mean, I've said things I've actually meant from the pulpit before, but well, never things that I meant as much as this. I said really, really bad things, Kit. Bad for a minister, I mean. Not bad for some anti-Christian, anti-Bible, not-liking-God person who just wandered in off the street and started spouting angry stuff for no reason except that they had an audience . . . and were insane. I basically called the Bible a book about how much God hates us all and said God is a fraud. At least that's better than saying God is a genuine person who hates us all, right? Do you think they'll see that? OK, OK, I am being incoherent. Maybe I was incoherent in the sermon too. In fact, I was incoherent. I started off talking about spending time with you on the island, and then for no reason that I can make out whatsoever, started trashing the Gideon Bible people. There isn't an obvious connection there, is there? Maybe that will save me. Maybe they didn't understand a word I said. I mean, I didn't really understand it all myself. I just . . . kept talking. I opened my mouth to preach on "The Greatest Gift," you know, some kind of happy-feel-good-God-loves-us-all-to-pieces-fluffy-bunny kind of sermon to kick off the Advent season, about all the nice things God gives us though God is so far above us and isn't that nice, and, I dunno, it's like I got a receipt with the gift and shipped it right back. That doesn't make sense. I mean, shipping it back doesn't, but the whole metaphor doesn't make sense. Is there something wrong when you're the minister and you feel the only good thing that can happen is for no one to understand what you're saying? I feel like I'm channelling my priest friend, Mark. I never met anyone with more talent for taking a perfectly understandable Biblical metaphor and wrestling it into incomprehensibility. Maybe they just didn't listen. I mean they were listening at the beginning when they thought I might be going to say something about sex in sleazy motels, but I think most of them dozed off when it became clear that I really wasn't. Most of them can't hear anything anyway. The only person who ever does hear is Margaret Ketchie, our token Stepford congregant. She's a lovely woman, really, she's just suffering like me from having too much time on her hands. She practically memorizes every sermon as I give it, follows me around all week afterward asking questions (believe me, every minister thinks they want congregants who ask questions right up to the point where they actually get them) and does every little volunteer thing and it's all perfect and you never have any real sense that she knows what the hell it's for. Or that it even matters. But you see, it matters to me, Kit. I need to know what it's for. I mean, whatever it is, I'll do it. George Bernard Shaw said, "The best place to find God is in a garden, you can dig for him there." Maybe that's what he meant. It's in the darkness where we have to look. I'll go there. Into the dark places. But I need to know it matters.

That it's not just snails on the wall. Kit, those words came out of somewhere that I don't know anything about. The sermon . . . was like I didn't even know who was talking. I'm afraid to call or e-mail Kelly or David. Kelly called me the other day about an e-mail I'd sent, asking me if there was something wrong because it was . . . it was a little odd and I didn't even remember writing it. Kit, what do you think is happening to me? In the late afternoons, the walls of the shell room pulse with firelight. Sometimes I just sit and don't think about anything. Sometimes I sit and think about why I came to this place. You remember when I showed you the book about Scotland and pointed out all the places where my family clan had been massacred? They would come hollering down from the Highlands, fall into battle with the Campbells or the MacDonalds or whoever were running the major fiefdoms at the time, they'd get slaughtered, more or less wiped out entirely, and then one or two lone survivors would drag themselves back into the hills, bleeding and spent, to start reproducing so they could do it all over in another fifty years. I recall that you had some respect for this, Kit. Called them "stupid but plucky." But they had a mission. They had a purpose. It was a really dumb, painful purpose, but isn't a dumb, painful purpose better than nothing at all? To feel that your dumb, painful purpose is going to mean something, that it's going to mat-ter at least a tiny bit, even if it's only to make the other side feel really superior every fifty years? I don't know. You also called them "lemmings in kilts." They at least had a purpose in trying. I need that now. I'm willing to bargain my soul for that. What do you think that means, "bargain my soul"? If

God wants me on His side, God's going to have to tell me so. Show Himself. Talk to me in words I can understand clearly, not in metaphors in an ancient book or by light falling on water or whatever. If God wants me, God's going to have to speak up. Explain Himself. Apologize for a ton of things. And if I believe Him, I'll help out. But none of this blind, unheeding trust anymore. As you would say so eloquently, "Screw that." You know, for a poet you could really use a larger vocabulary in everyday speech, Kit. You should be in my life right now. I say all kinds of things I wouldn't on an ordinary day. I say them from the pulpit now too, apparently. OK, I'm OK with this. I am ready to bargain for my soul. If God speaks to me Himself. But I'm not taking any "God moves in mysterious ways" nonsense this time. I haven't got enough of myself left to do that anymore.

In the late afternoons now, the minutes stretch before me so vast and empty I can hear the sound of my own breath. I have never heard anything so terrifying. Do you think King Solomon ever said anything about being terrified to hear your own breath, Kit? And it was just too honest for them to leave in?

Ruth

November 6, 2002

Dear Mark,

I don't know what you mean by saying that "faith is a flower that must discover itself." And why are you writing to me about the devil? We don't talk about the devil in the Unified Church. Then again, we don't always talk about God either. We certainly don't believe that people are possessed by demons, though thank you for your kind, reassuring assessment of my current condition. I'm aware, of course, that your church only dropped the ritual for exorcism sometime after the current Pope was elected. Timing I've considered suspicious given some of his actions while in office. But I'm not prepared to call all the bad stuff the devil and the good stuff God, Mark. It's becoming too hard to know where one leaves off and the other begins. And please stop telling me that I don't trust. I wish to God I didn't. You see, that's where the problem lies.

Ruth

PS~ You know, I have to believe that all the whispers and raving of the devil have never caused half as much suffering as the silence of God.

Rabbi Joseph Pinsker
Beth Aitz Chayyin
140 Glenview Street
Toronto, ON M4R 1R4

November 8, 2002

Dear Rabbi Pinsker,

I have no idea what you were talking about with the dietary restrictions and ritual slaughter information. I am, however, thinking that Hebrew scriptures have something to offer me in terms of dealing with a difficult God. My relationship is about to become Old Testament. I am ready to deal.

Yours,
Ruth Broggan
PS~ Proverbs 20:30 says, "Blows that wound cleanse away evil; strokes make clean the innermost parts." Do you think God would really do that? I need to know a.s.a.p.

RB

November 9, 2002

Dear Mark,

I have decided you're right. Well, partly right. You were right in a way. I know better than to sit here watching rain, complaining that I have nothing to do, no way to serve, no purpose to fulfill. It's ridiculous. I'm a minister after all. My faith and training tell me that there is only one sensible course of action. Don't worry, I'm not going to lock myself in the church and refuse to come out until God speaks to me. Church House would never allow it, for starters. I've locked myself into the manse.

Love,
Ruth

PS~ Nobody will notice if I'm not around for a couple of days, so I'm just not going to mention the whole thing. After all, I'm not crazy.

R

For Kit, message from the store
Wednesday, 14

Kit,

Your agent called. Says she's not a "lying, lazy toad," that's the best deal she could get you. Will call you Friday, 1 p.m. our time, please be at phone. That's going to be tricky because that's when Tim Ulley calls his mother at the rest home.

Message from Rachel. Is going into house to get books she left. Wanted you to know.

Message from someone called Elana. Is prepared to come at any time for any length of time and will get private boat if necessary. Says please respond this time. Sweet Jesus, girl, I should have your life.

Message from someone named Kelly. She read the newspapers about Ruth locking herself into the manse and saying she's not coming out until God talks to her. Cannot reach Ruth. Wants to know if it's true—says she didn't know who else to call. I tacked our copy of the newspaper article up on the board. No one thinks it's a very good likeness of Ruth.

Don't swear at the Whynot boy anymore or Jennifer won't let him bring your messages up. And the melons you wanted came in, so come down and get them today or I'm selling them to Gerrard.

All our love from the store,
McNelly

THREE

November 18, 2002

Notes to myself:

They still push letters through my mail slot so they must assume I'm still alive. Maybe Mark is right: the only answer is for me to leave the church. First, of course, I would have to leave the manse and then leave the church. I am not ready to do either quite yet. What would I do instead of being a minister? Private industry is not exactly crying out for someone who can put together effective liturgy or organize a hymn sing. Administering communion and preaching inoffensive sermons are not highly transferable skills. Not that I was much good at the latter

Someone has begun leaving flowers and casseroles on the doorstep. There were six casseroles and as many bouquets of flowers when I peeked out to look last night. There were more this morning. My front step is starting to resemble a small altar to some Polynesian goddess.

If God doesn't speak, does that mean She doesn't exist? I should have asked Mark that. A priest should know. He'd likely just give me some crap about how God speaks in many ways and through our relationship with others and yadda, yadda. I sold that one myself for years and where did it get me? Holed up in an ancient mausoleum of irrelevance demanding some unknown, maybe non-existent force speak to me and tell me what to do with the rest of my life. You'd think one simple answer wouldn't be too much to ask. "Seek and ye shall find, knock and the door shall be opened." Lock yourself in the manse and demand that God speak to you. The smart thing would have been to get in a few supplies before I started this.

I poked a hand out just now and brought in a casserole. It had a note on it. "We shall not be abandoned."

Well, that's good to know.

Unless, of course, we were alone to begin with.

November 21, 2002

Notes to myself:

Am making tremendous progress. Have alphabetized all books on bedroom shelf. Have tidied up all items in kitchen cupboards. Have cleaned out the linen closet. The shame of locking oneself in alone is that there is no one to admire these accomplishments. Have gone through that drawer in the bathroom, which seems to breed half-empty jars of hand cream and little sample pouches of foundation makeup. Tried out several of these and ended up looking like some kind of beige leopard. Was glad no one is here to see that. Began alphabetizing all items in kitchen cupboards. Stopped when it occurred to me that it was weird. Also, unable to decide if classification should be just "bowls" or "mixing bowls."

Have nothing to do again. Which I should be used to. Maybe I could vacuum.

November 28, 2002

Spent the afternoon cleaning around the kitchen taps with Q-tips. Try to read, but can't focus. Am wondering if ironed bedsheets really are nicer and whether it's worth the effort to find out. Have the strangest sensation that I am still managing to run away even though I do not leave the house. When Kit calls, maybe she will say something wise that will change the world. Am hoping she will do that soon. May have to put aside cleaning and trying to read and let whatever is trying to happen, happen. Am finding I am not as brave as I had hoped. You can tell you're not brave when you think ironing the sheets is the better alternative to being with yourself.

Excerpt from transcript of Sunday service, Glenview Unified Church, November 30, 2002. Mrs. Margaret Ketchie presiding.

I am standing before you this morning because we do not have a minister. Well, of course we do have a minister, but Reverend Broggan is . . . she is indisposed. She is . . . well, we all know where she is.

The lectionary calls for us to be reading about the Ten Commandments this morning. But I have here a note from Reverend Broggan, which she left in one of the empty casserole dishes. She had cleaned the dish out beautifully, by the way, it was just sparkling. Reverend Broggan says she doesn't want us to read the Ten Commandments today because if we haven't done anything about them after hearing them so many times before this, what's the point? I guess that might be true, though it doesn't sound quite right to me, coming from a minister. Of course I'm not up on all the latest theories of religion. For instance, I still think the Bible says two men of the same gender having . . . well, you know what they're having . . . together is just wrong, but apparently what this passage really refers to is an ancient practice of . . . well, you know what they were practising, and it says that people used to be able to actually go to the temple to hire these . . . friends . . . you know the word that sounds like "substitute" probably because the person is a substitute for who you should really be doing it with. Anyway, they used to have them in the temple for a reason that is not at all clear to me, and this passage is saying that that's not a thing we're supposed to do and I have to admit it's hard to argue with that.

As far as the Ten Commandments go, I know that no matter how many times a minister reads it to us, I've never really figured out the commandment that says, "Honour your father and mother." My mother passed away, of course, so I try to honour Paul's mother, but how do you do that when she insists on giving our son, Daniel, too much cake or getting her hair dyed orange again? I'm sorry to say it, Paul, your mother is a wonderful, Christian woman, but you have to admit she would test the patience of Job. I guess honouring people like that is what people call a "life's work," isn't it?

Instead of the Ten Commandments, Reverend Broggan wants me to tell you the story of Naaman the famous general, which is found in 2 Kings, Chapter 5. This is how the story goes:

Naaman was a famous general. A real soldier, you know, like you see on American television shows. I picture him a tall, broad-shouldered, kind of unshaven but still very healthy and handsome-looking man with nice clear blue eyes, except this is a Bible story so I suppose he must have had brown eyes. He was a Syrian. Does anyone know the colour of Syrian eyes? I think brown. All of the people in the Bible world were much browner generally than we are. I was very surprised to realize this because the picture of Jesus in our Sunday School rooms always showed him with the most beautiful, soulful blue eyes and kind of blond highlights in his hair. We know now, though, that he didn't really look that way. This is part of God's plan for our ever-growing acceptance of each other. Or, perhaps he did look that way after he got to heaven.

So, Naaman. I guess we don't know exactly what he looked like either, except that he was a great soldier. For his character, he was very practical and down-to-earth. I guess that makes sense for a general. You can't have someone who is all, "Oh, I don't really know what to do, I think I'll just look at the flowers for a while," or that kind of thing. When this story opens he's really doing very well being a general. He's doing that . . . the thing Paul says about golfers. Paul, honey, what is it you say about those golfers on television who are doing very well? Naaman was "at the top of his game." That's it. But you know, in Bible stories something always happens. I mean some of those people had the strangest things happen to them. It's like *General Hospital* where you just have to say, "I can't believe that happened!" even though it did, although that's a made-up thing, of course, and the Bible is real, though Reverend Broggan has explained to us that the stories in the Bible are possibly made up as well and just told to make us understand things better. Except for Jesus, of course.

So, Naaman. Now the thing that happens to Naaman when he's doing so well as a general is that he gets leprosy. Oh, that reminds me, the rummage sale will be held on the fourteenth, and the proceeds this year will go to agencies working to advance medicines for infectious diseases in Third World countries. Please try to bring in the best possible rummage you can find.

Now, Naaman. From what I've been able to gather, back in Bible times leprosy was just about the worst thing you could get if you were going to get something. You know there are all those stories about Jesus helping lepers by doing miracles for them. Leprosy was considered a judgment from God. Like AIDS used to be before normal people started to get it too. So Naaman naturally thought, "Why is God doing this to me? I have fought in God's army and done my job well, so why is this evil befalling me?" What he actually said, according to the Bible was, "Through me the Lord hath given deliverance unto Syria." I just love how they talked back then. What I don't quite understand is whether the Syrians were Jews or not. You would think so because the Old Testament is mostly about how God does good things to help the Jews like leading them into the promised land even though it probably meant someone else who was living there had a bad time. I guess that hasn't changed much today. But here I don't think these Syrians were Jews because Naaman's wife has a slave girl who is an "Israelite" who comes in a little later and that means the Syrians must have been against the Jews. I don't understand how the Lord was switching sides and not being in favour of the Jews in this story. Maybe this is one of the mysteries of the Bible. There never were any Jewish generals that I can remember. They were always prophets and high priests and slaves, things like that. Very specialized, you know, like now Jewish people are dentists and film directors. It's because they're a very scholarly people.

So, Naaman. He gets leprosy and he can't figure out why this would happen to him when everything has always gone fine and he thought he had God's favour to do what he was doing. Now this is the part where we're supposed to pause and think about what the character is really feeling. I mean he's this important general and he gets leprosy so he's going to become an outcast and have to live in a leprosy community an l not have a family or job or status or anything. Plus, he's going to die. It really could not be worse. It's like the time on *General Hospital* when Rachel catches Mac with Erica, plus her daughter elopes with that awful one, whatever his name was, and then she goes blind. Rachel does. This is like worse than the worse thing you can imagine happening to you. For Naaman, this would all be very hard because he was used to being so mainstream and celebrated.

So of course pretty soon people start to figure out that something's going on because, I don't know, Naaman starts to turn grey or something falls off. I guess nothing actually falls off because that's later, but his wife figures out that something is up and she suggests that they get help from a famous prophet, who was Jewish, you see, who lived in Samaria. Actually, this was his wife's servant girl's idea because she was Jewish, too, so she knew about this prophet. It doesn't say that they were related, just that she knew about him. The wife and the servant girl are the ones who come up with the bright idea of how to cure his leprosy. We don't know the name of Naaman's wife or the servant girl. I have to say that since Reverend Broggan mentioned about women in the Bible not usually having a name, it's really started to annoy me. I can tell you, my own mother who named me used to send cards addressed to Mrs. Paul Ketchie when we were first married and I told her more than once that I am not Paul Ketchie and she knows my name and I would like to be called by it. And Reverend Broggan has pointed out that this still happens because years from now people will be able to know the name of some man who brought down Enron but not his wife's name who raised their children and I will tell you which was a more important job. It just makes me mad. I think Reverend Broggan said that scholars are trying to address this, but I'd like to know how you do that because either the wife and the servant girl's names are down there or they're not, so what's left to address? It's not one of these silly feminist things that gets me on about it. I just think there should be credit where it's due.

So, Naaman. I guess he thinks he's got nothing to lose by seeing the prophet, and the king of Syria even writes him a letter to take to the king of Israel saying that he wants Naaman to get the best help they have available and Naaman goes off and delivers it. But the king of Israel thinks this is some kind of trick. He doesn't know how to cure someone of leprosy, so he thinks the king of Syria is just setting him up to look unhelpful and then attack him. It's just like the kind of thing you'd see in a James Bond movie. Isn't it interesting when you can see how a Bible story relates to your own life? I love that. So anyway, the king can't cure Naaman but the famous prophet, whose name was Elisha, who is not the same as Elijah, can you believe that? I thought they were the same person. So, Elisha, the other one, not the one with the crows, sends his own letter to the king of Israel and says this is not a problem, that he can cure Naaman's leprosy.

Naaman then goes to see Elisha who for some reason doesn't even come to the door of his house to see him. Isn't that strange? Naaman is at his door with a horse and chariot and maybe they saw that kind of thing all the time then, but really I think it's odd that he doesn't even come to the door. That's another one of those things we just don't understand, because stories about God are mysterious. Elisha sends out a messenger who tells Naaman that for him to be cured of the leprosy he has to go to the Jordan River and wash seven times and he'll be just fine.

Now here is the part where Naaman acts just like a man. He's been to the doctor. The prophet in this case. He's been told what to do. It's not all that complicated. Does he do it? No.

He complains about it. I think the writer of this story had men pegged exactly. I swear, it takes me a month to get Paul to the doctor no matter what he's coughing up and then he won't take the whole course of antibiotics because he says he's all better and he doesn't need them and you know the doctor always tells you to take them all. I would almost wonder if a woman didn't write this, except for leaving out the names of the wife and the servant girl, but maybe even a woman didn't think of those things back then. So, Naaman doesn't want to go. I will say, I looked on the map to see where the River Jordan actually is, and I think you'd have a better chance of catching leprosy than curing yourself of it from swimming there, but this was long ago so I assume it was cleaner even if they did wash in the river and dump bodies in it and whatnot. The thing is, this is not what Naaman wanted. He wanted Elijah, or no, it was the other one, to come out and see him and wave his arms around and call on God in some kind of impressive way and the leprosy would be gone. Plus, he thinks his own rivers, which are called Abana and Pharpar, are probably just as good to swim in if not better than the Jordan, which belongs to the Israelites. He just has to think he knows better, though he is not a prophet plus he's got leprosy. Instead he just gets mad and goes home.

You can imagine how happy Naaman's wife is about this. The Bible doesn't even tell us what she said, maybe because you don't print those things in a book which is holy, but the servants, who seem excellent, say to him if he'd been asked to do some big, difficult thing to get cured, he'd have done it, but instead all he has to do is this one little washing in the Jordan and he won't do it. This seems to work on Naaman and he goes to the River Jordan, where he could have just stopped on the way home in the first place and saved all this time and travel but no, he probably doesn't even think about what there is to do at home, he just makes another trip now and washes seven times and he's cured. Oh, and he says that the Israelite's God is the real God because he's cured, which is probably why this story is in a Jewish book. I hadn't thought of that before.

I don't have any idea why Reverend Broggan wanted me to read you the story of Naaman and his wife and servant whose names we don't know. This seems to me exactly the kind of story that we need a minister to explain to us. I mean, Naaman could have said the Israelite's god was the real one without all that information about seeing the king or not wanting to go to the River Jordan, I would think. I don't know, maybe this story is about how we're supposed to keep an open mind about how God can help us.

I wonder if that's it. I will say that I was very upset when Reverend Broggan said she wasn't going to be here today. We've already had one minister who . . . who became indisposed. But I also know that we don't choose to be ill. Our last minister was a lot like Naaman, if you ask me. He did lose his family and his job and then his life because of his illness. Maybe God didn't have a cure for him. Or maybe he knew what the cure was and he didn't want it. It did seem like he didn't want to be helped. I wouldn't have known how. Reverend Broggan doesn't have leprosy, of course, and I don't think she even drinks much, but clearly she is having some difficulty that we, or I'll speak for myself and say "I" don't understand. What I hope is that by this story she's telling us that she's asking for a cure. That seems to me the best that someone can do when they're having difficulties. I guess that and take the advice you're given when if comes. I, for one, am planning to do whatever I can to support Reverend Broggan while she finds out what it is she needs. This morning, I'm starting a sign-up sheet to help make casseroles. Anyone who has time should fill in a meal slot and make a casserole and bring it here to the church. We can just leave them on the step so we don't disturb her.

We're always being told that God works in mysterious ways and we're supposed to have trust and faith. I guess it's like the Ten Commandments. If we've heard this same thing over and over and aren't going to do anything about it, what's the point? I have faith that God will tell Reverend Broggan what she needs to cure herself and that Reverend Broggan will have the sense to do what she's told. I'm going to pray for it. Personally, I think prayers and casseroles go a long way.

December 2, 2002

Notes to myself:
1) Ritual smudging: Use much less sage. It is hard to surrender the soul to meditation when the damn fire alarm keeps going off every five minutes.

2) Consider words of Kelly's Buddhist guru, Lama Yeshe: "Realize that all beings want and need the same things. They are just seeking it through different ways." The man is an idiot. Who would want this? Perhaps the answer is to care less.

December 3, 2002

Notes to myself:
Blaise Pascal said, "All men's miseries derive from not being able to sit quiet in a room alone." That is so wrong. Misery is being forced to.
Possibly I am becoming a tad bitter.
Ironed sheets are OK. Maybe better if I actually ever slept anymore.

December 7, 2002
Note from Margaret Ketchie:

Dear Reverend Broggan,

I have read 2 Chronicles:8, but do not have a clue why you want me to talk on Sunday about all the things Solomon did to get ready to build the temple. It doesn't make sense. I also have to say that I am very busy at the moment looking after the people who are camping out on the front yard of the church. I hope you don't mind, I have been sharing some of the extra casseroles with them. Am trying to scare up some blankets and candles, and, well, I really am finding it a lot to do to take care of them and I don't have time to figure out what the Bible is trying to say. Please let me know who should speak instead, or if you don't I guess I will just have to figure out something.

Also, if you have any idea when you might be coming out again, it would be most helpful to know. There are tents being set up on the lawn now and the janitor is having a fit about what this will do to the grass. Not to rush you, of course. But just if you know. I will deal with the janitor if need be.

I hope you are well,
Margaret Ketchie

December 8, 2002

Notes to myself:
1) Under no circumstances must I scream. If I scream someone is sure to break down the door and come in and it will all be over. It'll be a miracle if they don't do it anyway.
2) This is not insane. Or maybe it is, but insane is just another way of looking at things.
3) When my predecessor glued shells onto this wall, did he think "just one more"? One more tiny, perfect spiral until the spirals were a wheel and the wheel the size of a pomegranate? Then across the whole wall. Then another. The light is so clear this afternoon, it looks like a lagoon. The shells are buried deep in a crystal pool of rose water. Kit could write about this and make it very beautiful and mysterious and like it made sense in some way. I will ask her to write something about it when she calls. Something about water and fire, empty shells and pomegranates

and enough love. Nature etching her Celtic knots onto the backs of tiny creatures. The shells are sea gems today.

4) I remember reading somewhere that the flower for this month is the chrysanthemum, the flower of the dead. But I read in one of the books Kelly sent that where Buddha walked, white chrysanthemums sprang up in his footprints. Don't you think that's just a different way of seeing the same thing? The flower book said that appropriate magic for this month is devotions to the dead, automatic writing, crystal ball gazing, working with trance state, and divination. How the hell do I remember all that when I've almost forgotten what day it is? This is a propitious time for seeking guidance and prophecies. If God won't speak to me, maybe someone else will. I think Mark is wrong about the devil, but beyond that I'm past the point of being picky.

December 9

Notes to myself:

1) I am so bored I could scream.

2) Ditto.

3) Must remember not to actually do that.

4) Casseroles do not take the place of coffee.

5) There is a reason why Kit has not called me, even though I asked her to. I just don't know what it is.

6) Mark has not become too religious to be saved.

7) There is a reason why they keep shoving newspaper clippings through my mail slot.

8) Could try calling McNelly again and make him go get Kit.

9) Could try reading newspaper clippings.

10) Mark may be too religious to be saved.

11) What are we saved from?

12) It is OK not to answer Kelly and David's calls. I do not have to be a mother all the time.

13) I think it's silly that the number thirteen is left out because it's bad luck when everyone knows that fourteen is just the same thing anyway.

14) Maybe fourteen is just another way of seeing the same thing.

15) I am not going to turn on the TV anymore. The last time I did I swear I saw Margaret Ketchie being interviewed. Maybe it was a cooking show.

At night, the walls of the house vibrate with sound. I think, after dark, people are chanting outside. When the house vibrates the door to the shell room won't stay closed.

December 12

Notes to myself:

I spend my time in this room. Sun washes over me when there is sun. By day, I bob and float amid opals. At night, I burrow deep with my snails into inky darkness and await the light once more.

If there is no God, there's no reason to go back to the world. I remember Kit once saying, "The cruelest thing is to be granted awareness but not faith." No Kit, the cruelest thing is to be granted faith but not purpose.

It would have been good if Kit had called. Or better still, got on a plane and come out here. I need something to hold onto.

I am so afraid.

Notes to Kit:

Where do you think all the old gods go? Odin, who hung on a tree three thousand years before Jesus, to bring wisdom to his people? Where did he go? Diana, the virgin goddess before Mary? Where? They are all just stories now. I have told people that knowing the stories that come before our own doesn't make ours less important. It means there's something there we need to hear over and over. Something vital, essential, that speaks to the core of us at every time and place. But where do you think our god will go, now that we need to be told something new?

It was September when I came here. Wet leaves blew against the screen door. The air in the hallways had the sour odour of whisky on an old man's breath. The church janitor told me that they removed seventy-eight Johnny Walker bottles from this room when my predecessor died. I put down my suitcase, sat down on the hall staircase, and wept.

Notes to myself:

If the phone rings, it will not be Kit. I do not answer the phone. I do not iron or clean or read or think. Light flickers, I can hear chanting outside every night now. I smell rosemary water, but it might just be the rain. I can no longer distinguish between sunlight and stars. Casserole dishes bloom like mushrooms on the front porch. I hear the chanting and smell rosemary.

"It is the glory of God to conceal things but the glory of kings to search things out." Proverbs 22: verse . . . something. It sounds like some kind of child's treasure hunt.

At night, I feel the energy of bodies pressed close to the

wall outside. Sometimes the heat of the bonfires. The chanting has become soothing. The smell of death is white. Sparkling white, like moonlight on the spiral backs of empty snail shells. Death smells like rosemary and flames and water. Sylvia Plath said that once you have children, suicide is no longer an option. Then she stuck her head in a gas oven. What happens to a woman when she stops doing the mother thing? The mother thing is not always enough to keep us from being ourselves. Or leaving ourselves. Maybe death is just another way of seeing the same thing. Rain is sunlight and stars. I thought death would be deep purple, like healing amethyst stones, but that's just what they tell you. It's sunlight and white stars on my study wall.

Despair was never yet so deep
In sinking, as in seeming
Despair is hope just dropped asleep,
For better chance of dreaming.

Ruth

Ruth

Ruth

And not.

Now we can begin.

Book Two

ONE

Tuesday, April 13, 2004

No letter from Ruth today. No letters at all since January. Just at the point when everyone stops caring, the ice splits and boats come again. Small craft first, weaving through a shifting obstacle course of bobbing mounds of frozen ocean, reminding us with a start that there is a world beyond the ice and fog. Letters only matter when they are from Ruth. It's hard to figure out why everyone else gets so excited about theirs.

I am sitting on my front verandah marking the passage of time. It is officially "Time of Enough Warmth," by which I mean it is temperate enough to sit in the little screened-in box I call a front porch, wrapped in a down comforter, warming my hands with fresh coffee. I am always glad when "Time of Enough Warmth" arrives. Being able to use my verandah increases my living space twofold.

This morning the sun slanted into the bedroom window at just the right angle to illuminate my bedroom clock. A really great clock made from a cross-section of wood with a picture of the Last Supper shellacked on it. I tell the women who come here that the wood was the last of an old growth forest. Someday, one of them is bound to get it.

After breakfast, I performed the ritual "Removal of the Tarp." Always a moving ceremony. When the plastic comes down from the porch windows I can see Gerrard's house across the way. Terrifies him. Sends him scuttling back into the dark and damp of his house, having just been released into the air after a long winter. I could see as I pulled down the first sheet of plastic that he'd already started hiding the garden gnomes he'd optimistically placed among his decorative rock garden yesterday. As if that will do him any good. I made another cup of coffee and stood in the now open verandah to inventory the view. Everything is still there. Fir trees tumbling down rocks into ocean. Some of them cling to boulders by a single root, the soil washed away by the rains of a hundred springs. They will never fall. Not for another hundred years at any rate, when the rest of the earth at last dissolves into saltwater. This island is slowly eroding into the sea. I've suggested that the anthem of our island church should be "Nearer My Cod to Thee."

A ferry far in the distance slides off to Vancouver. Still weeks before they begin their watery plod to our wharf. The return of the ferries also marks time here. Busy and important in the summer, trading neighbours and tourists at the dock. Slowing to a trickle like sap in autumn. Finally, the last one for the winter slogging off into grey waters gathering ice. Neighbours down at the store regretfully announce the departure, "The last one's just left," only to see one more wading in from the mists. "Why don't they leave us alone," someone will say by late November.

I came to this island because it discouraged the world. But, when I see the last ferry move off into the distance, soon lost forever, or until next spring, which is the same thing here, I have a sudden urge to run after it. Down the rock hill, along the path by Deirdre's shack and the boat houses, all the way to the end of the pier, calling it back. *Take me too.* I can't bear the silence again, can't bear shutting up the verandah when it's too cold even to sit wrapped in a blanket. I can't be alone here for one more winter or hour.

I am always glad that by that time the boat is far out at sea. Perhaps already vanished in the distance. There is no chance of them hearing my call.

Saturday, April 17, 2004

Today, I am reflecting on the question of loss. I am planning to let it consume me entirely so that I will have not a single brain cell available to reflect on the question of procrastination. This is a good day for woolgathering, not working. As so many are.

Loss. As in losing things. Things being gone. Usually we think of loss as misfortune. But the tarp is gone and now I can see Gerrard placing a gnome behind a boulder where he thinks I won't see it. The loss of the tarp is unfortunate for Gerrard. If I were working today I would try to find poetry in loss, pretend there was meaning and that I knew it. Nothing springs to mind except, "You should be working." Which must be avoided. Besides, I am working. No one understands how much of the creative process looks exactly like doing nothing at all. Or like reading trashy novels. Or finding ways to agitate Gerrard. How can poetry spring from the observation of the everyday unless I spend many, many hours drinking coffee and doing crosswords? Artists are continually misunderstood.

Loss. If it were fall I could do a "trappings of youth/gently into that good night" sort of thing, but nothing is lost in the passing of winter. Except, of course, the tarp. Someone wise wrote, "With every loss comes something found." I think it was probably me. I've gained a view and a blanket. And that gnome before nightfall if I have anything to do with it.

Cold in the walls and the floor. It will take a month of slanting, increasing sunlight before they are merely cool to the touch. I sit huddled in a Hudson's Bay blanket and drink instant coffee. No real coffee again until the first ferry comes. No room for such luxuries in the small store of goods that come over by snowmobile. Time is kind to us though. By January we've lost the memory of fresh brewed and this dingy water seems fine. Now, if time would only do the same for memories that matter.

Clouds begin to collect in the distance. The sunlight will not last. Soon rain will start and it will rain forever. So many things are forever on this island. Winter. Then the rain. The view. Me watching the view. Waiting for the "Time of Enough Warmth" to return. Gerrard's hope and gardens. These things are forever. Not Ruth. I tell myself that, and it's as if I'm running for the ferry again. Down the hill, across Deirdre's path, my heart sharp as my breath, to the dock, to the dock, to the dock, and I think, "Don't leave me," for God's sake, I almost pray, "Don't leave me with no one to love." This time, when I hit the pier, the ferry has not already left. It was never there.

Sunday, April 18

These few days of spring bring neighbours out of hibernation, scattering across rocks and bushes the watercolour painting, hemp plant hangers, shelled boxes and wool dreamcatchers made to keep them sane during the winter. Can't say it works. There are a few real artists on the island. People who do notable things on canvas or in stone. They are treated very badly by the crafters and poorer artists as a matter of principle. Egalitarianism is a sacred principle on this island, requiring the most delicate of balancing acts. The result being that the potters and flower soap-makers are treated with more respect than they deserve at the general store, and the recognized artists sometimes can't get served. I consider myself the most badly treated of all, but this may not have much to do with my art.

The tarp is down, the screens are now cleaned. I have had a talk with Gerrard about whether or not we will fence our property line this year. No one fences their property line, but I know Gerrard spends the winter months huddled like a hobbit in his den, crouched over his garden catalogues, dreaming of a barricade the size of the Jerusalem wall. As if that would stop me.

Gerrard titters like a chickadee about the plants and seeds he's ordered this year. Tiny green breaths of life destined to be nurtured and encouraged under his devoted care, which often wind up in a Mason jar on my verandah. He asks me not to take *all* the lilies this year. I might not. He asks if my worms were healthy this winter. He asks if Ruth is coming again this summer because he has forgotten. I tell him I fed my worms to the seagulls in February, trashed my Enviro-clean waste disposal and installed a pipe that directs sewage into the water cistern. Stupid. It'll be all over the island in an hour. And some people will believe it.

Reflecting on loss proves less desirable than avoiding work. From my little front room off the verandah, I write stories and poems, word pictures that conjure up the features and spirits of

ANNE HINES

people I have never known, women I have never slept with. Everyone on the island tries to recognize themselves in the poems and stories. McNelly wagging a finger at me across the counter in the general store and drawling joyfully, "You've been putting me in a story again, lass." McNelly is from the Bronx. He came here ten years ago for a week and never went home, acquiring first an accent then a general store. Perhaps he never went home because he would no longer have been comprehensible to anyone in New York. He is not always comprehensible to anyone here, as the accent he chose is Maritime and we are on the west coast.

Sometimes I write scathingly witty and insightful analysis of the world and what I find wrong with people in general. This is an excellent area of writing to be in. I am never short of material. *Time* magazine touted me "this generation's most versatile author," which I think is far more accurate than suggestions that I get bored quickly. I also write plays, but *Time* didn't mention that. My agent says she begged them not to. "The reason you should not write plays, Kit," she says, "is that you have never grasped the concept that successful dialogue involves listening." Generally, I just ignore her when she says that kind of thing.

I write my things, seal them in an envelope and then put them into a box that will be delivered to the mainland. Much, I have come to feel, like putting a message in a bottle and releasing it into the surf. The envelopes float over the ocean, and weeks later, by the magic of mermaids, or Canada Post, cheques float back. I turn these pieces of paper into packaged food and coffee at the general store. It's the one way of the world with which I find no fault.

Monday

Today, I put the blanket around my shoulders and find myself, after all, trying to draw a word picture of Ruth and loss. Of Ruth and presence. The two intermingle, the remains of love indistinguishable from the flower of it. Desire. Fear. The only thing no longer present is the object of love. And hope, of course.

The morning passes in a breath of cool air.

Wednesday

Sitting on my front porch, watching the afternoon sun tint the white frosted ocean to candy floss pink. Up the path comes Deirdre, leading a woman in city clothes, who claims she has permission to come and interview me about my work. I was ready to head right down to the store and call Lisa to complain that no one ever asks me about these things, except that it somehow always turns out that she did.

I think discussing my work should mean talking about taking down the tarp or tending the worm box. The word pictures don't usually feel like work. Railing at the world never does. I call it work though because it's impressive. Really, it's simply offerings required by the great cheque gods in order to make food and instant coffee appear. The people who are sent to interview me do not like it when I talk like that. They want to find me wise as my work. They know nothing about writers.

The interviewer that came this time is from a Montreal magazine. She arrived on the island wearing high heels, no coat. She had some cloth thing on that she called a coat but which

ANNE HINES

allowed you to see that there was a person inside it, and, believe me, around here that does not cut it as a coat.

Up she comes, taking the wrong street, the paved road instead of the unpaved one. Well, all right, they're both unpaved now, but one of them was paved in 1934 when, incredibly, the residents of this island voted for the Member of Parliament who actually got in. They were rewarded for this extraordinary act of conformity with one paved road, a gesture made not a whit less beneficent by the fact that this island has no cars. As it turned out, no one walked on the paved road either, there being a natural suspicion among the neighbours about accepting government favours. We never did vote again for the official who got elected. Winters and springs eventually dissolved the asphalt into grass and rubble once more. But you can tell it was paved once. Or you could have, had there not been a drift of new snow.

The journalist finally found me. Deirdre led her up by the hand, the two of them slipping together over the frost-slicked rocks. The high heels were ruined. The journalist was shaking all over, having been driven over from the next island by one of the Ray boys on his snowmobile. She huddled near the fire. In spite of sniffling deeply, she was glowing like my wood stove.

"I just love your work, Ms. Sheppard. I mean, I *love* it. I've read everything you've written. The poetry, the short stories, even the social criticism. I particularly love when you write something that speaks to the divine in all women. It's so . . . well, you really know what women want."

Happily, this is true.

She launches into the Questions.

"What motivates you to write?"

"I wish to eat and drink coffee."

"I mean, what motivates you to write such . . . with such insight and beauty?"

"I wish to drink good-quality coffee."

A pause. This is not what she expected.

"What's the one thing you'd do to make the world a better place?"

"You'd be sitting over here."

She almost drops her recorder. This could possibly be way more fun than I thought.

"Do you take your characters from real people?"

"Yes, I just call it fiction so I'll be eligible for awards."

"What word would you say best describes your work?"

"Peerless."

"Have you ever considered writing a novel?"

"A novelist is simply an inefficient writer."

Another pause. The journalist is confused.

"But . . . there are some great novels."

"Who told you that?"

"Everyone knows there are great novels . . . I mean, *Pride and Prejudice, East of Eden, Bridget Jones's Diary* . . . "

"Let me ask you something." I move my chair forward a bit, toward her. I gaze into her eyes. As if she were the only person alive. I sigh a wistful, half sigh that speaks of a lifetime of buried pain, loneliness, courage. Then I say softly, very softly, to her alone in the whole world: "If you read a Truth, something you know in the core of your being to be real, something that wakens in you what it is to be truly human, to feel and to breathe, to yearn, to love, wouldn't you know that truth immediately? Wouldn't you know it in less than ten words?"

"I . . . but I . . . but your poetry is more ten words. Your stories are more . . . "

Now I smile in that way that allows them to feel they've finally found the writer they fell in love with in my work. "Of course. I provide some commentary."

She ended up staying the night, so the whole thing turned out better than a lot of these interviews. When she left for the wharf in the morning, hoping to find someone other than the Rays to take her back across the ice, she asked me to get e-mail, or to call her, or to keep in touch in other ways that would simply ruin the memory of a perfectly pleasant night together. Also, it would mean having to run a line of some sort over from Gerrard's place. Thirty yards is thirty yards.

Monday, April 26, 2004

A letter from Ruth today.

The ice broke this morning. It has been heaving for days now, shot through with thin spider veins of black water. Yesterday the temperature soared to 4°C and the entire white plain erupted and split apart. This annual occurrence is cause for celebration among the neighbours. First sighting of an expanse of open water at the dock and the Thin Ice Festival begins. A pitiful affair. Breakup can start any time from March to June so there's no way to really plan anything except rescuing whichever Ray boy had to try one more ride on his snowmobile over the fracturing ice. One year, someone suggested marking the occasion by bringing a clown over from the mainland to entertain the kiddies, but there were fears he'd end up strapped to the back of a snowmobile, sunk in ten feet of water off the end of the wharf. A possibility that makes me suggest the clown every year.

Since there's no way to plan anything in advance, a strange kind of custom has developed to mark the breakup of the ice. A ritual of forced beneficence. Mandatory magnanimity. Conscripted kindness. We're all required to do one Nice Thing for someone else. There is really no way to tie in such an act with an event celebrating dissolving ice, though our Committee for Perpetual Cheerfulness waxes lyrical at the opening ceremony about re-establishing the "flow" of goodwill among neighbours with bits about global warming and spring fertility thrown in for good measure. I've never been able to follow it, but I go because someone always brings fresh muffins. Personally, I think there may be something in the idea that we've been huddled in our houses like animals in caves for five months and have to remind ourselves of what's required to be around other humans, but, to my mind, that does not necessarily translate into pleasantry. For some, taking a good long shower would be enough.

The main problem with the Thin Ice Festival is not the lack of planning or logic behind it, but the mental state of most of the participants. It's a fact of life here that we have a few basket cases among the neighbours. Not dangerous. Not psychotic, at least not what gets in your way, generally, if you don't mind just choosing another aisle at the general store when someone is there temporarily zoned out in contemplation of the colours on a cereal box. But if you listen to the talk at the store, or the Town Hall, most people here are nut cases. Gerrard, for instance, may coax a garden out of rocks, a garden which rivals

ANNE HINES

a Matisse, but he arranges his plastic gnomes in positions that give the tourists pause. Deirdre, who is my next neighbour just down the path toward the water, has a running commentary going on with fairies most of the time, and I'm not talking about the boats that come and go from the wharf. So really, if you take a bunch of people who are a little off at the edges anyway, have just been through a long winter, and ask them to act, well, like people, ask them to do something nice for each other, which requires skills most of us don't have much of at the best of times but certainly let slip over the winter, skills like, oh social interaction for instance, well, suffice it to say that things do not always go well. A number of neighbours make arrangements to go Off Island during the Thin Ice Festival; it's just safer.

Mostly, it's harmless stuff that happens, like the year Deirdre put a new coat of paint on Ian Duncan's shutters, which was charming, and Ian had a lot of chances to admire them since he had to sleep outside all summer on account of his windows being painted shut. Sometimes, though, it gets a little hairier, like the time the Ray boys decided to torch Gill Radley's outhouse. I'm not saying that wasn't an act of kindness, because it definitely was, though not necessarily to Gill Radley. It would have been even better if the boys had stopped to consider whether there was enough open water at the dock to make it possible to get the two hundred buckets of water we needed to put the fire out. Also, if Gill Radley hadn't been using his outhouse at the time.

Generally though, everybody's act of kindness is confined to whatever's quickest. A scrum of neighbours collects at the general store, waiting to pounce on anyone emerging with groceries that could be toted home for them. The neighbours amuse themselves while they're waiting by suggesting new items to add to the "Kit List." After I got banned from the store for a week for sharing my very interesting and insightful views on the Quebec separation issue, views which, I might add, everyone else in the country paid good money to read about in *Maclean's*, McNelly put up a list of topics that I may not venture an opinion on if I want to come into the store. He adds to this list on what I consider to be an unnecessarily frequent basis. At the moment, I'm not allowed to talk about politics, Gerrard's sexual orientation, anyone else's sexual orientation, any topic to do with other people, and dolphins. What the hell did I ever say about dolphins?

Sitting on the front step, listening to how the ice echoes, wondering if talking to Gerrard for a half-hour without calling him a perverted old tart could count as my Nice Thing. In my books, it's pretty damned angelic. Deirdre comes up the path. Not a pleasant sight at any time, but during the Thin Ice Festival, it's downright alarming. She has no paint cans.

"*Caid mille faid*, Kit!"

"Get away from me, Deirdre."

"*Caid mille faid*. That's Gaelic for 'May all your ice be thin.'"

"No, it isn't."

"It isn't? I've been saying it to everyone."

"Did they look at you funny?"

"About the same."

"What do you want, Deirdre?"

"You're my Nice Thing, Kit!"

"Forget it."

"You are! I've decided. You're my Nice Thing this year."

"I don't want to be your Nice Thing."

"You have to be. I've been planning this for months."

She rummages around under her coat in the copious pockets of one of those smock dresses she's always wearing. She beams.

"This is for you! A letter!"

"We haven't had mail in three weeks."

"I know. I saved it. McNelly gave it to me to bring to you, so I saved it so this could be my Nice Thing."

"You saved it for three weeks?"

"No, silly. Since last December. Well, I have to go report my Nice Thing to the committee. What's your Nice Thing this year, Kit?"

"I'm going to refrain from strangling every idiot on this island."

"I don't think the committee will accept that. You used it last year."

The letter was from Ruth, saying it was time for us to let go. I left it inside and went to do something nice for someone. By the end of the day, several people were not speaking to me.

April 27

My mother was always on at me about something: *Stay in school. Not that school. Don't sleep with women. If you have to sleep with women, don't let my friends find out. Stop sleeping with my friends. Get a job.* I did that. *A writer? Get a real job. Phone Ruth Chadwick. Who? Chadwick. She's Ruth Broggan now. You remember, your father and her father were in the Lions Club together in Port Hope.* I don't remember Port Hope. *Call her. I saw her mother today. Ruth's living in Toronto now and she doesn't know anyone. She wants to hear from you. She wants you to call.*

I called. She had no idea who I was.

"Who? Just a minute, sorry. The baby just got up from his . . . no, Kelly, sweetie, on the newspaper not the table. On the . . . get a cloth, honey. A cloth. Cloth. Never mind, Mommy will get it . . . I'm sorry, who?"

"Kit Sheppard. We knew each other at school. In Port Hope."

"Oh God. I've forgotten Port Hope."

I went over to drink coffee. When I left, I was in love.

Ruth Broggan is a luminescent being. She grocery shops. She knows where things are kept and how to do things and how to fix things if they don't do what they are supposed to do. She arranges people and things so that more things happen. She spreads out her hands and from them flow endless tissues to wipe runny noses, art supplies for school projects and, most miraculous of all, unfettered, unconditional love. Where Ruth passes, bake sales and used clothing drives spring into being. Groups of children are transported seemingly without effort to soccer tournaments and field trips, swarms of North Toronto mothers mystically separate themselves to form car pools and fundraising committees. The universe stirs itself into life and activity. To my mind, the only difference between Ruth and God is that after six days, God needed a rest.

Once Ruth and I arranged to meet at a restaurant and when I got there she was gone.

"Kit, you were over an hour late. If I say two o'clock, it has to be two o'clock. Maybe two-fifteen or two-twenty-five if you've been in a near-fatal car crash. I have library books to get back by three ten, ballet costumes to pick up at three-twenty, and I pick Kelly up at school at three-thirty."

"Do the books and costumes some other time."

"There isn't another time. I love seeing you, Kit, but I don't have an hour to sit waiting in a restaurant. Next time, you come to my place. I can do a phone tree if you're late."

So, I would go there. I would sit on a high stool at the kitchen counter with my cup of coffee, which Ruth had made, the new baby, David, screeching with joy from some kind of bouncing contraption in a doorway, Kelly laying out dolls in a careful line across the floor. Then, the two of them racing through the house, tracking toys in their wake. Soccer shoes and spelling tests. School projects on the life cycle of bees. David's bristol-board map of Canada, hand-drawn, with Manitoba missing.

"Why can't I hand it in like this? Kit says no one will care."

I am great with kids.

"Kit, Mom says that the main export of the United States *isn't* Bible-thumping, homophobic rednecks."

"Your mom is right, Kelly. They all stay home."

Then geography tests, calculus and Shakespeare.

"Kelly, honey, I know what Kit told you about her work, but I don't think your teacher will embrace an essay entitled *William Shakespeare: History's Second Greatest Playwright.*

David elated over making the football team. Kelly red-faced and teary over her first failed love. "Kelly, love falls into two categories," I consoled her, "brief and painful, or long and painful. You'll look back on this as the easy one." University brochures. A prom dress spread out like a sea of turquoise foam, the pins showing where Ruth would close the seams. Ruth's hands on each moment, each pulse, each heart, each tear, entirely available to who was in need.

When Kyle was there, he would come home to a clean house, dinner gently bubbling on the stove, the debris of the day already ticketed and stored away. I felt sorry for him then. Not to see how beautiful she was, knee-deep in celery chopped slant-ways, glue sticks, someone on the phone imploring her to make more things happen. Effortlessly turning the great wheel of all their lives.

I would ride my bike up the long hill that used to bank the lake of our city, to stay for dinner if Kyle was not home and she was lonely, or just sit with my coffee, and then ride back downtown. At night I would cry myself to sleep for love of her. I lied to my lover at the time that I'd had that dream again where I have to write something to suit popular taste.

This night after Ruth's letter stretches forever.

April 29

This morning, Gerrard pads over to ask who the letter was from. From my mother, I say. She, of course, is gone too.

Based on the success of this year's Thin Ice Festival (no one was hurt), the committee has decided to put on a festival of storytelling to entertain the tourists when they arrive. Gerrard's eyes are moist with artistic fervour. He says I will be asked to submit a story, being that I am a famous writer and all. I tell him the word pictures I create are not like the stories that people will be telling at this festival, in that they are not inane and incomprehensible. Maybe I'll go Off Island for a while. I wonder if it's too late to accept one of the speaking or reading invitations I've ignored since last fall, if I can still find them.

I take my blanket out to the front step of my verandah to look at the sea. Deirdre drifts in this direction, calling up the path to say she's going to the storytelling auditions. She forgets and wanders back down toward the wharf.

I am feeling low enough today that I decide to go and watch the auditions. Possibly, there will be muffins. The Town Hall is an echoing barn, damp and smelling of fish. Gerrard is up first. He remembers the title of his story and nothing else. One of the Ray boys wants to use this as a forum for complaining about the hour restrictions on snowmobiling and is shouted down. Carol Blass performs a story she wrote, which was read on CBC radio about ten years ago and by Carol at every community event ever since. There's no reason for Carol to read it, really, as any one of us could recite the damn thing word for word by now. The story is very earnest and very sincere, about Saskatchewan and snow. McNelly stands up next with "My Experiences in a General Store." This should be good. Maybe he'll "out" someone's *People* magazine habit.

"I remember the day Kit comes in for some instant coffee. Now, you'll all need to know two things here. First, Kit never comes in for coffee until she's been out for a few days and made sure that everyone around her is out too so there's none left to borrow. Loaves and fishes faith, our Kit has, she's always sure she'll find enough to fill one more pot. Second thing to know here is that, at the time, she's having trouble with one of her new poems. I know that for sure, 'cause there's not too many times when Kit is not having some trouble with a new poem.

Carpin' and complainin' she is to anybody who'll listen and a few more who won't. You'll all know what I mean. But today when she comes in, there's something different. She's quiet. Not rantin' about the weather or the PCs or the price of milk. Just, 'Some coffee, please.'"

I always say please.

"She never says please, so you know there's something up right there. I say, 'Well, Kit, I guess your writing must be going OK for you now.' And she says, 'No, it's not going at all. I just decided to give up writing for good. You can call up the Canada Council and tell them someone else can have the money for once.'"

This is such a lie. I have not applied for a Canada Council grant in ten years. Not a regular one. I get money every year, of course, to keep me writing. What the hell is it for, anyway? This story is pointless. I can't figure out why everyone else is enjoying it so much.

"Well, so, I says, 'That's going to be something then, isn't it? You not writing!' And we stand there and shake our heads for a while. Then she takes her coffee and goes. Three or four days later she comes in for another jar of coffee. I wait till she's finished kicking Buddy out of the way."

Buddy is his kid.

"'Kit, why don't you buy a few jars at a time? Then you won't have to come down so often.'"

Laughter.

"'Well, I might as well come down,' she says, 'since I've given up writing forever.' So, this goes on for another five or six days, with her mopin' and moonin' around, telling anyone she can how she's really decided to give up writing and isn't it a terrible thing for us all. It felt like months. Finally, when we're going to have to put 'Any talk at all about writing or not writing' on the Kit List, which I really didn't like to do because it means having to start another page, Deirdre pipes up that she's going up to Kit's house and have a talk with her and see if she can cheer her up a bit."

Deirdre has found her way into the hall. She is perched on a stray kitchen stool, macraméing something that looks like a groundsheet from old fish nets. She does not look up.

"I say, 'Well, thank goodness for goodness, because none of us will make it through another week with Kit fussing and mewling and whinin' and all.'"

This is a travesty. I have never mewled. I have, possibly, on very appropriate occasions and with genuine provocation, whined. Everyone is slapping each other on the back now, grinning and nodding. I could kick them all.

"So up goes Deirdre. Into the lion's den, as they say. She's gone one hour, then two, then it's most of the afternoon and she's still gone and we've been closed for lunch and opened again and all. Finally, it's nearly glommin' and there comes Deirdre in the door of the store, smiling like she spent the day pickin' berries. 'Kit's just fine now,' she says, 'By the time I left she was asking me if I had enough brains to not fall over.' So, we all says, 'Well, what did you say to her?'"

This is complete lies. I will sue everyone.

"'I said she shouldn't worry if she gives up writing forever, because even without her doing that the sun will still shine, the world will still turn round and people will get on with their lives.'"

"'So, how come it took six hours?'"

"'She didn't believe me.'"

Shouts of laughter. Applause. I stay for another few minutes to prove that I am not totally humiliated and do not think McNelly is a steaming rat turd, then go home, not stopping to pick up coffee at the store, which I really need. Later, I hear music coming from the hall. I write an evil, evil word picture using everyone's real name, and go to bed early.

Saturday, May 1, 2004

When Kyle left Ruth, I was the first person she called.

"Maybe he just went golfing."

"It's February, Kit. There's two feet of snow out there. He's not golfing. He's gone."

Her voice told me that this was a bad thing.

"Do you want me to come up?"

"Yes, yes please, come up."

So, I finished my work and got some groceries, and then I had a dentist appointment, which was kind of ironic if you think about it, and the anesthetic made me feel a little funny so I had a nap, and then I was out of it when I got up, so I watched some TV and went to bed. A couple of days later, bright and early, I went up to Ruth's place. She was gone. The woman next door said she thought Ruth had taken the kids to her mother's place in Port Hope. Why the hell did she tell me to come up then? I waited a few days to see if she would come back, and then I called her.

"When are you coming home?"

"I don't know. I don't know what I'm doing ten minutes from now. I can't think about it."

"Don't the kids have school?"

"I told them we're taking a break. They can study for their exams here."

"You should come and stay with me. The kids can live with Kyle."

"Look, Kit, I'll call you when I figure out what I'm doing, OK?"

"I don't think I can wait that long."

"I'll call you."

I didn't hear from her for eight years.

Sunday, May 2

The rain holds off and the sun continues to return by inches. Every morning when I get up and look through where the plastic used to be, another small patch of my walk is illuminated.

Went down to the general store today, in need of company. The storytelling festival is off, apparently. Everybody heard each other's stories and that was enough. Not a lot of news. Someone wants to open a B&B. Neighbours are afraid for the eco-toilet system if tourists start staying overnight. "The worms, what about the worms?" they all moan. We are enthusiastic about our worms here. There was a movement once, if I can call it that, to designate a Worm Appreciation Day. Nobody could figure out exactly what that would entail. Possibly eating more fibre. Eventually, it was decided that as long as dried fruit is readily available on the island, every day is Worm Appreciation Day. Deirdre claims to have named every one of hers. The worms, that is.

Stayed at the general store all afternoon. Drinking coffee. No worries for my worms. I said my coffee maker was broken.

Everyone says the same thing when they feel like hanging out at
the store. The only decent thing the neighbours ever did was not
to point out that I don't have electricity. I think they really like
having me there. Livens things up. Went home in a thin, cold,
five o'clock light and the first beads of rain. Put on a good fire.
And watched Ruth's letter glow.

Monday

When Ruth finally called I had moved into a new place, one I
owned this time, in the Annex. Everybody talks about buying a
house like it's such a chore. I walked into that one, it was empty,
there was a room to work in and a room to sleep in and a bunch
of other rooms and that was that.

Ruth didn't actually call. We met on the street. I think I had
just started living with the Anthropology Student. I was in a
restaurant having lunch with her and arguing about something.
Or maybe I was having lunch with that actress, so the fight with
the Anthropology Student would have come later. I explained
very rationally the philosophical concept of deepening our pri-
mary relationship through thoughtful, caring associations with
secondary partners, and she yelled, "The problem with
polyamoury, Kit, is that it's really hard to tell it apart from just
sleeping around." I might have got away with the "Poets are
nonmonogamous by nature," if it weren't for Elizabeth-Frigid-
Barrett-Tight-Ass-Browning. That's probably what made her
sick. I saw Ruth walk by outside, so I ran out onto the sidewalk,
called her name, and she stopped and turned around and smiled
at me. Just like nothing had ever happened. Like she'd never
walked out and deserted me. I didn't care. I forgave her on the

spot. We talked about a couple of things, I don't remember. She said she'd call me.

I walked home somehow, like I was flying. Didn't remember till an hour later that I should have gone back into the restaurant, at least to pay part of the bill. The Anthropology Student came home around then. That must have been when the fight started.

Ruth called a week later. Which was good 'cause I'd been making up all kinds of excuses for not leaving the house, and I was running low on everything, even using writing paper in the bathroom although I did not use the Anthropology Student's Goddamned thesis like she said. Maybe a draft page.

Ruth called.

"Where have you been? It's been eight years!"

"I've been getting my life together, Kit."

"For eight years? God, I cleaned out my filing cabinet and tossed my dead underwear once and it took twenty minutes."

"I've been getting my emotional and spiritual life together."

"Oh." I figured there was murky water ahead. "How are the kids doing at university?"

"They're both finished university."

"Oh." I had a feeling this wasn't going well somehow.

"David's selling computer software in Calgary and Kelly's moved to Halifax. She's a Reiki practitioner."

There was some silence. I could think of several things to say about Reiki practitioners, but I didn't think any of them would be well received.

"I read one of your poems in the *Atlantic Monthly*. It was wonderful."

"Yeah, it was."

"Kit, I've missed you."

"I love you too. When can you come over?"

"I'm the minister at a church in Markham now. I don't get downtown very often."

"That sounds really, really interesting. Come over and tell me about it."

Silence again.

"Kit, I've missed you. I've missed your . . . I've missed . . . whatever it about us that just seems to connect."

(Yes! Yes!)

"But nothing has changed. I mean, I have, so I guess how I love you must have . . . "

(Yes! Yes! Yes!)

"But, what I want is . . . still not what you want."

"What I want is for you to dump whatever you're doing out there in the suburbs and come live with me forever."

Another pause. I thought it was a nice, cozy, anticipating-good-things kind of pause which might be followed by Ruth suggesting that she call a moving company.

"Listen, Kit, maybe we could have a coffee sometime. I have to come down to Church House in a few weeks. Maybe then."

"What is this? Are you leaving me again?"

"I want to have coffee. I don't want to move in with you. I do want to have coffee. How is that leaving you? Look, why don't you . . . tell me about your new house?"

We talked about the renovations to my workroom, made a plan to get together in two weeks, and I went shopping for toilet paper and orange juice, feeling like it might be going well after all.

Over coffee, Ruth explained to me about her becoming a minister. I don't believe in God. Except, of course, when I'm writing. I certainly don't believe in God as an institution. Institutions don't allow for unfettered creative expression and so I have learned that they are not very good places for me. Or for God.

"Ruth, the reason you buy into institutionalized religion is that you're still in spiritual enslavement to patriarchal and hetero ideology."

"I just want to help people, Kit."

"By perpetuating spiritual enslavement to patriarchal and hetero ideology?"

"Kit, you're not understanding what I'm trying to say."

So I tried really hard to understand. I really listened to her talk even though thinking about other people's lives usually gives me a headache. I think that's why I'm so good at being in relationships. Not thinking too much about other people gives them a lot of space. I'm good that way. The women I've lived with never appreciated that. But with Ruth, I tried really, really hard to understand what she was saying. Which was even harder than normal because I ached for her. I longed for her. I did things for her I would never dream of doing for another person. Like saying I thought it was possible that the single most socially entrenched promotion of violence against women is not organized religion's continued use of a language of male dominancy. I didn't recognize myself when I was with her.

I met her for coffee about once every two or three weeks after that, sometimes for a beer. Once she brought lunch over to my house and I figured this was the start of something, but it wasn't yet. I even put all the Anthropology Student's stuff in the hall closet, which I guess was pointless since Ruth already knew all about her. The first thing she said was, "Where's all Rachel's stuff?"

I just kept being in love with Ruth. Not with her body, though I would have loved her that way, too, in a second. With her. The Anthropology Student said I was just fascinated by someone so different and unobtainable. I slammed an ashtray onto a pub table and said Ruth and I were not different. The ashtray slid off the table and smashed into twenty pieces. I should have bought ashtrays in bulk for that bar. I had trouble explaining the ways Ruth and I were the same, but it was the end of a very long evening and I was tired. I said we should just go home, reflecting all the way there that being in a relationship seems a very high price to pay for not being lonely.

When we got to the house, the Anthropology Student was mad because I forgot to take her things out of the hall closet before she got home. She put her Crete statuettes back on the mantel-piece, banging each one significantly as she set it down. My head hurt. She shouted helpful things like, "Guess if someone's unob-tainable, it saves you the trouble of driving them away."

I tried to do some work that evening, but it was no good. Between the drums beating in my head and the Anthropology Student pounding about the house, slamming doors, thumping books, I wondered painfully if she might be right. Not right as in me being wrong, but right as in maybe there was something, a small thing, that was true about what she said about Ruth and I being so different. Ruth had kids. I had a cat. She'd had one long relationship. I'd had, well, a lot of shorter ones. She was always doing things that were good for other people. That is not really how I would have described my life. Ruth considered the world to be a fairly pleasant place. I found it frustrating at best. Of course we both love women, but Ruth is so far in the closet she could spend the afternoon cataloguing the Anthropology Student's statuette collection. I heard a definition of lesbian once as a woman who responds emotionally to other women. Hell, Ruth does that. She does that more than me, and I can attest to the fact that I am a true blue, dyed-in-the-wool lesbian. Mind you, she responds emotionally to everyone. I was willing to admit that, possibly, there was nothing the same about Ruth and me. I could live with that. If opposites attract, it meant we'd be together forever. Maybe she was also unobtainable. I didn't choose to be in love with someone unobtainable. Different from me was OK. Different from me was actually probably the only way I could be in relationship with someone. Unobtainable was . . . likely a misinterpretation of "not just yet."

The Anthropology Student stopped banging things by about midnight. She made me a cup of tea before we went to bed. Then she lay beside me and cried for an hour.

"Kit, do you know what it's like to love someone who doesn't seem to see you?"

"Rachel, I was wrong."

"Oh Kit . . . "

"I thought you had no idea what I was going through."

She got out of bed, packed a few things and was gone for a week.

Wednesday

The first thing that happened after the Anthropology Student moved back in was that she called up Ruth and invited her over for dinner.

"You called her? How could you call her?"

"I picked up the phone and called her. Why not? She's coming Friday night. I'm going to do a real Shabbat dinner. She'll find it interesting."

"How the hell do you know?"

"Because she's a theology student and also she told me so. I live here, Kit. I feel like having Ruth over for Shabbus dinner. If you're not sleeping with her, what's your problem?"

My problem is that I'm not sleeping with her, of course.

"My problem is that I'd like to be asked."

"So would I, before all my stuff gets shoved into the hall closet."

I got coffee, stomped upstairs, furious, cursing. Wondering what shirt I would wear Friday night.

The Anthropology Student made tons of food, didn't sleep with me for three days and answered the door herself when Ruth arrived. They stood in front of the fireplace and admired her statuettes from Crete. I hovered in the kitchen, not actually doing anything with the food, but wondering how you make a great entrance into a room that contains your lover and the woman you're in love with, when they're two different people. Ruth didn't sound like she was embarrassed. She and Rachel seemed right at home together. I thought of going out for a beer. The Anthropology Student came into the kitchen for the wine.

"We have a guest. Get out there."

"You invited her."

"Fine. Don't get out there. I'm about to light the candles."

I went into the dining room and sat down and, incredibly, the world did not explode.

The Anthropology Student said blessings over the candles

and wine and bread and then she served us some chicken soup. She and Ruth talked about ritual and the things we need to feel grounded. The whole thing was weird. Especially since I was why they were both there, and everybody ignored me, the Anthropology Student, pointedly, and Ruth, by just not paying attention. They seemed to have a lot to talk about. I decided to go out for a beer after all.

In the bar, I let a truck driver talk to me. He might have been a truck driver. He was wearing a baseball hat. He said, "I love how you downtown girls wear nothing but black." I crinkled my nose, let him pay for the beer, and went home.

The house was dark. Ruth had gone home a while ago from the look of it. The kitchen was clean. They must have cut the evening short after I left. Of course it was one-thirty by the time I got in. The Anthropology Student was asleep in the spare room again; I went in and sat on the bed, and looked surprised when she woke up.

"I guess you're really mad," I said. I had had a lot of beer.

"Not at all. We had a really nice evening. We're going to the ballet next week." She rolled over in a very unencouraging way, and went back to sleep.

I called my agent and told her I had reached an emotional epoch.

"It's two a.m. in the Goddamned morning, Kit. For Christ's sake, go to sleep."

I went to bed, hoping every one of them felt at least as bad in the morning as I was going to feel.

Friday, May 7

Snow again today. Just a few feathers that dissolved into dew, but I consider snow in May a personal affront. Small boats have started appearing regularly now, bobbing through the ice wafers in the harbour, bringing manna in the form of milk and mail. Some cheques today, and a letter from *The New Yorker* asking for a piece about democracy for their November issue. Maybe I'll write something in favour of it this time. A notice that I've been nominated for a Delacroix Award. What the hell is a Delacroix Award? And why don't they just tell me if I win or not? The letter includes an invitation to the awards dinner. The ceremony is in Moncton, so obviously they can't expect me to attend. There is also a rejection letter from a theatrical producer for a really great play I wrote. The rejection letter says, in the nicest possible way, that I should screw off and die. That's about what I am going to say to the Delacroix people. I head down to the store to call my agent singing "The Circle of Life."

Afternoon. Still Goddamned Friday.

Banned from the store again for two days. Seems people do not appreciate my reaching out to them to share my most intimate feelings. Some people just can't do "close." It's possible they will have forgotten it by tomorrow, which would be good, because I forgot to pick up milk before I got thrown out. Someday someone is bound to remember to put "rejection letters" on the Kit List. Did manage to get a call in to my agent, Lisa, who said she'd explain to the Delacroix people about my reclusive nature. I have to admit Lisa has a knack for this. "Reclusive" is a better word than "lazy." Asked her to deal with the theatre producer who sent me the rejection letter, too, but she says she told me to stop writing plays. I do not understand that. I write excellent plays. Nobody has realized this yet. Lisa says I should stop letting small theatres, who are impressed by my name, produce my plays, because it's embarrassing. I said, "To who?" and she said the actors, to begin with. How the hell can you embarrass an actor? They'll dress up like celery if you pay them, or tell them it's art. I suggested to Lisa that she is not supportive of my theatrical career, and she said, "No shit." I suggested to Lisa that I was going to get a new agent and she said maybe that could be my birthday present to her. I have a play I'm working on now and no way is she getting 20 percent. I think it will be brilliant if I make it much, much longer.

Went home and got out the letters I have saved from Ruth. Misery loves more of the same.

> "Dear Kit,
> I am having trouble understanding from your letter if you are blaming the recent US congressional support of gun ownership on me, or the entire Christian clergy, or everyone in the world. Please clarify.
> Forever,
> Ruth"

> "Dear Kit,
> Thank you, thank you for your note. I swear, I haven't laughed in three months. Maybe longer. You used to complain that I laughed all the time. Please Kit, write me something else funny and horrendous and true. Or call me.

Please call me, I need to talk to someone who doesn't expect me to be anything except possibly in love with them.
    Ruth"

"Dear Kit,
    I don't think the fact that you're not eligible for a Pulitzer, because you're not American, is actually discriminatory. And the fact that Mary Oliver got one does not prove any marginally talented lab rat can get a poetry award in that country. Besides, either you can rail against them for not recognizing your brilliance, in spite of the fact that it goes against all of their rules, or you can complain that they throw Pulitzers around like cheese to clever rodents, but I'm not sure you can do both. No one else's success, including the very deserving Miss Oliver's, takes anything away from you. There is always, and forever only one Kit, thank the gods. Go polish your Governor General's medal, Kit, my dearest darling, and I am sure you'll feel better. Remember, Mary Oliver will never get one of those.
    Love,
    Ruth
    PS~ Kelly was here for a Healing Touch workshop, and sends love too.
    R"

"Dear Kit,
    The ferry schedule you sent me is from 1972. I found a current one on-line. No, you don't have to meet me at the wharf if you're in the middle of work. I have a feeling I'll

be able to find someone who can tell me where you live. Kit, I can't wait! I'm going to put all this behind me and become refreshed and renewed before I start my new post. I'm going to sleep late every morning and wiggle my toes in clear water. God, I so need that.

See you in three weeks!

Ruth"

"Dear Kit,

I've been thinking about what you said, 'Religion used as a tool is helpful, but used as an answer is lethal.' I don't think it's always lethal. Sometimes it's merely limiting. But that's still problematic for a woman who makes her living pushing it as an answer, isn't it?

Bless you for keeping me uncomfortable.

Love you ever and always,

Ruth"

Monday, May 10

Wind today. Comes with the warmer weather and the approach of rain. It sweeps the last of the ice and chill of winter away, ushering in patches of cloud and sunshine across the island. Wind is worse than cold. Wind seeps through cracks in my walls, whistles in the living room. Cold, I can combat with a fire in the wood stove, or another blanket. Wind has no natural enemies. Neighbours scuttle back inside. I drag on my winter jacket and run down to the store for milk then back again. Wrap up in a blanket that smells like wind and sit down to drink my coffee. Today I will begin a new word picture. A story about wind and trees and what turns solitude into loneliness. I have no idea where it will go. Creating is like free fall. Where you land is largely up to luck, weather and how much coffee you feel is required.

May 11

The Anthropology Student and Ruth went to the ballet. They went to an Andrew Lloyd Webber play for which Rachel's parents had given her tickets. I was so pissed off I couldn't even say anything derisive. They went to some kind of women's spirituality thing that involved talking to invisible animals. They went to see Rachel's father preside at the synagogue. I could hardly talk. Throughout, they were endlessly patient and kind to me, and I was charming and entertaining in a way that makes people want to throw things at me. Finally, the Anthropology Student announced that she was going away for the summer to study comparative mystical traditions in Israel. Before she came back, I had moved to this island.

The cabin was a bequest from a writer I had never met and never heard of. His wife called and said he had left me a cabin on Bolin Island. "My husband always said that no writer should have to live in Toronto."

I said, "That's what the ones say who can't afford to."

She didn't like that much, but it was in the will that I got the cabin, so I walked out the door of my house in the Annex, got on a plane and three ferries, and arrived here late in May. The Anthropology Student arrived about eight weeks later. She just came walking up the path one day.

"Kit, what the hell are you doing? I thought we were living together."

"Yeah, well, you left."

"I had a return ticket."

"How's Ruth?"

"Shut up about Ruth, Kit. The people next door to the house called the police. I thought you were dead."

"I guess you're pretty glad to find out I'm not."

"I'm still deciding. I just had to come out and see for myself that you could leave our home, travel three thousand miles away and stay here without telling me. Without telling anyone."

"I told Lisa."

"I was thinking more along the lines of someone who might feed the cat."

I had forgotten about the cat.

"I had the newspapers stopped."

"No, Kit, you did not have the newspapers stopped. They were piled up all over the porch. That's why the people next door finally had a policeman break down the door to see if you were lying dead inside."

"Did they get him to feed the cat?"

"I called the house about four hundred times. Finally, I got smart and called Lisa."

"I'm sure she wasn't worried."

"Of course not. She's enjoying the quiet."

"I told her I was coming here for a few days."

"Eight weeks ago, Kit. Eight Goddamned weeks ago. I left my course before the exam to come here."

She sat down on the front step and put her head in her hands. I started to rub her shoulders and she slapped me, hard.

That seemed a bit harsh. She pulled out a package of cigarettes.

"You don't smoke, Rachel."

"How the hell would you know?"

That was pretty much it for a long time. A few people came and went on the path. The Anthropology Student smoked hard and proficiently. She stared out at the ocean. Finally she got up, crushed the last cigarette under her heel, and walked off in the direction of the wharf. That was the last I saw of her. She came thousands of miles and then left without even saying goodbye.

Lisa sent me a letter the next spring saying that my lawn had reached a state where people were starting to complain, and the city was planning to add lawn cutting to the bill they had already sent for snow removal. I went back to Toronto to sell the house.

The Anthropology Student had left notes all over: "You can't sell these plates. You borrowed them from Dionne." And, "Do not tell people Chagall painted the mural in the dining room. No one has ever believed you." Finally, it just seemed easier to lock the door and pay someone to take care of the lawn and the snow. I left the electricity on so the stuff in the fridge would be OK. Margarine keeps forever. I don't know what happened to the cat. I guess the Anthropology Student took it.

May 20

The wind drops. Stillness before the rain. The morning sun tilts through my window too early now, waking me long before my day should begin. I sit on my verandah without a blanket, before the noon sun has warmed the ground. Pale green buds dot the branches of our few maple trees. The sea has melted into the colour of sky. Ferries appear, and soon we will forget that once fresh fruit and newspapers were luxuries. Here on the island we get the newspaper a day late when it comes at all. By the time we read what's happening, the world has already moved on. No one seems to care. After a few winters and springs here, time becomes merely an idea.

Gerrard fusses about his bare patches of garden, cajoling perennials back to life. Down the path, the boulders by Deirdre's shack are festooned with colour, a decaying patchwork quilt draped over them to air, smock dresses in hues of orchid and parrot; as if someone newly arrived from exotic realms had emptied out their sea chest. Deirdre stands at her front door, staring at the ocean, not moving. In her hand is a length of garden hose. There is no tap on her shack.

A few hardy, early tourists stray toward my cabin, pausing far enough down the path to claim to be polite. Usually by the time they've walked this close to my place someone has told them not to. Very few come the last few yards off the path and up to the door. Ruth suggested I put a note out saying simply, "Writing/Please do not disturb." I came up with a version I thought was much more explanatory, but she reminded me that these are people who might in future buy my books.

Deirdre came up to have lunch with me. Not that I'd invited her. She brought sandwiches she'd made for herself and two for me. Feeling generous of spirit, I let Deirdre stay and sit on the front step to eat hers. I asked her what the filling of the sandwiches was and she said she wasn't sure, but she hoped it was tuna because that's her favourite. I heated up some canned soup instead. We sat watching swatches of sun and cloud over the water, Deirdre's dresses rustling turquoise and fuchsia in the breeze.

Deirdre asks me if I am doing any spring cleaning before the rain comes. I sit in early afternoon sun, pushing aside cobwebs. Maybe this is spring cleaning.

When Ruth got fired from Markham, she called to say she was coming to the island for a whole month, before her next job. I figured, having been fired, she was going to be very vulnerable. In need of some selfless kindness. I could do this. I considered cleaning out part of a drawer for her stuff and went down to the store to tell everyone that my lover was coming to live with me.

So began the Summer of Ruth. Our Lady of Every Virtue Possible. From the moment her foot touched land here, Ruth was embraced as some kind of goddess. There was something a little fragile and vulnerable about her, but it just made her more . . . Ruth. The luminescent, universe-embracing Ruth I remembered from before Kyle left. She wandered the island barefoot, trailing radiance in her wake. She held neighbours' hands, smiled into faces, laughed and encouraged. Everyone except me. To every other Goddamned person on this Goddamned island, the entire month was Ruthfest. Ruthorama. Some kind of Ruth religious crusade, with no religion, ironically, involved. Neighbours adored her. Invitations were issued for dinner or lunch, burnt offerings of BBQ tofu, or lentil burgers, or a cup of coffee, sometimes given so eagerly they offered to include me. They let her leave her own mug at the general store, for God's sake. I haven't been able to leave my mug there since the creamer incident two years ago. Children placed daisy chains on the doorstep. For one entire month, ecstasy poured over the island like August sunshine or ritual wine.

She would come back to the cabin, red-nosed from sitting on the rocks with someone else all afternoon, the lines around her eyes and mouth more deeply etched by salt wind, her hair pulled back in a ponytail, loose strands straying across her neck. She, who was never with a hair out of place, simply pushed them back, laughing. If I ever felt inclined to answer when someone asks me, "Why do you sleep with women?" I would draw them a word picture of Ruth brushing the hair away from her eyes.

Ruth came home to me every night. Standing at the sink doing my dishes, telling me where she'd been and who she'd talked with. How the sun and the salty wind had felt against her face. "Come with me tomorrow, Kit. If you think we're not spending enough time together, come with me." After she'd talked for a while, we would go to bed. Me in the bedroom. Ruth on the couch she'd dragged out onto the verandah. The next morning she'd go off on her own again.

Maybe that should have been enough for me. The coming home. The talking. But it wasn't. It wasn't nearly enough.

"Kit, I just don't love you that way."

"You could. You haven't tried. You'd like it. Trust me, everyone likes it."

"It's got nothing to do with liking it."

"You just think that, 'cause of sleeping with men."

"I mean, it's not about how it feels, Kit. Not how it feels to touch you with my fingers."

Yes!

"I won't be sucked into you, Kit. I can love you better from the outside. And it's the only way you can love me at all."

We would have this discussion now and then, or every night, I can't remember. I think she began to get frustrated. It was hard to tell with her. I mean, when someone boxes up their books once again, takes their Crete statuettes and says anyone who wants her can call her at the dorm, you pretty well know. The whole leading-up-to-frustration process I've never really figured out. I once thought that people should wear mood T-shirts, so that those of us with important things happening in our lives would have some way of keeping tabs on what was going on. I mean, without having to think about it. The Anthropology Student said there was a way for me to know—it was called seeing her leaving the room, crying. But that's so open to interpretation, you know? Anyway, Ruth never took her things and went anywhere, in spite of neighbours trying to lure her away with promises of monstrous luxuries, like electricity, or a real bed.

Ruth and our days were always the same. She was out every morning, singing. Neighbours wandered around wrapped in the wonder of her. Then at night she'd talk and I'd listen. Mostly I just liked the sound of her voice. The details of what she said didn't register so much. "I can say anything to you, Kit," she'd laugh, ocean and music in her voice. "You never judge because you never listen." Then I'd say it was time for bed and she'd head out to the verandah. I was ready to scream.

Ruth came to my room one night. Window open in my sea-dark cave. Cool breeze against my skin where I lay sweating, naked in the August heat. The walls of my cabin absorb warmth like a paper towel, holding it in, just as they sponge up cold in winter and release it slowly, long after the frost outside has passed.

Ruth came in, standing in the doorway, moonlight flooding from the verandah behind her.

"Kit, I want you."

Crossing two steps to my bed. Her robe falling onto bare floorboards.

I knew what Ruth's body would feel like before I touched her. Years of longing prepared me for shoulders too slight to have carried the weight of so many people's lives, breasts tender and softened by nurture and time. I knew how my fingertips would feel tracing desire across the downy skin on her back. The warm pulse of her breath when my lips found her throat. What it is to be human, to crave the closeness of another's body. The ancient promise of wholeness. To not be alone.

Ruth dropped her robe, moved into me and we both cried for the rightness of it. What separated us dropped away, melting into tears and sweat, the wet of our bodies and our love. I knew we would never sleep apart again.

At least that's how I figured it would be if she ever did come in my room. Every night I would sleep naked just in case, even though I hate how my thighs always feel sticky in the morning.

May 22, 2004

More wind, and for a few days I feel that I removed my tarp too early. Stray raindrops spot the front verandah. In a week, pines and earth and sky will dissolve into a seamless shroud of grey. The path down to Deirdre's cabin will become a wash of dark floods. It will be hard to remember that sunlight ever existed. Or that the swatch of mud and rubble that is Gerrard's garden will soon burst into pink and violet foam. Gerrard used to plant more earthy colours—burnt gold sunflowers and dusky crimson mums, which I liked better. They looked much more vibrant than those pink things on my kitchen table.

Gerrard came over this morning, pushing through the wind, wrapped in a clear, plastic, women's raincoat. He remembered about Ruth and wants to talk about it. Gerrard wants to know if I think death is final. I say of course it's final, but Ruth is not dead. Gerrard asks, "What's the difference between being dead and being gone forever?"

At the end of August, Ruth went back to Toronto. Neighbours arrived in a throng to help carry her one suitcase down to the wharf. Gifts were presented, wrapped in newspaper and bright squares of hand-loomed cloth. Ruth smiled and hugged and made promises to come back the next summer, and then stood shading her eyes, watching the ferry chug out of the morning mist toward the island. I stood beside her, deeply resenting that we were not alone. That she was leaving me.

"I don't see why you can't stay here."

"I have a job, Kit. People are counting on me."

"They might fire you from this place too. How can you work for ungrateful people? If they fire you, you could come back here to live."

"Thanks for the optimistic thought."

I'm helpful that way.

"Why don't you come to Toronto?"

"And do what?"

"Visit me?"

A deep, low blast from the ferry sounded across the water. Gulls screeched and left off ravaging fish heads on the rocks. The sounds of missing Ruth. How could I be missing someone who was standing beside me?

"I don't think it's going to be the same this time, Kit. I have a feeling that something really amazing is going to happen."

"With us?"

"With my work."

"Oh."

"Ruth, stay here with me. I'll really try."

"You always try."

"I mean . . . I'll try to be whatever it is you want me to be."

Ruth smiled and brushed a hand against her eyes.

"You already are, Kit. Just exactly."

The ferry sidled to the wharf, let out the last tourists of the summer, took on neighbours headed for shopping in the city, one of the Ray boys to see his parole officer over on the next island, and Ruth. The Anthropology Student told me that when her father died she couldn't understand how the sun could rise the next morning just like usual, or people go about their day as if the world had not changed profoundly and forever. The ferry did not sway under the weight of Ruth leaving me. The horn did not blow more mournfully as it pulled away. I sat at the edge of the wharf long after the ferry had disappeared from sight. Deirdre came drifting up the pier and plopped down beside me.

"The committee is going to hire a medium, Kit."

"What for?"

"To find out why the water in the cistern is tasting funny."

"Couldn't they afford an 'excellent'?"

"What?"

"Never mind, Deirdre. You know, anywhere else it might occur to someone to bring in a water specialist."

"I know," she beamed. "Isn't it wonderful?"

We sat in silence for a few moments.

"Where is Ruth?" she asked.

"She left on the ferry."

"I know that. But where is she?"

"I don't know. Maybe somewhere around Hornby Island by now."

"I think Ruth is at the end of the world."

I had a therapist once who said that we move when it becomes less painful than staying where we are. I got up and walked up to the general store to see who felt sorry for me. McNelly was Off Island at a bagpipe festival so "Any mention of Ruth leaving" was not added to the Kit List for a whole twenty-four hours.

May 23

In the first days after Ruth left, all I could really think about was trying not to think about her. I wrote to every woman I'd ever held hands with, inviting them to come to the island for three or four days. I could stand having someone here for three or four days. I got nothing back at all. You know, every time I leave a woman they're always, "I'll love you forever," or "Oh Kit, I've never loved anyone like this before." And I usually say, "Really? You mean that's the best you can do?" You know, just to help make the healing process go faster. I'm good that way. So after swearing all this undying affection, not one of them wrote back. Women are so inconstant. Except for me. I am very constant. I would have had any one of those women again for three or four days. Three would be good. McNelly said my mistake was photocopying the letter. Screw him. Personally, I blame it all on the absence of some kind of cosmic seven-second-delay rule, the provision of which, to my mind, would be proof enough of a truly caring deity. Live television airs seven seconds behind to give producers the opportunity to slice out anything said that might be troublesome. In a properly ordered universe, we'd have a similar delay available to us in any number of treacherous situations—I think of those first seven seconds after orgasm, for instance, brief, brief seconds of contentment when I, for one, am likely to spout all kinds of things that can cause any amount of trouble later. A similar seven-second delay would be useful for parents of gay children, for those first perilous moments following the all important coming out speech. For some parents, it should be seven minutes. Or seven years. In the case of my mother, longer than that. Anyway, I finally did get one letter back from the ones I sent. The Anthropology Student wrote to tell me exactly what she'd like to do to me if she came, but it wasn't really what I had in mind. I decided that maybe the rest of them just needed a little time to think about it.

Fortunately, being a writer, I've cultivated the life skills that see one through times of significant trial. Mostly, "distraction." I did crosswords. I looked at the view. I watched the Ray boys engage in an occasional friendly round of "elf toss." The best part of this game is not the nice heave you get with one of those things, or seeing their pointy heads sticking up from the water just off shore, but waiting for the shriek when Gerrard finally looks up from whatever flower bed he's half buried in and sees what's happening to his garden gnomes. It's a fine sight, Gerrard wading about in knee-deep seas, pants and shirt sleeves carefully rolled up, gathering up his dripping elves and repositioning them in Saturnalian poses in the garden, all the time wittering

on about how we've somehow debased his precious lawn orna-
ments. All I can say is that what I do to them is a lot less debas-
ing than what Gerrard has them doing with each other.

Elf toss was not an entirely satisfying diversion. I kept
thinking about Ruth and how she felt about my tormenting
Gerrard. I felt almost ashamed.

In the evening, I found myself waiting for her to come up
the path, cheeks burnt and hands full of wildflowers she'd
picked for our Mason jar. I crouched by the wood stove, roar-
ing in spite of the heat still hanging in the early autumn air, and
wondered what she was doing and who she now shared the map
of her thoughts and feelings with at the end of the day.

The days did pass and finally my order from Good
Vibrations arrived and I was glad no one was coming to stay even
for three or four days. If God had intended us to depend on each
other for comfort, he definitely wouldn't have given us batteries.

May 25, 2004

Ruth wrote me letters about her new job.

"Dear Kit,
Finally, and at long last, as much of the manse as I
plan to use is unpacked, the staff and I have come to terms
of a sort and now I'm ready for something to . . . happen!
I must have relaxed too much on the island, because I've
been back in the city for weeks and can't seem to feel
'geared up' again. I know, theoretically, that this should be
a good thing. The truth is, there really isn't much for me to
sink my teeth into here as yet. I miss the island and how

time seemed like a gift instead of a challenge.

    Call me so we can talk about this!

    Sending you love,

    Ruth"

This sounded promising to me. If they fired her by November, she could still get the last ferry here.

In her letters, Ruth always asked if I would call her so we could talk. My experience with a woman saying they want to talk is that it's hardly ever going to be pleasurable for me. I had every intention of calling Ruth, if I had ever remembered to take her number with me when I went down to the general store. And if long-distance phone charges weren't such a scam.

Then a new book of my poetry came out, so I was occupied with that. The best part of the writing process is the moment you hold your new book in your hands for the first time—a perfect yin/yang of potential and fulfillment. I've heard women writers say it's like holding your first baby, but that seems unlikely. A book just has to be better. The sleepless nights and heartache are over. The future is all possibility. Maybe this will be the one that changes your world forever. Maybe this will be the one that realizes everything you are. The one that remains when everything else slips away. That feeling lasts for a whole twenty seconds until the reviews come out. If you get reviewed. Not getting reviewed is better. Try explaining that, though, to writers who can't expect a page in the *Globe* every time they pen a memo. Getting reviewed means some frustrated graduate of journalism or creative writing, who can't make a living doing what you do, belches out a few hundred words missing entirely the point of what you were trying to say, or missing that this is the ultimate gift humankind will ever receive, or even saying that it *is* the ultimate gift but missing that somehow, that's just not enough for you to hear. They are strange things, reviews. I mean, here I am, normally a very easygoing person, inclined to let the little unhappinesses of life just roll off my back unremarked, but in a review of twelve hundred words festooned with adjectives such as "stellar," "genius," or "virtuoso," the words "the last poem, 'Cassandra,' was possibly the only weak link in an otherwise superlative collection," are branded on my confidence forever. So, you write another book, because this time you will show them what you mean, so the idiot reviewer, who can hammer on your psyche as easily as his keyboard, will finally understand.

This time the twenty seconds of bliss lasted longer, because the reviews almost said what they should have. Interviewers appeared at the cabin, sent by newspapers and magazines to discuss my work until the November winds chilled the ocean into ice. Then the last ferries of the year came chugging to the wharf laden with art-and-craft supplies for the winter. It was too cold to sit on my verandah, even with my Hudson's Bay blanket. Too much to do to think about writing letters or making phone calls. Time to put the plastic on the verandah windows again, sealing myself back into my cave of warmth and dim light for the winter. "Time of Return to the Wood Stove." It was at that point that McNelly came up to the cabin for the second time ever.

Saturday

The rains began this morning. The floorboards on the verandah are soaked and black within an hour. I huddle by the stove, listening to pounding overhead.

Only two times in history has McNelly ever braved the path to my cabin. Both times it was fall. The first time I was in the kitchen trying to figure out what I could take down to the Town Hall as a generous donation to our Autumnal Equinox celebration, something that I wouldn't miss. The committee presents a festive display to mark the change in season, entitled "The Bounty of the Island." We're all supposed to file reverently past it on the twenty-second of September, murmuring appreciative things about food, our hope for a good harvest, with prayers to whatever deity we have most truck with. It's stupid, really, because we don't actually have any kind of harvest here, unless you count the mangy clump of marijuana the Ray boys have been cultivating behind their shack. You can barely grow moss on this island, let alone anything to eat. Only Gerrard seems to possess the magic, or the pigheadedness, to coax flowers into sprouting from stone. Displaying the potential bounty of the season means decorating the meeting table with an assortment of dried blueberries, some dead fish, packaged pasta and canned goods, which conjures up less a portrait of nature's potential bounty and more a vision of a checkout line at No Frills. Of course, if you mention this pretty obvious fact, the neighbours are all over it. Now I say nothing and just hand over some canned goods. I am thankful for canned goods. Until about the middle of February anyway. I think the neighbours could stand to be a little more thankful, frankly. When it comes time to open the cans and share a harvest meal, my traditional donation of creamed corn is always rejected.

The first time I saw McNelly coming up the path, I figured

the committee had sent him to demand that I not donate the same expired can of creamed corn again.

Instead, he told me that my mother had died.

"This must be a terrible shock, lass."

"It is. I thought she'd been dead for years."

"I take it you didn't get along?"

"We got along perfectly. We never spoke to each other."

"Did she find it hard to accept your . . . lifestyle?"

"Yeah. She hated the writing thing. Then I moved in with a Jew and she went off the deep end."

"I guess you'll be going Off Island?"

"What for?"

"Well . . . to make the arrangements."

"What do you think concierges are for?"

Turns out, I had to leave the cabin and fly to Toronto to bury my mother. I didn't even get to see Ruth, because she was in Halifax at the time trying to talk Kelly out of joining some religious cult or something and then going to see her priest friend who was having some kind of nervous breakdown. Everything bad happens to me.

So, when McNelly arrived at my door again this time, I guessed he wasn't coming to apologize for . . . well, everything. This time it was November. Raining, like today.

"Kit girl, you need to come down. I've got Rachel on the telephone at the store. She says she needs to tell you something about Ruth."

My blood ran colder than the sea.

"Hello, Rachel? Is she OK?"

"Kit, thank God I got you. She's OK. I mean, she's not sick or anything."

Thank God. Thank God.

"Kit, Ruth has locked herself in her house. She's locked herself in and says she's not coming out until God talks to her."

"Are you sure?"

"Of course I'm sure. It was in the newspaper this morning. Reverend Ruth Broggan, Glenview Unified Church, Toronto. Kit, do you know what this is all about? Why does she want God to talk to her?"

"Isn't that what we all want?"

"Listen, you've got to call her."

"What, and tie up the line?"

"This is nothing to joke about, Kit. The newspaper says people are starting to camp out around her house, like spiritual pilgrims or something. Like they're expecting the second coming of Christ."

"I think in that neighbourhood it would be the first coming."

"There's television crews arriving and everything. It was on the radio too. I'm afraid she needs help."

"So, go help her."

"I think she needs to talk to someone she trusts."

"Other than God."

"Kit, stop it. I am serious. I'm really worried. This doesn't seem like the kind of thing Ruth would do at all."

"A minister would like God to communicate with her. Wouldn't it be strange behaviour if that *wasn't* the case? God, Rachel, Abraham Joshua Heschel said, 'Faith is awareness of divine mutuality and companionship, a form of communication between God and man.' He's one of the brightest lights in Jewish philosophy in the last hundred years, so I would think you'd know that. What's the big deal if Ruth is looking for a little tangible mutuality—asking God to hold up her end of the conversation? Seems to me that if you're going to be religious, this is one of the most entirely reasonable things you could be doing. Maybe you should stop telling other people how to live their lives."

"At least I'm aware that they have them. For God's sake, Kit, the woman you idolize, the woman you claim to love better than any other human being on the face of the earth except yourself may be in real trouble. Are you going to pick up the telephone and call her, or not?"

I'd have to think about it.

"Kit, doesn't Ruth write to you? Has she said anything unusual?"

"I live on Looney Island, Rachel. I don't have a clue anymore what's unusual. She's been saying some things about light and shellfish lately. It actually sounded pretty good to me. Listen, there's something I need you to do for me. An alternative theatre group in Toronto is doing one of my plays next month. I want you to go."

"Why?"

"Because I'd like to show Lisa-Don't-Write-Any-More-Plays-Or-You'll-Be-Looking-For-A-New-Agent Sellers and the rest of the Goddamned world that my plays can be a success, and success in alternative theatre means having people in the audience that you're not related to."

"I'll think about it. If you promise you'll call Ruth. Ask her if she needs help. Just let her know she's not alone."

"God, Rachel. She knows she's not alone. It's the rest of us that need to be reassured."

The next day the paper arrived with mention of the

Toronto minister who had locked herself into the manse and was refusing to come out until she was told what God wanted her to do. I thought over what I remembered of the Bible, and couldn't recall any times when what God commanded was, "Realize you're a lesbian and go immediately to live with Kit." Probably got bumped when they made up the canon.

I talked to Kelly.

"Kit, I'm so glad you called back."

"The receptionist said this is an ashram. Is this an ashram?"

"I live in a Buddhist meditation centre. My mother must have told you that."

This sounds plausible.

"What's happening with her, Kit?"

"Apparently, she wants God to talk to her."

"Is she crazy? Do you think she's crazy?"

"I have to say I find it a little discouraging that so far a devout Jew and a practising Buddhist have both suggested that the idea of God actually being present is insane. It's becoming very difficult to tell the atheists from the enthusiasts, Kelly."

"But . . . well, God, if you want to call it that, Enlightenment, comes from within. Divine energy doesn't speak to you."

"I guess your mother thinks it might."

"That's why I think she might be insane."

"Which is insane, Kelly? To believe there's a God or Divine Energy, but that it never speaks to us in any way that we can really comprehend? Or to believe there is a God or Divine Energy that might?"

"I told you, Kit, it doesn't work that way."

"Kelly, you're young. Only someone very young thinks they know how things work."

"Look, none of this is helping my mother."

"Isn't the only way to help her by encouraging her to follow her own path, or something Zen like that?"

"Well, yes, but . . . I'm afraid she might really harm herself."

"Kelly, if I'm not mistaken, Buddhism says that the kind of birth you have in your next life is determined by the nature of your actions in this one, right?"

"Yes, of course, but . . . "

"If you're really concerned for your mother, if what you truly seek is her happiness and not your own peace of mind, why don't you spend your energy wishing her clarity and strength for the path, rather than trying to stop her from going down it?"

"So . . . what do you think we should do?"

"We should do nothing."

There is a pause. I wonder if it's sinking in that being Zen and just not caring look suspiciously like the same thing. The Anthropology Student was always confusing the two.

"I . . . guess you're right."

"Well, Kelly, *He in whose heart the words of the master have entered, sees the truth like treasure in his own palm.*"

"Of course. You're right. You're entirely right. We'll send her white light and wish her strength and clarity, won't we? Thank you, Kit."

I should have been a priest or something.

I did not call Ruth, because I was thinking of possibly going to Toronto to see her. Then I had to think about who I could count on, if I did go, to get me back to the island since the ferries were sure to stop running soon. Then it snowed a bit and I had to think about how safe a ferry is when the ice is going to start forming any moment. Then I got a letter from someone named Margaret Ketchie who said she's one of Ruth's congregants and could I please come and talk Ruth into ending this stunt, my being her closest friend that they know of, because the governing council of the church are about to have the door knocked in and everyone removed from the lawn where they are camping. So, I had to think about that for a while. In the meantime, McNelly had a new article about Ruth tacked up on the bulletin board every day: "Religious Pilgrims Flock to Unified Church," "Divine Conflict: Minister Challenges God," "Church Leaders Decry Challenge to God." One photo showed a cluster of tents, oddly dressed people huddled around trash-can fires. It looked like a convention of homeless people, or a tailgate party.

The neighbours loved it. There was a general sense that Ruth belonged to the island, ownership based on the flimsy reasoning that she'd spent twenty-nine whole days on our soil. I was livid. She belonged to me. For reasons I couldn't quite come up with but I knew were true.

A couple letters came from Ruth.

"November 27, 2002
Dear Kit,
Can you come to Toronto? Let me put that another way. Please, please, Kit, come here and be with me. Remember how you used to quote Thomas Mann to me when I suggested your island was a little isolated? That it's

one more way for you to keep people at bay? What was it? 'Solitude gives birth to the original in us, to beauty unfamiliar and perilous.' I seem to be becoming entirely familiar with the perilous part. Kit, I've locked myself into my house. I've been here for nineteen days. Alone. I had this sudden inspiration that there was no point toiling away at my life until I had a clue as to what it was all about. What I was supposed to do. But . . . all I'm finding is nothingness, Kit. I have less idea what it's all about than I did nineteen days ago. Then, at least, I had hope. I need you to come here. You can show me how to do this alone thing and be creative and find beauty. How to be naked with my own thoughts and self. You can explain to me how it's possible. Please Kit, I'm in a very bad way.

Ruth"

My feeling, at that point, was that it was better not to interfere in what was clearly a very personal struggle. You can really mess people around if you step in when they're feeling vulnerable and needy. I have a lot of integrity that way.

"December 7, 2002

Dear Kit,

I am hoping you got my last letter. I asked one of our congregants who delivers food to me to mail it. Margaret is very efficient so I believed she would do that. A river of scarlet is washing over the shells tonight, staining them poppy red. The walls are lit by fires burning outside my window. Maybe someone is burning witches or books or Joan of Arc outside my window. Maybe the church is on fire. There was a famous rabbi who said that humankind should burn all our sacred books every fifty years, otherwise each generation just squabbles over what was found by those long dead and gone, and does not search for wisdom of their own. I believe in wisdom passed down, Kit. I believe I must discover it for myself too. I won't worry about that anymore. I don't have the inclination. Isn't that a good word? Inclination. Feels good on the roof of my mouth.

It would be very helpful if you came here, Kit. Maybe you could come here and keep me from vanishing from my own life. I still have the inclination to worry about that from time to time. I might vanish into scarlet water over shells. I might get burned in that water like Joan of Arc. Gerrard could plant poppies to remember me, Kit. Scarlet drops on my open hands. I have no inclination to think of anything at all.

Ruth"

This didn't necessarily sound too good. Clearly it was the kind of thing she needed to sort out for herself.

The woman named Margaret wrote to me.

"December 12, 2002
Dear Miss Sheppard,

I am writing to you as a person that we know to be a close friend of Reverend Broggan, and you are the only person she has contacted. I am wondering if you can do anything to persuade her to come out of the manse and stop waiting for God to talk to her. We have tried to be patient and supportive but it's been going on for over four weeks now and there are at least two hundred people camped out on the church lawn waiting to see if God *will* speak, and television camera people here almost every day, and everyone arguing with each other at all hours about whether someone who thinks God might communicate with us today the way He did with Moses is a kook, or whether there really can be miracles even in modern times, even though we do not live in the age of miracles any more as our former minister explained to us, and this is not a time any longer when God makes it clear to us what we are to do. It is all very disturbing. Particularly as our congregation looks to the church as a place where we do not have to think much. We must seem like nuts to our Jewish neighbours, and I have to say that I used to think that about them when they put up those little shanties in the fall and ate outside even in the freezing cold. Well, it's the middle of December and the people on our lawn have less than shanties, I can tell you.

But also, I like her, Miss Sheppard. I think Reverend Broggan came to us for a reason. I know that sounds silly and I don't believe in fortune telling or "feelings" or anything like that. But, I like her. I feel a little lost somehow now that she's not with us.

We're very worried that Church House is starting to think there's something wrong with us because we can't keep our ministers . . . well . . . in a good frame of mind. We know they're upset about the tent people and the bonfires and the arguing and singing. Maybe they'll want to close Glenview Unified altogether. If there is anything you can do to get Reverend Broggan to change her mind about this and stop this whole thing before it gets out of hand, our congregation would be most grateful.

Respectfully,

Margaret Ketchie

PS~ I am taking this opportunity to enclose some poems written by my son Daniel who is only ten but very advanced for his age. His father and I don't wish to encourage him to write too much poetry, because of course we want him to grow up to have a useful profession, but we are quite struck by his writing ("Dreaming in Aubergine," for instance, seems particularly sensitive for a boy his age) and we are wondering if you, as a real writer, can tell us if you see anything in them.

With our many thanks,

Margaret Ketchie"

"December 17, 2002

Dear Margaret,

If I could persuade Ruth to do anything, she and I would be in bed together right now.

Regards,

Kit Sheppard

PS~ The poems are not awful. Your son is gay."

I figured it wouldn't kill me to be helpful just this once.

McNelly ran out of room on the bulletin board and began taping newspaper clippings onto the back of the cash register and across the milk fridge. "God Watch: Week Four. Crowd of Pilgrims Swells at Glenview Unified. 'We believe God has new message for the world.'" "Pope Condemns Religious

Extremism." "Unified Church House Moves to Have Minister Declared Insane." "Week Five: Pilgrims Clash With Police, Church Officials—Form Human Barricade To Keep Authorities Out of Manse."

I started to wonder if maybe I should give Ruth a call and see if everything was OK.

Then my agent called.

"Kit, am I right that you know this woman minister who's holed up in her house until God talks to her? I've got a television producer on the other line who's interested in booking her for a talk show. Could you get him an interview?"

"Lisa, if she wanted to talk to some random journalist, there's about two hundred on her front lawn right now. She wants to talk to the Almighty."

"Well, the television booking is for *Oprah*, so she'd be pretty close."

"Could you leave me alone? I'm having a hard time with this."

"Really? Now that's interesting, because I would have thought this was one of those rare events that are actually about other people. Does your friend Rachel know her? I'll try calling Rachel. By the way, *Vanity Fair* wants that story by the twenty-first. And don't even think about writing a play about this."

I hung up the phone feeling worse than I ever had. Deirdre pushed open the door, lugging a blanket and pillow into the store. "I'm going to camp out under Ruth's pictures. Just like I'm a pilgrim."

"If you want to be a pilgrim, Deirdre, take a very long hike."

I walked back to the cabin in darkness. I would call Ruth

tomorrow. I would go to Toronto. I had that piece due on the twenty-first, though. And three ferries just to get to the plane. Then there was the whole travelling before Christmas thing, which would just be a nightmare. Probably she was fine. She didn't really mean that I should come. It would all blow over soon, anyway. I would go if she sent one more letter saying that was still what she wanted. The letter came the next morning. Then just before I had finally decided for sure what I'd do, it was suddenly too late.

Two days short of six weeks, Ruth came out of the manse.

TWO

January 12, 2003

Dear Kit,

The best part of this is how I see the details in life now. My coffee cup is so blue. The kitchen floor is a miracle of suds and water when I wash it. I'd be happy to wash it every day, just to marvel at the rainbow suds and water, the movement of my muscles beneath my skin, but as soon as I start, someone always rings the bell and I have to figure out how to get across the part I've washed in order to answer. I never mind, because every person around me is fascinating. The lines between me and the coffee cup, the kitchen floor and the people are less and less apparent. Am wondering what makes you happy these days, Kit. My list is too long to get into. And changes hourly!

Love and bright blessings,

Ruth

Dear Valerie,

I didn't forget to prepare the Order of Service for this week. We're not having an Order of Service. It tends to limit the possibilities, don't you think?

> *Cheers!*
> *Reverend Broggan*

Valerie,

I'm so sorry, this miscommunication was entirely my fault. When I wrote "Re: sermon title: No more sermons," "No More Sermons" isn't the title. I mean I really won't be preaching a sermon anymore. I don't know what the janitor should put on the signboard outside this week. Perhaps just "We don't preach." Unless you think it will still be misread.

> *Knowing you'll do whatever is best with this,*

> *Reverend Broggan*

Margaret,

We will need:
> *Purple candles. Purple is a healing colour.*
> *Lavender (dried or fresh).*
> *At least a bushel of apples. Please explain to Valerie one more time that in every culture in the world and history, apples are a symbol of fecundity and plenty, rebirth and possibility. That's what we're going for here. Only Medieval Christians considered them the fruit of Satan, and I doubt there will be any Medieval Christians in attendance. We're not expecting representatives from Church House, are we?*
> *About 6,000 snail shells. Will that be a problem?*

Pine cones might do.
A frog. At least, I think a frog. Maybe a frog. A frog.
Also, do you know anyone who can play a zither?

Ruth

February 1, 2003

Valerie,

You are entirely right that tradespeople just don't listen. I did not call a locksmith to change the locks on the church. I expressly told him to remove them altogether. Please get him back a.s.a.p.

Reverend Broggan

Dear Valerie,

Yes, I know this might mean some of the people outside will start camping in the church where it's warm. Let us remember the words from Saint Matthew, Valerie . . . well, sort of from Matthew . . . Matthew-esque. "It profiteth a religious institution nothing if it adheres to all the insurance regulations but loses one soul." Please get the locksmith back today.

Reverend Broggan

February 8, 2003

Dear Mark,

Do you know any Latin? I mean other than that which Ezra Pound stuck through his poetry that just annoys people because no one knows what he's talking about? We've been using the King James version in services lately, so that the poetry can speak to our soul, but I'm feeling we ought to offer something in another language altogether. The words are getting in the way of our comprehension. What do you think? Maybe Polish?

    Love,
    Ruth

February 12, 2003

Reverend Broggan,

The "Question Everything" group isn't meeting anymore. They were having trouble establishing an agenda. I've suggested their time spot to the "Over-50 Lesbian Wiccan Gardeners" group. By the way, they have lovely things planned for a "healing herb garden" on the side lawn this spring.

    Margaret

March 4, 2003

Dear Valerie,

First of all, it is not called the "Sing Any Damn Thing You Want" program. The correct title is "Sing Any Damn

*Thing You Want Really, Really Loudly 'Cause We Might
All Die Before Morning." I think the context is key, don't
you? And yes, I think if you're concerned about the fact
that some participants are performing hip-hop songs in the
church, then absolutely you should contact our congrega-
tional president. After all, he runs the group. He does a
rendition of "Never Let Em C U Sweat" that brings the
house down. Every time.*

Reverend Broggan

PS~ We're still waiting on the locksmith.

March 7, 2003

Dear Valerie,

*Further to the subject of fairly loud noises, just a reminder
that the Wolf Howl will be taking place some time this
afternoon. Or tomorrow. Or whenever they feel moved.
Wanted to give fair warning because I recall it was surpris-
ing to you the last time.*

*Also, no need to call the locksmith after all. Someone
has simply removed the hinges. Isn't it wonderful how
these things just seem to take care of themselves?*

*Cheers,
Reverend Broggan*

March 8, 2003

Dear Margaret

Alas, I regret to inform you that Valerie has resigned. She came back from the photocopier yesterday and there were people squatting on her desk, howling. It seems that Valerie did not feel this is the sort of thing she signed on for as a church secretary. My guess is that this isn't the last we'll hear from her, though. I understand she's joined the "Over-50 Lesbian Wiccan Gardeners" group.

March 18, 2003
To: Unified Church of Canada, Church House
From: Margaret Ketchie

Dear Sirs and Madams,

I know it has been weeks since you asked me to share my impressions of what's been going on here at Glenview. Honestly, I've been so busy that I haven't had a moment to write. I was even late for my son Daniel's dance recital last week, and that's the first time that's happened, I can tell you.

Things are just fine here. I had the largest group yet at my cake decorating and creative writing class this past week. I call it "Poetry and Pastry." It's simply an integrative personal exploration of the soul/body connection through sound and a nice, light Bundt cake. That kind of thing. Also, we do creative dance. The whole thing was my son Daniel's idea, and it's become very popular. This week's session was preparation for our upcoming Spring Equinox gathering—I called it "Fertility and the Feminine." We read nineteenth-century romance poets who celebrate goddess imagery and made ladyfingers. The next one might not be until April, when I think something traditionally Christian would be appropriate for the Easter season. Sacred poetry on the theme of resurrection. We'll make angel food cake.

I cannot really answer your question about who currently makes up our congregation. There are so many people I don't know now, more and more arriving all the time, it seems. We're managing to keep the ones who stay here fed and housed more easily than you'd expect. Actually, I was working out a new schedule of casserole donations with the local Hadassah group over at Beth Aitz Chayyin, which is why I was late for the recital. What we'd do without their kitchen, I don't know. Once Passover is finished, the Hadassah group is going to lead a "Poetry and Pastry" session, reading the poetry of Carol Rose and making blintzes. I have no idea what the connection is between the two, but as our Hadassah sisters say, "Im l'ashon b'chutz!" I'm sure you'll agree.

There are lineups to get into the shell room, particularly in the afternoon, of course, but even there we seem to be all getting along without too much trouble. I think you should probably leave us as we are for now. No one used to come to evening hymn sing of a Sunday night at all: now we're seating them in lawn chairs in the aisles. We don't sing many actual hymns, of course. But it seems good anyway, don't you think?

I will try to send an update when everything has settled down from the Spring Equinox gathering. But that might be weeks.

Sincerely,
Margaret Ketchie

March 30, 2003

Dear Mark,

You see? This is a perfect example of how the media gets the facts wrong and starts all kinds of rumours. I did not give a group of Druids permission to erect a replica of Stonehenge inside the sanctuary. No one needs permission anymore.

Ruth

April 12, 2003

Dear Mark,

I need you to come here! I need a partner for the next "Doctrinal Diversions" competition. A bunch of local clergypeople sit around trying to one-up each other with examples of the most dubious doctrines we've ever bought into. Extra points if you've actually preached it during a service. There was a bit of difficulty at first, because the Buddhists felt they were being excluded on account of their not having any doctrine, but we finally agreed that they're not discriminated against, just lucky. Now it's all just a good time. Margaret arranges casseroles for afterwards. Last time it lasted all night, so we ate them for breakfast. I have

no idea when the next contest is, so just come!
Blessings of the goddess, or whoever,

Ruth

April 20, 2003

Rosemary for joy,
Larkspur to encourage growth,
Willows to celebrate water,
Oak leaves for wisdom,
Alder wood to call up the north wind.

We have delighted in the potted mums your shop has provided to Glenview Unified for the last twenty years, as per
our standing order, but we really are trying to go in a different direction.

Looking forward to seeing what you come up with.

Reverend Ruth Broggan

April 27, 2003
To: Unified Church of Canada, Church House
From: Reverend Ruth Broggan

Abraham Joshua Heschel wrote:

"We do not leave the shore of the known in search of
adventure or suspense or because of the failure of reason to
answer our questions. We sail because our mind is like a

fantastic seashell, and when applying our ear to its lips we hear a perpetual murmur from the waves beyond the shore."

I hope this helps explain the nature of our ministry here. Also, why there are people applying shells to the outside walls of the church.

Reverend Broggan

Dear Margaret,

Please tell the Druids that since Stonehenge takes up so much of the sanctuary, the only way we'd be able to get actual trees in would be to take out all the pews.

Choice is a terrifying thing, which is why religion works, in a way. It removes so many choices. We still have free will, but often a narrow list of ways to express it. It's funny, you know, how we want more choice in cars, clothes, ketchup, and less in the things that really matter.

Ruth Broggan

May 12, 2003
To: The Unified Church of Canada, Church House

What is upsetting you about my saying that institutional religion is humankind's most effective weapon of mass destruction? That it's true?

Ruth Broggan

June 9, 2003
To: Unified Church of Canada, Church House

Absolutely, you have been patient. You've been more than patient. I realize that Glenview Unified is still the responsibility of the greater Unified Church of Canada and you have every reason to insist on a full explanation of what's going on here. I am very happy to say that we now have some solid doctrine for our ministry to share with you.

We favour play.

I hope this clears up any misunderstandings.

Reverend Ruth Broggan

PS~ I have thought of another doctrine. Possibly doctrine. Doctrine-ish. Jung said that religion is a defence against a religious experience, I would say that is what we are trying to avoid.

RB

June 15, 2003
To: Unified Church of Canada, Church House

I no longer refer to God as He or She or even Father or Mother, because gendering God limits God and limiting God is idolatrous and I do not wish to be idolatrous. Not because it's a sin. Because it's a shame.

Ruth Broggan

June 28, 2003
To: Unified Church of Canada, Church House
From: Margaret Ketchie

Thank you for your suggestion that everyone using the building keep minutes of their meetings and that I put them in a nice binder and have them delivered to you every week or so. I have to say, it's possible that such minutes would not entirely clear up your confusion. Instead, I suggest asking everyone to create a mandala of their hopes and dreams. Would that be helpful for you to see?

I can report that things are very peaceful and quiet here. Except for the Thursday night group, who will be using pyrotechnics for the next few weeks.

I hope this report puts your mind at rest.

Sincerely,

Margaret

To: mduggan@jesuit.com
From: feralpastor@ucc.ca
Subject: I blame you

Mark,

Beth Aitz Chayyin trounced us again last night in "Doctrinal Diversions." Rabbi Pinsker pulled out an ancient rule of Kashrut once again: If a plate designated for either meat or dairy touches the other substance it is defiled and must be broken. But if the plate is expensive china, you can just put it away for a year and then it's OK. How do we compete with that? Rabbi Pinsker admits that it's not a fair contest, since they've had a few thousand more years of stockpiling doctrine than the rest of us. Shauna Singh, team leader for the Muslim contingent, is working out a handicap scale for the next go round. I'm already planning my entry: Two thousand years of Christians arguing, excommunicating and even killing one another over whether Jesus was more divine than human, or more human than divine. That's got to be a winner, right? I mean, if I can get it to sound dubious and not just plain horrific.

Please come here immediately. You're Catholic. You could take this for me.

And no, I don't see this as irreverent. Hasn't the harm always occurred when we took these things too seriously?

Blessings,
Ruth

July 4, 2003
To: Unified Church of Canada, Church House

What I am trying to tell you is that the trees are not in the church, so much as the trees are the church. I'm not sure how else I can explain this to you. I realize you find it subtle.

Reverend Broggan

July 5, 2003

Dear Kelly,

In answer to your question, nothing happens here most of the time. People sit on the pews that remain. They listen to the water splashing in the fountain. Sometimes there are birds. Always there is silence and space to simply be. Yes, this could all be outside, but there is power in a place where one thousand people have prayed. Just as there is power in a prayer that's been said one thousand times. Or one that gushes from a glad heart or broken soul finding words for the first time. We have all of that here.

There are still TV cameras around, but I'm so used to them now that I simply don't see them any longer. Mostly, I think they're the documentary makers now. I trip over abandoned equipment from time to time, left by someone who found a group or a song or just a mood that spoke to them more than the difficult art of making art. Margaret has a place to store it all until someone is ready to speak again and comes back for it.

I'm having a good time, possibly for the first time in my life. Every morning I open the church doors and people flood in, smiling. They come early. Well, they used to come early; after we replaced the front door with tarps it became hard to tell which of them simply hadn't left from the night before. Prayers start before the sun comes up. The wonder of another chance. We had to pass a rule: No chanting out loud until 7 a.m. It disturbs those of the neighbours who don't come to join in. It's the only rule we have so far.

I am managing to preserve a little space for myself. The shell room is full of people most of the day, of course, so after all these years with grown children, I sometimes find myself locking myself in the bathroom once again to get a half-hour alone.

We've enrolled most of the children in school for the fall, and a few of the parents are planning a kind of home school, well, a tent school really, for the rest of them. I think everyone will have to move to the church basement when the weather turns again, though, even if they did make it through the winter outside.

But they'll have to take responsibility for that themselves. I'm not here to solve their problems. Just to be with them.

So don't worry about me. I'm being joyous and that's so much better than being sensible, isn't it? It occurred to me that when people insist I be practical, they're really saying, "Don't imagine you might get what you want." And where would that kind of thinking have got me?

Love from your mother, honey!

PS~ Don't believe most of what you see in the media about us. For instance, we did not do anything with goats. Well, there were a few goats. There were goats. But we certainly didn't do what they said we did with them. People are so quick to apply "the devil" to something they just don't understand. In my opinion "Satanic worship" is simply not wanting to take responsibility for your own bad behaviour. You may, however, believe the article that described me as "vibrant and youthful at 59." It's all true!

Mom

July 10, 2003
To: Unified Church of Canada, Church House

I am finding it difficult to explain something that exists beyond explanation. That is the point, you see? Obviously, the way our mind works is by comparing something new to something it already understands. And we who are religious know that whatever the God thing is, it outreaches our mental capacity to comprehend it. There is nothing that may be accurately compared. We label this impossibility "mystery." And then we try to explain it anyway. Or at least to contain it in theory.

What I believe now is that metaphors for God are useful, but only as long as we present a plethora of them. What the church should be championing is not what God is, but how many things God is. The divine spirit present in all that lives and breathes and all that does neither. God in all things, in all creation, all theology. More present in diversity than conformity. More evident in silence than in words. You have asked if anything we say or do here is heretical. I hope so. I hope it questions all things, embraces all things, makes possible all things, acknowledges that all that exists is holy.

I understand that you are still finding all this a little confusing. But really, certainty is just another word for stagnation, isn't it? Confusion is a very good place to be. It means we're still thinking.

Respectfully,
Reverend Ruth Broggan

July 11, 2003

Dear Mark,

You are right, I do change my mind. Isn't it wonderful? We of the church have made such a virtue of consistency and yet I believe with Bernard Berenson that "consistency requires you to be as ignorant today as you were a year ago." The only thing I'm consistent about now is knowing that whatever I believe is true this morning may be entirely different by this afternoon.

It keeps life interesting, don't you think?

With love,
Ruth

July 30, 2003
To: Unified Church of Canada, Church House

Yes, of course we perform same-sex marriages here. In the first place, love is too precious a gift to quibble about what sex it comes in. In the second place, if our challenge is to love without judgment, how can we do that if everyone is the same?

Margaret—This is absolutely the draft I sent. I did not add "Duh" at the end.

Able to take helpful suggestions,
Ruth

August 12, 2003

Dear Kit,

There were over 10,000 people at our Summer Solstice gathering—twice the number we had at the Equinox event. Yet somehow, everything that needed to happen did happen by magic, or Margaret—I have come to equate the two. Strange to think that the world is turning back toward darkness, even though our days are filled with sunlight.

I walk in a vacuum of stillness. Noise no longer hurts me physically as it did when I first left the manse. I seem to carry it with me now, feel it washing over me in continuous waves like the tides at sea. In such a silence the wicked in hell would find peace.

Yesterday I sat for a while with the men who come in the late afternoon to play bocchi down the back hallway of the church. One elderly gentleman described making tea for his wife, every night for the forty-eight years of their marriage, until she died. At the same hour of the evening, he would take the same cup from the same cupboard, remove the tea canister from the same spot on the counter, boil the water, fill the tea pot, place it side by side with the cup and saucer on a tray. "A Japanese tea ceremony," I suggested. But the man, who was Italian said, "A way to remember that I loved her."

Stillness in rites recreated, moments of stepping outside of time, offering the sacraments, remembering which songs are sung on a particular day, making tea as love. An hour spent in silence and simply being, in our sanctuary, or in the shell room. Bringing the mind and body back to the soul. Nothing separates us from ourselves, from each other, really, but the illusion of separateness, the mirage of time.

I do very little now. Am required to do little. A journalist compared me to a furnace recently, providing a constant, steady unseen comfort, which allows for all other activity. I simply walk all day, stop, listen, walk. I don't go to meetings. Or read the newspaper. I don't try to determine how the events of the day can be explained away by scripture. I haven't written a sermon or anything much at all besides notes to Margaret, letters to you or Kelly. I don't do anything you might consider of note at all.

Funny to find out that what matters, after all, is the scrubbing of floors, Kit. All the philosophy in the world isn't bigger than that.

With love,
Ruth

September 1, 2003

Dear Kit,

Couldn't you come out for a visit? Just a few days? I am

happy here, happy every moment and full and have a sense of purpose, though I'm beginning to wonder if purpose really matters. Wouldn't that be interesting? But, I could use a friend, Kit. My hero of the Celtic church, Palagius, had an idea that, better than a priest, we all needed a "soul friend." Not someone who tells us how to make our journey, but someone who travels beside us, sharing our learning, sharing our fear. You and I have not exactly appeared to travel in step, Kit. But we do give each other this—we witness each other's journey. I feel, in some way, that we have always done that.

Come and visit, Kit. A thousand new people to love can't take the place of one old friend. I'll even keep people out of the spare room of the manse for you. The Africana healing circle can move down to the parlour for a few days.

With all my love,
Ruth

September 6, 2003

Dear Kyle,

I know you're a dentist and this isn't your line of expertise. In fact, I suppose in a way it's as far away from your area of expertise as you can get, but I need someone to look at my feet. A doctor. I wondered if you could recommend anyone. Someone discreet. My general practitioner usually wants to talk to me about her past-life regressions now, which is fine but not quite what I need in terms of medical attention. I'm writing to you because I can't think of who else to ask. I do need to do something about this soon, as our Winter Solstice gathering is coming up in a little over three months and, well, I'd like to try to avoid bedlam, if at all possible. Worst comes to worst, I'm just going to have to find a long robe.

Hoping you and Heidi are very well. Kelly tells me that Mia is a camp counsellor this year. They grow up so fast!

Yours,
Ruth

September 24, 2003
To: Unified Church of Canada, Church House

In answer to your latest query, I believe in immanence, interconnection, community and the temperance of time. If you can tell me that's what I was taught in church school, I will say I still believe.

I must ask you to address your questions to Margaret Ketchie from now on. She is really the one who knows what is going on.

Ruth Broggan

October 30, 2003

Dear Kelly,

Yes, I think you should go and visit Kit if she's invited you. No, she and I are not fighting. It's impossible to fight with someone you never hear from. Your idea of taking to her aromatherapy oils is lovely, but you might want to consider something a little less, well, esoteric, and a little more "Kit." Take her some good coffee. Take trashy magazines. She will pretend to be appalled and then stay up all night reading *People* after she thinks you're asleep. Take her a *New York Times* crossword puzzle book and you'll be a hero. Don't take wine; she gave up drinking years ago. Said alcohol made her lose her "edge." I'm surprised they haven't tried to force-feed her Jameson's out there. Cigarettes will either deify you or condemn you to hell, depending on which side of the issue she's on at the moment. But, perhaps Buddhists don't give alcohol or cigarettes. Take blankets. I swear the woman is oblivious to the fact that ice forms on her kitchen walls by November. And be sure to check if there are ferries still running. Take lots to read. Kit writes from about 7 a.m. to noon. Then she'll want to follow you around and make you crazy. Take a mug. If the ferry has stopped, you'll have to go by water taxi or snowmobile. Do not, under any circumstances, get on a snowmobile owned by anyone with the last name "Ray." It's enough to shatter the composure of the Dalai Lama. Trust me on this one, honey. Do you need money? I have money. I don't spend it anymore. I guess I should arrange to give it away.

Did I tell you your father called? He's being wonderful about helping me with something. He and Heidi want to come to a service if they can find a day when Mia doesn't need to be taken to horseback riding or band practice. This is when scheduling would be helpful. I could only say we have them "from time to time."

OK, I have to go. A group of women in orange tunics is outside my door. They've been hovering for twenty minutes. I expect they want time in the building. I will have to say what I say to everyone, "Come! Where you can find space, use it!" We haven't scheduled anything for months. Even Margaret admits there's no point. Groups just appear and disappear, form and disband, and since everyone sweeps up after themselves, it's really not a problem at all. Mind you, Margaret is a marvel at manoeuvring people alongside each other. She moved the drumming circle into the same room as the senior's bridge club. The older people can't hear anyway so it works like a dream.

Let me know if you do decide to visit Kit. I miss her, Kelly. I might send a note with you. I do write, but maybe a hand-delivered note would actually get a response. Her former partner, Rachel, is here quite often. She's brought students from one of the courses she teaches at the university—"Forgotten Flames: Lesbian Sexuality in a Jewish Context." They do a combination Shabbat candlelight service and coming-out ceremony almost every Friday night. I suppose your father and Heidi could come to that. I suggested they attend our Winter Solstice gathering, but we're beginning to think it might be quite large.

Love from your mother!

PS~ Mark has just arrived! He's been sent by the Catholic Church to spy on us! I mean, to observe our practices of ministry, of course. Margaret is taking him with her to hand out casseroles. I have got to see if I can rustle up participants for a round of "Doctrinal Diversions."

Mom

November 15, 2003
Message for Father Duggan,
from Margaret Ketchie

Dear Father Duggan,

Reverend Broggan says you are going to be staying for the Winter Solstice gathering and I should give you something to do. You should know that we're expecting over 20,000 participants and it can get pretty hairy at these events, so you might want to take that into consideration. Being a Catholic clergyperson, I do not know if you have any experience dealing with large groups.

This is what I've figured out so far:

If we don't provide chairs (we can seat the elderly on the pews that were left among the trees), we can get 2,000 people into the sanctuary, at the most. Another 1,000 if we use the narthex, the basement rooms and the gym. We'll have to use a PA system, but I think we'd realized that anyway. So the problem is that the building is just not going to be nearly big enough. We can't have it on the front lawn because of the tent city, and we can't use the side lawn or the herb garden will get trampled, unless there's a lot of snow between now and then. I'm thinking we might go with some kind of system of "celebration stations." I think it's kind of like the Catholic idea of "Stations of the Cross" except people will be dancing and singing instead of weeping and being morose. We just rotate people through the stations. In the parking lot we will write down our regrets on little pieces of paper and throw them into the fire, the other side lawn can be for chanting to bring back the sun, we'll use the sanctuary for dancing if I can persuade the water blessers to do their Solstice prayers a day earlier. And we can make the holly head wreaths down in the gym. I think that covers it. Oh, I forgot about the Christmas pageant someone wants to put on. I'll have to figure out where that can be, because we sure heard about it from Church House when I didn't leave space for the Passion play last Easter. They seem to think we can accommodate everything. So do you want to organize the wreath making or talk to the water blessers?

Margaret

November 19, 2003
To: Father Mark Duggan
From: Margaret Ketchie

Father Duggan,

Please stop telling the vendors who have kiosks on our sidewalk that they are defiling a sacred place with commerce. Reverend Broggan says that truly sacred places cannot be defiled. Also, Reverend Broggan says that people have a right to make a living. If you would talk to them, you would see they are deeply spiritual people, even if they are selling coffee mugs with Reverend Broggan's picture on *them. One of them told me yesterday that he ran out of merchandise four months ago and simply never got around to ordering more or going home. He leads our "Reflections on Rumi" group now.*

I am hoping that as a person with experience in religious ceremonies, you will stop telling people what to do and start focusing on what really matters. Have you made arrangements for the holly?

Margaret

November 21, 2003

Margaret,

Ruth is still resisting the need for a platform in the sanctuary for the presiding party. Of course people should be allowed to do their own thing, but they certainly still need to know where their guidance is coming from or they'll end up believing God knows what. Like Rumi is worth reflecting on, for instance. The spirit is a garden, dear Margaret, which, untended, becomes a lost sheep. This is the history of religion at its worst. People want a personalized relationship with God but won't take the time to have what that should look like explained to them. Can you try to make her understand why we need to demonstrate who the leadership is here? You'd think after almost an entire year of this kind of "intuitive spirituality" ministry, there would start to be some structure. As for the vendors, I suppose they can stay if they're providing a service people really need. As far as I'm concerned, the Turkish guy selling Tylenol fits into that category.

Oh, I did not order the holly. I'm sure you didn't realize, being a layperson, but it smacks of goddess worship. I'm planning a mass to the Holy Virgin Mary in that space instead.

Father Mark

November 28, 2003

Reverend Broggan,

I have tried not to bother you with this, because I can tell that you've been distracted lately, but I finally have to let you know that Father Duggan has promised the sanctuary to the group doing the Christmas pageant. He has also suggested we ought to restrict entrance to the shell room to dignitaries and celebrities during prime viewing times. He made everyone stand out in the hall for an hour and a half yesterday while he took Madonna in. There were other people there who needed to be in the room. Some of them had been waiting all morning. I know I am supposed to trust that Father Duggan is being true to his own path. I am trying to embrace that thought. Thank goodness Madonna isn't staying for the Solstice gathering or he'd have her up on that stage he's having built.

And please, Reverend Broggan, if there is anything at all the matter, anything you need to talk over, please consider me someone willing to hear. It worries me to feel that you're a little distant. But maybe we're all tired already, and still over three weeks to go.

Our best estimate now is about 40,000 people. I've applied to have the street closed off between the nineteenth and twenty-third of December. I'm not concerned about whether they'll issue the permit. The street will be impassable either way.

I'm bringing you a chili casserole tonight. Buck you right up.

Margaret

December 1

Dearest Mark,

Of course we will be giving the hot beverage vendors space. Margaret will look after it. If the other vendors complain, tell them they have to learn the concept of sharing. In fact, tell them I have specifically instructed them to read the Book of Daniel, beginning to end, before they whine about preferential treatment. The Book of Daniel has nothing to do with sharing, of course, but it's a great read and should give them lots to think about.

I do like the newspaper ad, though I imagine people would know the event is occurring anyway. I did notice you forgot to mention about sewing in name tags. It's really the only thing we absolutely need people to do.

Have I mentioned that I love having you here? There's symmetry to your presence, Mark. We were together at Emmanuel College all those years ago. Remember how we had an idea then that anything was possible? Who could have known that we were right?

Ruth

December 1

Dear Margaret,

Be patient with Mark. You both want the same thing. You're just going about it in different ways.

Ruth

Reverend Broggan,

You have to eat. And you have to sleep sometime. And whatever is on your mind, surely it would be better if you share it? Also, I am worried about the foot thing. It's a miracle no one else has noticed. Other than that, everything is fine. We're guessing there might be 60,000 people coming. I have a lead on toilets.

Margaret

December 2, 2003

Dear Mr. Richmond,

Thank you so much for your company's very generous loan of two hundred Enviro-potties. I enclose a map of the street site, with our preferred location indicated in pink, and the best times for delivery and pickup in green. Reverend Broggan asked me to tell you specifically that she is very pleased to have worms. I am hoping that means something to you. She says also that she will be delighted to bless the Enviro-potties, but you know you can do this yourself whenever you feel it's needed.

Also, if you have any idea of a toilet paper company who might be equally kind, please let me know.

With our deepest thanks,
Margaret Ketchie

December 3, 2003
To: Unified Church of Canada, Church House

Dear Sirs and Madams,

I'm sorry, I really don't have time to answer all those questions right now. We're expecting upwards of 70,000 people on our doorstep between now and the 19th, and I have things to do like asking to borrow another eight hundred Enviro-potties and expand our food network and find several thousand rolls of toilet paper and you would not believe what else.

I can tell you that, yes, we are observing Christmas here at Glenview. Of course we're observing Christmas. We're a church. How could we not be observing Christmas? We're just calling it a Winter Solstice gathering instead. It's the rebirth of light. Isn't that what it's all about? Reverend Broggan says it doesn't have to be on December 25th since that's not when Jesus was born anyway, because at that time of year shepherds would not have been abiding in the fields, keeping watch over their flocks by night. So we observe at the time of greatest darkness, from the 19th to the 22nd, when light is returning to the world. At least that makes some sense, whereas the 25th does not. We also like that everyone has a story for the return of the light: Demeter gives birth to Persephone, Isis rebirths Horis, Amaterasu comes out of her cave. Everyone here can celebrate together. Also, the 19th is when Reverend Broggan finally came out of the manse last year, so that's something for us to mark as well. Everyone is very excited. We go into darkness. Light returns. When I'm not too busy, I get quite breathless about the whole thing. Also, I haven't had to be in a single mall this year at Christmas. That's got to be good for the soul right there, don't you think? Why is this a problem, when we've been singing "The Holly and the Ivy" for years and no one ever complained about that?

By the way, have you been bothering Reverend Broggan lately? I mean, more than usual? I wish you would stop badgering her about things until after the gathering at least. She has seemed very distracted lately and we need her all here. Or as much here as we can get.

I hope this report will satisfy you that the best you can do for us is just to let things be. But if you know anyone in portable toilets, please, please let me know.

Yours sincerely,
Margaret Ketchie

December 4, 2003

Dear Kyle,

Unfortunately, your latest recommendation could not be helpful to me either. Is there another doctor you can think of? Someone less inclined to hysteria would be good.

Ruth

December 5, 2003
To: Unified Church of Canada, Church House
From: Reverend Ruth Broggan

I have reviewed your conditions, and understand that you would like my decision by the 12th. In the meantime, I wish to address one of the statements made in your letter. You say that our ministry here makes Church House increasingly uncomfortable. Of course it does. Religion is founded on the feeling of being uncomfortable. Discomfort is a gift. It's what compels us to search.

There is not a person on the face of the earth who hasn't wondered, at least for a moment, "Why am I?" Not even, "Why am I here?" I think, but "Why am I?" That is what makes us search. Possibly it is even what makes us human. It's also what tells us there is a God, because we're born into this world knowing from our first heartbeat that there is something missing.

The question speaks to our aloneness. As if, knowing purpose, we could feel connection. I know that aloneness. I know the other, too. It's what I've seen occur here at Glenview. People finding an answer for themselves, by letting the truth speak to them in the language they best can hear.

Is it still religion? I think so, though I'm not sure why the labels matter so much. What we call Christianity today is a patchwork of ideas and images, stories and myths, from different cultures, from many times. I remember being in history class at Emmanuel College when some of my fellow classmates first encountered the idea that Christianity didn't spring fully formed from the lips of Christ or the pen of Paul. That "Easter" takes its name from the festival of a Germanic goddess of fertility and rebirth. That the placement of Jesus' crucifixion at Passover may have more to do with Biblical authors wishing to identify him with the widely known, deeply revered, image of a sacrificial lamb and less to do with authentic timing. I remember the outrage that poured out when our professor observed that no rigorous historian would call the Last Supper a Passover seder, since no ritual meal of that kind was known to take place until around AD 600. And if Jesus were arrested during this most sacred of Jewish holidays, there would have been no court in session to try him. You would have thought that poor teacher had suggested the Bible had as much authority as a cookbook, for all the anger he engendered in class. I didn't believe he was saying that. He was saying that faith is anchored in something more meaningful than facts. Two weeks later, the same professor suggested that the Church endorsed the cult of Mary mainly because it was unable to eradicate goddess worship among the people it sought to convert. Best to bring the Divine Mother under the control of the Church where she at least can be aligned to a correct doctrine and dogma. Three students dropped out of the seminary entirely after that class. And only one of them was Catholic.

There was no truth for them in religion if it wasn't exactly the truth they'd been brought up with.

I thought at the time, Isn't that what it's all about? I know perfectly well that when a culture or religious faith moves into a new area, it takes into itself whatever serves its purpose or it simply can't get rid of. Isn't that the point? That how we think about God changes? How we respond to God grows and develops as we do? In that, I have found a truth of sorts for myself.

I found it through the confusion of sifting through many ideas and listening to many voices. Those of my upbringing, those of my experience, my happiness, my pain, what I learned and unlearned at school and mostly by finding that every time I thought I had a place for myself, something changed and I had to look again. I have been uncomfortable for most of my life. Until a little over a year ago, when I did something so foolish as locking myself into my house and refusing to come out until God spoke to me. Spoke clearly, through the jumble of voices. And explained what it was all for. In that foolish act, I was given the gift of rethinking the Divine from the ground up. But the truth is, since then, my understanding, my response has never stopped changing. I am learning to embrace the growing. And to tolerate the falling away.

Glenview Unified is not a place that offers answers. It is a place that supports each person in their search. That's naturally going to look different for each person, because we are all different. Maybe it looks like chaos to you. I'm not sure who promised that a search for God would be orderly.

What I do wish to ask of you is that, whether or not I agree to your conditions, that you please, not shut Glenview Unified, or ask the police to clear the tent city, or remove people from the street until our Winter Solstice gathering is over. You are entirely right that there are safety issues at stake here, but please consider what the danger to safety might be if several thousand people were suddenly told that this event is not going to take place. This is not a threat. It's what I know from experience happens to people when you stand between them and their deepest need.

Yours respectfully,
Ruth Broggan

PS~ It occurs to me that my friend, Rabbi Pinsker, shared a story with me the other day that I could have simply related to you and saved the trouble of writing all of the above! It goes:

A rabbi, passing by a farmer's field, heard the farmer singing as he worked. "Dearest God," the man bellowed joyously, "if I could give you a radish, I'd give you the biggest radish in my garden." The rabbi was shocked, and, going over to the farmer, he admonished him, "That is no way to address our King! Let me teach you a proper prayer so that your words may be acceptable to God's ears." So the rabbi taught the man a very formal and ancient prayer. The next week, the rabbi was passing the farmer's field again and saw the man hard at work, but this time no sound escaped the man's lips. The same thing happened the next week, and the next. The farmer never sang again. Finally, the rabbi died. He arrived at the gates of heaven and was greeted by the sound of angels singing loudly, proclaiming their love and devotion to God. The angels sang, "Dearest God, if we could give you a radish, we would give you the biggest radish in the garden."

RB

December 7

Carl,

4,500 postcards. The ones of Broggan, or the shell room, are the only ones that sell.

2,500 T-shirts with pine cones, shells, or poppies. Those Celtic knot ones go well too. I'm sending back the ones with the sunflowers. Seems they're just a circle. Who knew, eh? Also returning the ones of the Pope holding a shell. We couldn't move them.

500 of those mugs with the frogs on them. What's with frogs, anyway? Somebody said they were a symbol of fertility. Why don't they use rabbits then? Also, I'm sending back the frog snow globes. People keep complaining that frogs hibernate in winter. Bunch of religious literalists. You got any with trees? They might go. They might have to be evergreens, I guess.

I heard there's mouse pads. You heard about mouse pads? Send me about 500 of those too. Unless they've got sunflowers or the Pope on them.

Ray

December 8, 2003

Dear Kit,

I can't believe that when you read this letter it will mean that Kelly is on the island with you. She's promised to give it to you the moment she arrives, so you can read my list of things you *have* to do while she's there. Show her the standing rock down by Ewen's cabin and make sure she meets the Whynots, because I know she'll love them. Send her over to talk gardens with Gerrard one afternoon, because it will please him no end and she'll be surprised by what she learns. And please, please make sure that she gets to go into the store at least once when you're not with her so she can get the flavour of what the place is like when everyone's relaxed. Oh, I asked her to bring out chocolates for Deirdre, so please make sure she takes them right over, or we both know you'll eat them yourself.

In spite of the fervor of pre-gathering activity here, I am learning slowly still, every day, what you began to teach me about solitude. Blaise Pascal was right after all; all men's miseries *do* derive from "not being able to sit quiet in a room alone." These days the only misery I feel is when I'm *not* able to do that. I realize now that the quote from Kafka on your kitchen wall, which I accused of being at best anti-social, at worse narcissistic, is actually wonderful and wise: "You do not need to leave your room. Remain sitting at your table and listen. Do not even listen, simply wait. Do not even wait, be quite still and solitary. The world will freely offer itself to you unasked. It has no choice. It will roll at your feet in ecstasy." The world does roll at my feet in ecstasy, Kit. In fact, at the moment it occasionally rolls right under them—which I will have to save for another letter.

Along with silence, Kafka and ecstasy, I even realized the other day that I know nothing about Solomon, though preaching Proverbs is what got me into trouble, a lifetime ago, back in Markham. Solomon was all wrong. Or I was. Or both. The troublesome woman in the mansion is not railing against life, Kit. She's railing in favour of it. Refusing to accept that the comfort of life in a mansion is enough. Without that troublesome woman inside who prods me, badgers me, demands that I go further, where would I be? I'd be back in Markham thinking I had a clue what life was about. Instead, here I am, at the beginning and entirely uncertain of the future once again. What could be more exciting? I need that troublesome woman inside me, Kit. I bless her. She keeps me searching.

I've been struggling with a decision and am amused to realize today that the only reason I haven't found an answer is that I didn't want to listen to that troublesome woman one more time. But this morning I was walking across the lawn to the church and I noticed that the herb garden that was planted last spring had a dusting of snow on it. Most of the herbs have been harvested for healing balms and tinctures, but a few dried sprigs of lavender poked through the new snow. It reminded me of a conversation I had with Deirdre during my month on the island. We were looking at Gerrard's gardens and I commented that he must be so sad when frost comes again and all the careful devotion he had shown to his gardens seems to vanish into the earth with the last fall flowers. Deirdre said that plants don't die, really. They become food in the soil and their spirits infuse the seeds that grow in the spring. At the time, of course, I thought she was nuts.

Do we learn, Kit? Yes, but oh so slowly!

This I do know to be true, that all things pass away. Purpose fulfilled. And we are back at the beginning again. Life returns to life. It's only our sense of separation that gives us cause to mourn.

Enjoy your time with Kelly, Kit. You know she loves you as I do. And please don't let your ruthless insistence on solitude keep you from letting a little ecstasy roll around your feet. It's an odd thing that happens when you do, but very interesting!

Love to you both!
Ruth

December 11, 2003
To: Reverend Broggan
From: Margaret

A woman called from the Forest Hill library information desk. She said the person you were trying to find out about was likely Saint Teresa of Avila, who lived from 1515 to 1582 and founded a convent. Reverend Broggan, if you're going to found a convent, you will have to get someone other than me to do it. I do not think I would be very good dealing with Catholics, although Father Duggan is really the only one I have dealt with, but it's just very annoying that he keeps trying to change everything. I know you said that most Catholic priests are not like that. Also, those nuns who come sometimes to lead the yoga breathing classes are really lovely. But we do not have time for some-

*thing like starting a convent. I cannot take it on. You will
have to ask someone else, if that's what you're thinking of.
I am up to my ears in arranging for tents and food and we
still don't have enough toilet paper. Also, I have run out of
ways to explain these projects to Paul and have them
sound reasonable. Mind you, we could house a few nuns
in the manse if we moved the clothing bank into Valerie's
old office. And it's no trouble to scare up a few extra
casseroles to feed them. When we do get toilet paper, we
could give them some of that too. And they could look
after the shell room, because you know we keep losing
whoever goes to supervise there to the silent meditation
circle. We could have a convent if you think we need one.
We should have a convent. I could explain it to Paul. I've
explained stranger things than this. Let me know when the
nuns will be arriving.*

*And, any luck yesterday with the doctor? Did you tell
him it's happening all the time now, and not just when
you're around trees?*

Margaret

Dear Reverend Broggan,

*I would like to thank you for the blankets you brought us
last night. It's cooler here than in Victoria for sure. I'm
bringing them back now, because a truck came in today
with a whole load. I'm sorry we do not have the facilities
to clean these ones. The casserole we had for breakfast was
very good. My wife wonders if there's some way to get the*

recipe, though we understand that it came up from a church group in Vermont.

Yours sincerely,
Lewis Kingston

December 12

Margaret,

No, I cannot help you find toilet paper. Do you have any idea what it's like to organize twenty different media groups? They all want to be embedded with a group of pilgrims and no one will take the ones with religious prohibitions against bathing.

As for your worry that there's been something odd about Ruth lately. Margaret, my child, the woman is about to lead a Solstice gathering for 150,000 people, gathered here together because they're nuts. And, her feet hover a couple inches above the ground most of the time. You think there's something unusual about her, do you?

Father Duggan

To: Christians for a More Understood Merton Society
From: Margaret Ketchie

Thank you so very much for volunteering to help round up supplies for the gathering. As you must have heard, we're

ANNE HINES

expecting over 100,000 people in the next ten days. We did have an associate of Reverend Broggan's helping out, but he's been unavailable for anything else since the 20/20 crew arrived.

I've attached a list of things we still need. The most pressing are sweet grass and toilet paper. The difficulty with the sweet grass is that it's a sacred substance to the native people so they're not supposed to sell it. They can, however, exchange it in trade. So far, I've got twenty of the forty-five pounds we need and I've handed over two DVD players, a Cuisinart and our lawn mower. My husband is not happy about the lawn mower, even though I've asked him if one lawn mower is really too high a price to pay to ritually purify an area of ten city blocks and the hearts of over 100,000 people. I think he's still weighing it. It was a riding mower. I also traded four packages of photos of Reverend Broggan in the shell room, which I suppose we shouldn't technically sell either, but maybe one bunch of sacred stuff traded for another is even-steven, don't you think? See if you can scare up anything else to trade.

I talked to the Humane Society about the frogs. It's OK to use them if they're kept safely in aquariums, so it won't be the same effect as we had at the Summer Solstice, but it's better to avoid what happened when someone mis-stepped during the native dancing session, because the effect certainly wasn't conducive to freeing the spirit. Except, I suppose, for that frog. If you can rustle up about two hundred aquariums, it would be wonderful.

The last thing we desperately need is a robe for Reverend Broggan. She does not normally wear robes except . . . well, lately. It needs to be very long. At least three or four inches longer than you'd think. Down past the floor. I have a few other people looking as well. It would be most helpful if you kept this request within your group. People are inclined to tell all sorts of stories. And you know how people try to get ahold of anything she wears. One of the vendors cut up a rag she used to clean the floor and sold it on e-Bay. So we'd like to just keep this whole robe idea quiet.

Thank you all so much again. Your help is more appreciated than I can tell you.

Wishing you a joyous Winter Solstice,
Margaret Ketchie

To: Father Mark Duggan
From: Margaret Ketchie

The play isn't happening in the sanctuary because I told them it wasn't happening in the sanctuary. And, a couple hundred pounds of holly is going to be dropped into the room where you're planning to conduct mass. And we will be making wreaths with it. There is a time and place for everyone's beliefs, but the third week of December is no time to be making a big deal about Christmas.

Margaret

To: *Casserole dispersion team #51*
From: *Margaret Ketchie*
Re: *Dispensing at Shamanic Divining site*

The first casseroles will be delivered to your section this evening. Please separate them into meat, vegetarian, vegan, wheat-free, dairy-free, sugar-free and nut-free. Also, sort out the ones with mushrooms. Some people just don't like mushrooms. Don't worry, there's nothing to this once you get going.

    MK

Father Duggan,

Also, some boxes of folders arrived that look like they might be press kits. Or maybe travel brochures. It says, "Ruth Celebrates Rome" on the front. Do you know anything about this?

    And no, of course you can't mention the foot thing to Fox News. Are you out of your mind? The best we can do is continue to pray that no one else notices.

To: *Constable Kevin Durie, 42nd Division, Metropolitan Toronto Police Force*
From: *Margaret Ketchie, Glenview Unified Church*

Dear Constable Durie,

Thank you so much for going over the site of the gathering with me. I agree entirely that we should double the number of police in attendance, even though our gatherings are traditionally entirely peaceful. If nothing else, we need them to help distribute casseroles. We are now anticipating a crowd of 200,000. But as I say, I can't think of anything that would cause them to be disruptive. Not really.

Many thanks,

Margaret Ketchie

Mory,

Couldn't we just do a Pepsi spread across the side of the church wall? Isn't there some kind of open access rule about churches? I mean 'cause they don't pay taxes? And who cares what denomination they are. I don't think they have a denomination.

Brad

December 15, 2003
To: Dan Coo, RCMP, Region 4
From: Constable Kevin Durie

Thank you for agreeing to provide backup at the Glenview site, beginning immediately. The street is currently closed to traffic between residence numbers 16 through 420 and will remain closed until the gathering concludes at midnight on December 22. I always thought a Solstice was twenty-four hours long, but it seems it's forty-eight. Something new every day. The majority of the homeowners have either vacated their properties and rented them to participants, or are staying to take part in the event. So far, no homeowner has complained about the street closure. I guess they've got used to their street being used by these people; pilgrims—they call them. Given the number of people on the street already, we're anticipating a crowd of about 300,000. So far, everything is entirely peaceful. After 10 p.m. you can hear a pin drop, except for a group called "The Star Callers." They chant as soon as the sun goes down and just keep at it. Apparently they're helping the stars maintain their correct course by offering encouragement. Seems to be working as far as anyone can make out. We've been trying to get them to stay off the roofs, but that's a losing battle. There is also a gang here studying the effects of the Zodiac on local compost heaps. No chanting involved there, so we've pretty much left them alone.

We're not expecting much trouble here. The Reverend in charge, Broggan is her name, is an interesting woman to talk to. She spent an hour with me yesterday, talking police work and stuff you wouldn't think she'd care about. Feel like it's good if we make this all happen without trouble, just for her.

Let me know if you have any trouble making out the map. The blue dots are where the "cleansing fires" are going to be. Didn't even ask about that one.

KD

Mags,

A woman named Kelly called. Is that her daughter? Says she's on some island and there's no phone, so you have to call again and leave a message about when she can get you.

Says she doesn't understand what you mean about Ruth being "absent." Says they get the paper where she is and she's seen photos of Ruth getting ready for the event and other than the robe, which just makes her look huge, she seems fine. I didn't know what you meant either. She always seems weird to me. Are you coming home tonight? Daniel's rhythmic gymnastics practice has been changed to 7 p.m. If you're not going to be there to pick him up, you'd better let me know soon. I ordered KFC for dinner. I'm with the kid who said that one more casserole would make him puke.

Paul

December 16

Margaret,

I can't tell you what's going to happen during the main part of the gathering because it hasn't happened yet. Why does anyone worry about this?

And yes, you were right to inform me that Mark has set up a website selling fridge magnets with my sayings on them. I had no idea I had sayings. Could you order me some?

Ruth

December 17

Dear Margaret,

"Sufficient unto the day, is the toilet paper thereof!" A

gentleman called from New To You Recycled Papers, promising all the supplies we could possibly need, arriving tomorrow.

Ruth

PS~ I keep meaning to tell you that we are not starting a convent. Not that I've heard. I am interested in Saint Teresa because—I am interested in knowing what happened to her. Apparently, she was visited with foot issues as well and—the parts of me which cannot simply accept are wondering.

Carl,

Forget the mouse pads. Everyone wants a shot of the foot thing. I don't care if it's real or not, they'll believe anything here at the moment. Someone told me that one photo sold for six figures. It must be on the Net. Get it on a poster, or shirts, and get them here by morning and we'll sell a million.

Ray

PS~ You know what, though? You can't help wanting it to be true, eh?

December 15, 2003
To: Unified Church of Canada, Church House
From: Margaret Ketchie

I don't know what you've heard exactly about Reverend Broggan, but I can assure you that the media blows everything out of pro-portion. We certainly learned that with the whole "naked Druids painted blue" rumour. I mean, when it turned out to be red.

Really, what do you think the possibilities are that this story is true?

We are thinking of starting a convent.

Margaret Ketchie

Dear Reverend Broggan,

I've sent Church House a note that I think will distract them for a bit. Maybe you should just stay inside until the gathering begins.

Margaret

Dear Kit,

I felt a hand on my arm yesterday, like an electric shock through sheet metal. I told the woman who touched me, "I can't do anything for you." She said, "You already have."

Waves of light pass through me, like continual breath. And always the question, "What is required?" Nothing. Nothing at all.

Love,

Ruth

PS~ You know, I think when it all comes down to it,

the only real failing of organized religion is that it's not a good place to find God.

R

December 18

Dearest Kit,

Kelly called this evening, crying. She didn't have to tell me what happened. You don't have to tell me why. She is on her way to Toronto, but before she comes, I think I will not be here anymore.

I have left a letter for Kelly. One for David. Instructions for Margaret, though she would always know what needs to be done. Reassurance for Mark. I thought of leaving instructions for you, too, but you will do whatever you want and of course that's exactly what you should do. I am afraid they will try to explain it all, Kit. If you ever do want to do something for me, see if you can keep that from happening.

Peace in this room tonight. A tiny island of calm. Even the shells are dreaming.

I can feel breathing outside the walls again tonight. Margaret says there are 500,000 people camped on the yard and all down the street. I smell new snow falling. Feel the world sinking into sleep. The shoring up of energy before rebirth. A new baby must experience this, just before it begins its hard journey through the birth canal. Fully formed, cocooned in darkness, about to be cast into a world it cannot imagine. What I hope is that when the time comes, I will know how to breathe.

The person who made this room applied a million tiny spirals to a blank wall. An act of insanity, I am certain. As if he had simply set his mind to the side for a time, become unbound from this world, this reality. Creating something of such brilliant beauty. I don't feel ready to leave here. Though I recognize the miracle that Church House hasn't simply hauled me away months ago.

Don't worry about Kelly, Kit. She's a smart, sane woman and can make her own choices. Don't worry about me either. I am ready for what comes next and know that whatever I need will be supplied in abundance. It just probably won't look the way I expect.

So, on this night when the world rests in the deepest darkness, before new light returns, I am releasing you at last, my dearest, darling Kit. A relationship based simply on each of us withholding what the other most desired would never have lasted this long. In fact, we got exactly what was needed. Just exactly.

It just sure didn't look the way you'd expect.

My love always,
Ruth

PS~ If things turn out differently than I think, maybe I can come back to the island this summer and we can sit on the front step, listen to the waves, and laugh about what we think we know. If not, then you'll have to imagine me there.

Ruth

Dear Margaret,

1) Please let Mark read first at the service, or he'll never get over it. Tell him not, under any circumstances, to speak in Latin. No one understands it, and it makes most of our participants nervous. He could read one of Kit's poems, perhaps. "Passage by Water" would be lovely.

2) If at all possible, try to keep people from singing "Lord of the Dance." It's supposed to cheer everyone up, but someone always ends up sobbing.

3) If it seems absolutely necessary, get some ashes out of the fireplace in the manse and scatter them around on the front yard of the church or something. We were told in our "Dying Rituals" class that the process of cremation is so hot that all human remains basically burn into air, and all that's left is the ash from the container anyway, so I don't see a problem with this, really. You don't need to explain.

I am counting on you to keep doing what you always do, which is everything. Holding things together, holding others up. You have a gift for that, Margaret. You are the rock on which this ministry is built. I know a period of settling in will be necessary. But I also know that you will carry on the way you have been, very beautifully. Please try to keep the stories within reason, if you can. It will not be easy. And be patient with Mark. He is helping with our work, even if you cannot see it.

Bright blessings,
Ruth

Dear Kelly,

Years ago, I was sitting in the library at school, gazing out through the casement window at rain dripping onto red and orange leaves in the quadrangle. I saw something. Heard something. Sensed something. And left myself behind to go looking for it. I have not stopped leaving since. Every moment of the day, I seem to head out. Learning not to be terrified while I'm waiting to see what my new self will look like. There's no use longing for what no longer exists, Kelly. You'd be the first, with your Buddhist wisdom, to tell me that.

I guess this is a strange message to get from your mother. Please know that I am more proud of you than I can say. Not because I made you who you are, but, because you did. Remember that. When you find yourself needing the courage to leave again too.

All my love,
Mom

To: Constable Kevin Durie
From: Dan Coo, RCMP, Region 4

Have received your estimate of 600,000 people camping on the street tonight. I advise that we send over another fifty officers. Have notified St. John Ambulance crew that a second site has been located for them. Please confirm that this is "across from the tarot readers." In the meantime, we're all hoping the snow will keep up so no more people arrive during the night.

Someone in the department said it won't snow at all if Reverend Broggan prays for sun. Says, if she prays hard enough, the sun won't ever set. The whole thing is too weird for me. Do you happen to know if they do anything with healing, though? Like that place out by the airport? My arthritis has been giving me the devil lately. Unless I hear from you by midnight, I'll assume we should dispatch those additional officers.

Dan Coo

Excerpt from speech / official interview, by Reverend Ruth Broggan, Glenview Unified Church, December 19, 2003

A year ago, I was given a gift, a chance to rethink God from the ground up, and what I found is what my soul had always known to be true. I walked out of my house, crunching across new snow on frozen ground, much like the snow we have this evening. I opened the great front doors of Glenview Unified and said, "This is a place for whoever needs it." It didn't seem like such a profound gesture at the time. After all, we're a church.

As it turned out, people did need it. Together we made a place for singing, dancing, eating, sometimes fighting, mostly sharing; some of you even chose to live here. But remember, this is not sacred ground. Sacred ground is what we hold within us. What is sacred is how we are able to approach each other, without judgment, without fear, without expectation of how things ought to be.

When space was needed, we removed the pews. They make wonderful benches under our indoor forest, and line the street, so the elderly, the nursing, or the just plain tired can rest on their way to us. When we needed food, my comrade-in-arms, my right hand support, Margaret Ketchie, between scaring up tents and blankets and leading courses in the art of the spiritual soufflé, organized a casserole network that has amazed the world. When we needed God, we made space for God to occur in the hush of sunset as we stood together around evening fires, or in the afternoon sun washing silently over the backs of shells.

What matters is not what we made here. Certainly not whatever I have been able to provide you. I have nothing to give which you do not already possess, no love to offer which we do not already share and nothing to teach which your own souls have not known since time began. There is no teacher here and no student. We have been masters together.

What does matter is that each of you continue to seek the truth you need to lead you further. And wherever you go, know that what you need will be provided just as it has been here at Glenview. It just may look a little different than what you expect at the moment. Or hope for.

> *Deep peace of running wave to you.*
> *Deep peace of flowing air to you.*
> *Deep peace of quiet earth to you.*
> *Deep peace of shining stars to you.*
> *May the stars pour forth their healing light on you.*
> *Deep peace of this night of peace to you.*

The wheel of the year is turning.
Darkness ushers in the return of light.

We die and are reborn
Fear will be lost to the night
Fear will be lost to the night

We die and are reborn
What must we lose to the night?

I left the gathering and went into the church. Everyone was outside on the street, chanting. That was how it began. I am tired of telling you over and over.

Official transcript:

Father Duggan? Pick up! Pick up! They've been into the church and arrested her. There are a million people on the street. What in God's name are we going to do?

This building is closed by order of the Unified Church of Canada. For information, please call Church House at 416-231-5931.

Paul,

I will not be home again tonight. It's all totally confusing still and I can't get a straight answer from anyone. As far as I can make out, they've charged her with so many different things it's a miracle she ever had time to use the bathroom. Trespassing, ignoring a court order from Church House. Effecting medical treatment without a licence seems to be the big one, but no one is saying what this medical treatment was. And they keep saying the child was never dead in the first place, so how does this make sense?

I managed to find a lawyer who was here for the gathering, who says he can represent her. Another lawyer arrived from Texas about four hours after the arrest. He says the Mormons are paying his bill. I'm not even trying to figure out that one.

Maybe if I can persuade people on the street to calm down, they'd let her go, or at least let me in to see her. There are things she's going to want, like her Starhawk book, or a stone or something, because I'm sure there's nothing in a detention centre that isn't man-made. There's a Constable Durie who says he might be able to get a plant in to her.

I'm sorry I can't get home right now. Oh, could you call Kit Sheppard for me again? Her number is in my book beside the phone. If she came out here, I'm sure they'd let her in to see Ruth since the woman is considered a national treasure or something. If the RCMP have already taken my phone book, then call directory assistance for British Columbia. I know they've already got everything out of the manse and they've taken Mark's diary and phone book as well. I'm sure Reverend Broggan would want us to co-operate with the police. Please be sure to do that—though you might just slip my phone book under the mattress first, OK? Also, could you leave me a message about whether or not those extra blankets came? There's no way we have enough for all the people who are saying they're planning to stay. Thank *you, Paul. You have no idea what this means to me.*

All my love,
Your Mags

December 24, 2003

This is my statement about what happened between me and Reverend Broggan. I am writing this down myself so that you will stop sending people to me every hour so that I can watch them write it down.

I came up to Glenview Unified on Sunday night. I came up because I heard on the television that Reverend Broggan had helped some woman get cured from her cancer or something. I'd heard a lot of crazy stories about Reverend Broggan, how she's some kind of New Age person and how her feet don't touch the ground, and I never paid any attention to it. But then when it happened, I remembered hearing about that woman, so I came to the church. It was a long walk from Women's College Hospital, all the way up Avenue Road and then across to Bathurst Street and up again, and it was snowing pretty hard, but I kept thinking the whole time about how Mary and Joseph walked to Bethlehem, you know, because it was almost Christmas then too, and it just felt like if I got there something good would happen. I was so cold, though. I didn't dress for the cold, because I just left the hospital when I remembered that woman.

When I got near the place, I thought I would hear all this noise, because there were supposed to be like a million people here to see the minister, but it was really still and quiet. There were campfires burning all along the street where I walked through, and people sitting together singing like they were whispering. Some of them were singing "Silent Night." The music kind of floated on the dark, cold air. It made me feel really nice even though I was so cold and tired from walking.

I walked right up to the church and went up the front steps. There were no doors, just a kind of tarp hanging in the doorway, so I lifted that up and went in.

At first, I thought I wasn't inside at all. The big room, which I guess is where the church services are, has these giant trees growing in pots and a big fountain in the middle. I could only kind of see the outlines of the trees, 'cause there wasn't any moon, just some light flickering through the stained-glass windows from the campfires outside. It made patterns on the trees like splashes of blood. I didn't know what to do then, so I just went and sat down on one of the benches. I guess I was worn out from worrying and then from walking so far and not being used to carrying anything heavy. I figured when I had rested a bit, I would go and ask someone where Reverend Broggan was.

Just when I was thinking that, a lady came out of the shadows by the doorway. I wasn't scared or anything. Not like you'd expect. She just walked up the centre aisle to where I was sitting and I said, "You're Reverend Broggan, aren't you? I saw you on TV." Then I held out my arms and just said, "I need you to do this."

I could tell she knew right away the baby was dead. My little shrivelled girl child, just grey and naked. But she didn't say anything, just looked at the baby. So I said, "They brought her to me to hold. So I brought her here."

Reverend Broggan sat down beside me. This peace and silence just went through me, like I knew everything was going to be OK, no matter what happened. She reached out her hand, touched the baby's forehead, the little chest swelled and sucked in air and my baby cried. Just like she was supposed to do in the hospital, but never did. It was a cry like she had all of a sudden decided to live. I tried to say something, anything, to say thank you, but Reverend Broggan said that the baby was just crying out her "yes" in answer to doubt, and that it had nothing to do with her. I guess I have to think about that.

We sat on the bench together and I let the baby nurse. Then the police arrived, I'm not even sure they knew what they were looking for. They looked embarrassed. One of the officers apologized to her. Reverend Broggan had to tell them it was OK. There were no handcuffs, that much was made up by the papers. They were very respectful.

That's really what happened. But they say I can have my baby back if I say she was already breathing when I went into the church. I am going to do that.

Kit,

I can't tell you what's happening because they won't let me into the detention centre to see her. They keep saying that *she* won't see *me*. I'm finding it a struggle to stay balanced and simply observe all of this instead of yelling my lungs out at every one of them. Dad put me in touch with a lawyer and even offered to pay the fee, but when I showed up with him I was told she already had legal representation. Some person from Texas. Do you know anything about this?

I still have no idea what she's being charged with. I thought it was violating an order to stay out of the church, but now I hear they didn't put up that sign until after she was arrested. The medical stuff is as ridiculous as confusing. They give me all this technical jargon and won't provide anyone to explain it properly. Apparently, they took the woman's baby away, saying she denied it proper medical attention, but the nurse on duty is saying it had already been pronounced dead. She's been suspended and the PR person for the hospital is trying to explain to us that "dead" is a relative term. As a Buddhist, I'd be all in favour of that, if they hadn't arrested my mother because of it. The doctor who signed the death certificate isn't speaking to anyone. They found the father of the baby somewhere, but he's not talking because he's already sold the book rights. And Mark tells me that there was a joke about the whole thing last night on *Leno*.

Kit, don't you think that, if you came here, they'd let you see her? Mom told me once that "Call me, Kit" was like a mantra in her life, so I'm sure she must need you now more than ever. What happened between you and me was, well, it's between you and me. Don't let it keep you from coming out here to be with her. I'll leave a message when I hear anything more.

Kelly

Reverend Broggan,

Constable Durie says he can get a message to you, so I am hoping this is the case. I want you to know that things are fine here. I am getting along with Father Duggan, as he has left us for a while. I know you said the road to compassion lies in knowing that we all want the same things, but I do not want to do a media tour about what is going on with you, and apparently he does. I am trying to remember to breathe, to relax, to see all of this as temporary. But it is hard when there are so many people here to feed, and so many hurting because you are not here with us. There is a lot of anger some days. Sometimes the anger is mine. But, "Failure is not falling down, it's refusing to get up again." I will try to keep getting up.

That American lawyer came over to see me this morning and he says we can expect a change very soon. I guess that's not news here. But I hope this one is what we are hoping for. Just to have you back safe and sound.

> *Sincerely,*
> *Margaret*

Carl,

1,000 postcards of the feet thing. Those are still going like hotcakes.

1,000 of the T-shirts. The ones that say "Free Ruth."

Any more pieces of that robe, if you can get your hands on it. I don't really think people care if it's the real one anymore or not.

100 copies of any book by some chick named Kit Sheppard. She was here, and there was a big fuss about it. Some police constable even took her into the house and the church to look around. I don't see what the hoopla about her is about. It must be some woman kind of thing. Oh, can you pretend they're autographed?

Also, I heard there were diaries. Are there diaries? Anything like that would be gold. Even a few pages. I'll just cut them up and sell the bits.

Ray

Official transcript:

I: Reverend Broggan, do you believe that God speaks to you?
B: Yes.
I: How do you know it isn't just you talking to yourself?
B: It is me talking to myself.
I: God is generally understood as an external presence.
B: Yes, that's true.
I: Is it true that you made a statement that you are God?
B: Yes.
I: You seem quite rational to me, Reverend Broggan. Is that something a rational person would believe?
B: I don't think you mean a rational person. I think you mean a person who thinks as you do. That's not sanity, it's just one way of thinking.
I: Well, that seems to be just about how we're using words.
B: I'm afraid it usually is. Which is why I don't recommend them.

I: I see. So, doesn't God speak to you in words?

B: More in the spaces where I am able to allow silence.

I: And how can God speak to you if you are God?

B: That's entirely the point.

I: Reverend Broggan, I have a list of quotations here that are attributed to you. A list of your teachings. Would you care to comment on them?

B: I never taught anything.

I: But you're a teacher. A religious leader, right?

B: You can't teach anyone. Not anything that matters. You can only say what they already know and are ready to hear, or not.

I: But don't you know more than anyone else? I mean, particularly if you're God?

B: But so are they.

I: Surely the reason people come to a religious leader, the reason people have flocked to your ministry, is to hear something new?

B: I don't know. Sometimes I think it's just to hear the same thing again instead of having to act on it.

I: Reverend Broggan, you've had several visitors wanting to see you. Your daughter. Your colleague, Margaret Ketchie, who I'm told has been instrumental in getting your message out. Your friend, Kit Sheppard.

B: I heard there was a riot when Kit came.

I: There were about a thousand agitated women outside.

B: And she signed their arms?

I: Well, and other places. Ms. Sheppard came a long way to see you, I'm told. Your daughter has been here every day. Why have you refused to see anyone?

B: To return to silence. To allow the falling away. We all have to begin learning to be together without the physical part. Did Kit talk to Constable Durie?

I: The police officer? I think so. I think he gave her a tour of the church. Is that important?

B: No. It's not important.

I: Now, what you said about "falling away" . . .

B: Do you think we could be finished for now?

I: OK. We'll continue tomorrow.

I have begun to draw shell patterns on the walls of this small room. I tell them it's meditation. That was the problem, wasn't it? That we didn't have a name for it.

The year is turning. The flames of the hearth are rekindled. The ancient Romans designated December 31st Hecate's Day, honouring the great mother goddess who decreed the destinies of humankind. Candles brighten the winter nights. "Banish fear, raise joy." The colour is red. The tree is pine. The flower is holly. The creature is rock. To endure, to die, to be reborn. Give thanks for the experiences of this lifetime. Our journey around the sun is complete.

> I believe in God, one energy in us all
> I believe in existence eternal
> The good race
> I entrust my soul

> *Amen*

Reverend Ruth Broggan, controversial leader of Glenview Unified Church, pronounced dead in Toronto, January 1, 2004 at 7:25 a.m. Details to follow.

Authorities say the fire, which broke out at the Don Jail around midnight, is clearly the work of arson. Chief Inspector Ryan Shank reports that the fire was deliberately set in the furnace room of the building and spread quickly to the floors above. About a third of the hundred-year-old building has been destroyed. Inmates were evacuated without incident to nearby Grace Hospital. No injuries have been reported. The jail has been in the news since it became the holding place for New Age preacher and healer, Ruth Broggan, as she awaits trial on a number of charges. Crowds of up to 10,000 people have brought traffic to a standstill around the jail and have hampered the efforts of firefighters, who struggled to put out the flames. In spite of the extremely cold weather, the crowds have been on-site since the arrest of Reverend Broggan, December 19th, protesting Reverend Broggan's arrest and detention with an ongoing twenty-four-hour vigil. No one has stepped forward to claim responsibility for the fire, and it is not known if it was set by supporters or opponents of Reverend Broggan. Rumours circulated this morning claimed that Reverend Broggan had, in fact, died in the blaze, but as yet there has been no official confirmation.

Meanwhile, rioting has been taking place in the area of Glenview Unified Church, the site of Reverend Broggan's popular ministry. Police reports say that upwards of 100,000 people have been camping out on the street for the past two weeks with relative calm, but erupted violently when news of Reverend Broggan's death began to circulate. Police are warning people to stay out of the area. RCMP have been called in to provide reinforcements.

Dad,

They won't let me see the body. They just keep saying no information is available. The news report says she's dead. If she's dead, why the hell can't I see the body?

    Kelly

January 2, 2004

Ruth Broggan, spiritual leader of the breakaway Christian community of Glenview Unified Church, Toronto, was officially pronounced dead yesterday at 2:55 p.m. Reverend Broggan died of smoke inhalation in the fire that broke out just after midnight at the Don Jail detention centre where she was being held on charges of trespassing. More information will be provided as it becomes available.

Religious leader, guru, Ruth Broggan, aged 59, dead at 2:55 p.m. They can't clear the streets.

Paul,

I can't come home. The shell room has been destroyed. I don't know who did it. There's enough anger on both sides. I'll be home tomorrow, I think. There's just so much to do here.

    Margaret

To: Unified Church of Canada, Church House
From: Margaret Ketchie

I'm sorry, but I have no idea how to keep several hundred people from entering the church in spite of your notice, do you?

Respectfully,
Margaret Ketchie

"I am here because I know my mother would wish me to come and speak with you. Our family, friends and the members of the congregation of Glenview Unified Church share your distress at my mother's passing. We appreciate your sympathy and concern. Nothing can bring her back to us, and we must begin, each of us, to live our lives again, remembering her ideals, her love of life and her dedication to the happiness and well-being of others. Let us take that with us as we go back into the world.

I have been assured that no one will be charged if you all leave now. Please, I'm told there are many thousands here at the church and around the jail. For the safety of each of you, in the memory of my mother's struggle to bring peace, it is important that you vacate the street and go home."

Margaret, I have said exactly what they told me to say, and they still won't show me her body. They showed me some dental records, but even Dad said it didn't prove anything. I have no idea where we go from here.

Kelly

Dear David,

Please come here immediately. We've decided to have a memorial service to see if that helps quiet people down. Besides, it's possible that it's appropriate to have a memorial service. And yes, there is absolutely a tradition among the great Buddhist masters, that when they feel the time had come to die, they are able to simply release their spirit from their body. But you see, that leaves a body, David. That's where this thing falls down.

   Kelly

January 4, 2004

Margaret,

Mom is gone. Not dead, just gone. The reason they wouldn't show me the body is that there isn't one. They can't find that lawyer either. One of the police officers took me into the jail tonight. He showed up in a cruiser around midnight and drove me over to look at the room where they had kept her. There's no evidence of . . . anything. It was like one minute she was drawing on the wall and the next . . . well, they have no idea what happened next. Just one small bare patch of wall by the door. Anyway, that's why they took all her papers. They wanted to know if I have any idea where she might be. My feeling is that we should not tell anyone about this. I don't know what else to do. Can you think where she might have gone?

   I think we should go ahead with the service tomorrow. Also, I know I told you that spreading ashes outside the manse was foolish, but I think you might be right. One way or another, we have to encourage people to move on. At least until we hear from her.

    Kelly

Ms. Ketchie,

Our magazine is looking for details of Reverend Broggan's life prior to her original sit-in in the manse. Family bios. Photos. That kind of thing. We'd also love photos of the memorial service, since no press was allowed in. If you have a clear photo of the foot phenomenon, we'd be very interested. The one in *The Times* was very grainy. We've been told you're the one to ask. We can offer an attractive fee, of course.

Kelly,

You do not have to thank me for my part in the service. I could not have let Ruth go without honouring her commitment to the traditions of faith, with a proper Latin benediction. No one shares your grief at your mother's loss more than I. She was my friend and a friend is a gift that rivals the angels.

    Now that things have quieted down a little, someone needs to go into the manse immediately and retrieve whatever personal papers your mother might have left. I'd come and do it myself, but I've got four more stops lined up on this tour, and I'm not sure I could get past the police barricade anyway. I'm sure they'll let her daughter through to get her personal possessions. I mean, the ones that aren't already turning up on e-Bay. I'm happy to take care of anything you find, notes, sermons, letters. I will make sure they are properly protected until we see exactly what they say.

May the blessing of Christ be with you in your grief,

Mark

To: His Eminence, Bishop Noble
From: Father Mark Duggan
February 15, 2004

In answer to your query, my presence at Glenview Unified Church has always and only been as a personal friend of the late Reverend Ruth Broggan, and as the eyes and ears of my church in observing her ministry here. Reverend Broggan and I were students at Emmanuel College together. I had no idea, at the time, of her becoming a spiritual leader of some stature. As I recall, she usually only got Bs.

During my few weeks at Glenview, Ruth naturally called upon me to fulfill certain tasks, which required a trained clergyperson—liaisoning with media, escorting visitors of particular note through the famous shell room, spearheading the collection of supplies to meet the most basic needs of her followers. She also entrusted me with saying a mass for the Catholic participants who came to participate in the Christmas season gathering, though the very small turnout proves that we did not sufficiently publicize the Catholic perspective of the event. The rest of the gathering had rather more of a free flow than we are used to in the Catholic tradition, but I generally found them theologically innocuous, if vague.

I am amazed that my relationship with Reverend Broggan continues to attract such attention. You may, of course, dismiss suggestions that I was Ruth's consort, a view which is being widely circulated, and which I consider beneath my dignity to even refute. It was explained to me in my most recent meeting at Alliance Atlantis that such rumours will help make the movie more sellable, anyway. I am now being turned to by such pundits as Oprah and Sting, as the person who, being closest to Reverend Broggan, can most genuinely share with the world the message she brought. I believe that by appearing on *Letterman* and the like, I am able to clarify Reverend Broggan's deep commitment to the precepts of Christianity, particularly as expressed through the doctrines and rites of the Catholic Church. In fact, it has been my mission to inform people that, in her very last days on earth, Ruth apparently turned to the study of the life of Saint Teresa of Avila for guidance and comfort. I assure the public that Ruth never lost her profound respect for religious order and obedience to God's law. I can almost hear the words on her lips, "God leads me on with a firm hand, as I walk before him in praise and worship."

Without my continued participation, it will be entirely possible for people to get the wrong idea, particularly as interest in Reverend Broggan's story is still considerable, the newspaper reports being flamed, I think, by continued speculation that she did not actually perish in the fire. My task is to make what is obtuse shine, or people will misunderstand her devotion to church doctrine.

The networks pick up the tab when I travel. Rumours that I have signed a book deal are simply that. We're still talking. I am presently ministering to my agent by sharing with her the doctrine of Saint Augustine regarding money, "If the mind cannot clearly perceive whether it despises the possession of riches, best to test this by giving them away." She's getting 10 percent, tops.

To: Father Mark Duggan
From: Margaret

I don't know why you're worrying about a bunch of papers when there are people on our doorstep who need food and clothing. I did write to Kit Sheppard and said that, if she had anything of Ruth's it was her duty to share it, just as you asked, but I have to say I did not receive a very favourable reply, and am not feeling like writing again. But what matters is Ruth's concern for the basic human needs and physical well-being of the people. If you actually want to be of service, you might see where we can get about two hundred shovels. The snow will melt in a few weeks, and if we don't get trenches around the tent city, it'll be underwater again this year.

Also, I am thinking of starting a convent in the manse. Do you know how one goes about that? I mean, particularly if you're Protestant?

Margaret

March 14, 2004
To: Unified Church of Canada, Church House
From: Margaret Ketchie, Director, Teresa's Mission, Glenview
Unified Church

I do not like to tell Church House how to run its business, but it seems to me that if you don't like people using a crowbar on the front doors of the church, you should stop putting new doors on. One of our members almost pinched his knuckles the last time.

There is nothing broken here, so I think you should leave us as we are. You will be pleased to hear that, since the rioting subsided, we have created an actual committee to get our homeless program back on track. So far, they have hammered out criteria for helping us to tell the homeless from our own members. I know you're concerned about the vendors still on the street, but that really has nothing to do with us, and frankly I don't see a problem with selling T-shirts that say "Make casseroles, not religious edicts." I suppose, if you really think it's an issue, I could stop wearing one myself.

I don't think you should give another thought about what's going on here. I know you're anxious to install a new pastor at Glenview, so perhaps you should just concentrate your attention on beginning the prescribed Needs Assessment Process. If Church House proceeds with your usual efficiency, I'm sure that will suit us here just fine.

Wishing you all abundance,

Margaret Ketchie

March 30, 2004
Miss Deirdre Casson
Bolin Island, British Columbia
V1E 1E0

Dear Ms. Casson,

Thank you for your most interesting suggestion that we instate the late Reverend Ruth Broggan as a saint. I admit, it had not occurred to me that the reason rumours surrounding Reverend Broggan's death still abound is due to her having been "assumed" into heaven. You are right in thinking that assumption is considered a possibility in the Catholic Church, but it is an honour reserved only for a very, very few, exceptionally divine souls. The Virgin Mary, Handmaid of the Lord, Theotokas, Mother of God, for example, was carried bodily into heaven. Much as I esteemed Reverend Broggan, I would not really characterize her in this way. Elijah, the most holy and venerated of the Old Testament prophets, was also assumed, carried up to heaven by "a chariot of fire and horses of fire," which appeared out of a whirlwind. Whatever stories have been circulating concerning the final hours of Reverend Broggan, I cannot recall anything of this kind, can you? Finally, our Lord Jesus Christ was, of course, assumed. I'm sure you're familiar with the account of the empty tomb. I don't think anyone is comparing Reverend Broggan to Christ. Well, except for that misguided columnist for *Time*, but I've sent a firm letter off to him. That's pretty much it for those deemed worthy of bypassing the normal process of death. I believe the Koran attests to Mohammed having been assumed, but of course that's outside of the jurisdiction of the Catholic Church.

I can assure you, Miss Casson, that however extraordinary and full of grace Reverend Broggan may have been, real people do not get assumed. Of course, the Virgin Mary, Elijah and Christ were real people, but what I mean is that we no longer live in a time when that kind of miracle occurs. We have different kinds of miracles today. I don't know why.

With blessings of the spirit,

Father Mark Duggan

To: Bishop Noble
From: Father Mark Duggan

Your Eminence,

It occurs to me that, given that the Holy Catholic Church has recently seen fit to install the first saint who had been a layperson rather than a religious, perhaps we might now wish to consider our first saint from the Protestant tradition. It would recognize that God calls even those not technically from our church to join in spreading the true values and doctrines of Catholicism. Frankly, it might also go some way toward reversing the bad press we've had in the last while, accusing us of being insular and self-interested. As the closest advisor, and now official biographer, of Reverend Ruth Broggan, I can attest to the many ways and means employed in her ministry in support of the traditional doctrines of our church. Of course, we would also need to prove that she was responsible for miracles, but with so much continued liveliness (you may read "hysteria") surrounding her life and death, I'm sure that will be forthcoming. I think, in fact, it would be best to take Ruth into the fold so that her teachings may be given the proper bent. The Broggan thing is simply not going away. And if the one true church does not step into a leadership role, heaven only knows what people will choose to think.

Looking forward to hearing your thoughts on this.

Father Mark Duggan

To: margaretk@stteresamission.ca
From: rachelrosen@utoronto.ca
May 9, 2004

Margaret,

I was really hoping you'd have more luck with Kit, or that priest, than I have. They're both still swearing they don't have anything or know anything, though the priest managed to turn out an entire biography on the basis of some information or other. Surely they realize that anything Ruth wrote is an important historic document and should be in the hands of a qualified community of scholars. I keep being told that my own documents will be returned to me "when the investigation is terminated." I mean, the woman is dead, you would think that would be grounds enough for terminating an investigation, don't you think? Duggan said they even took the stubs for his dry cleaning, which is amazing, because I read his book and assumed that was what he used as the basis for his in-depth observations. I have to talk to that Constable Durie again. I'm convinced he knows something and isn't saying. Classic white-male control issues.

It's particularly annoying, because interest in her work is so intense and the whole thing just screams "Major Research Grant" if I could get my hands on any material to research. God, if any actual letters show up in Duggan's next Book-of-the-Month-Club follow-up to "Ruth Broggan: A Handmaid's Journey" or "The Orthodox Ruth," I'll just spit. I hear he's contracted to do a workbook version of "Reimagining Ruth," so hopefully that will keep him busy for a while. Where does the man find enough hours in the day to churn out this stuff? I guess by not taking time to bother checking a dictionary or he'd realize that "reimagining" is not a word. Nor is "visioning." God, how can they pay humongous sums of money for this shit when I can't get anyone more impressive than the University of Wichita Press interested in "The Social Context of Feminist Spirituality in Broggian Theology"?

My current work is on the history of the spiral as symbol in science, culture and religion, with reflections on how that plays out in the teachings of Ruth. My contention is that the oldest religious symbols are drawn from recurring patterns in nature which speak to the foundational experiences of life. The spiral is used as a symbol, or "picture lesson" if you will, of the continuous cycle of life and rebirth found in the natural world and applied to human experience in all religions. Celtic knots, roses, I remember my father referring to the netivot as spiralling. Netivot are the thirty-two mystical paths of the Zohar which an individual must discover in herself, leading her to wisdom. I remember the priest telling me that even the Vatican has a huge bronze pine cone displayed in one of their outdoor squares, lifted from a pagan temple. This is really interesting because even though it had been used as a symbol for a faith the church abhorred and wished to eradicate, they still took the pine cone, one of nature's perfect spirals, and placed it in a prominent position in their new grounds. Interpretations sometimes differ slightly, but this motif occurs in the art and religion of practically every civilization, and mirrors nature.

In our modern, scientific world, of course, we've discovered that the spiral is the shape of the DNA molecule, so the image takes on another whole layer of meaning. Inner resonance of the outward experience. We also know that energy itself flows in spirals. This is incredibly heady stuff. Thank God I'm dating a physics prof, because I can't believe all the stuff I'm reading and have to get her to keep assuring me that it's true.

She also says that energy cannot be exerted indefinitely in one direction. It will always reach a peak, a climax, and then turn. Building up, then falling away. A time of perceived passivity or "waning" always follows an exercise of growth. My idea is that we see this everywhere, not just in nature or our own bodies, but also socially, politically and in organized faith paths. Movement toward greater freedom is usually followed by movement toward greater security.

My intention is to use the spiral as the basis of hypothesis that freedom and security are not mutually exclusive states, but rather essential phases of a whole. My working title is "A Deconstruction of Metaphorical Imagery in the Post-Christian Theology of Broggan, With Attention to Sociological and

Economic Patterns of Growth." If that's not a best-seller, then I don't know what people want to buy these days.

Oh my God, as I write this I wonder if the concept of climax/passivity explains why we always want to be cuddled after orgasm. I mean women do. I don't know about men. Maybe I should find out about men. One wishes to be academically rigorous. This opens up a whole new area of study. Internalized metaphor in sexual relations. "Principals of Broggian Theology in Context of Human Intercourse." Or maybe just "The Broggan Guide to Great Sex." I mean, to make the ideas accessible to laypeople. I think I might put the spiral imagery idea on hold while I figure this out. This might be the only way to steal a march on the priest. Not that I can count on that.

In the meantime, please keep looking. I'll take any material you can find. Anything at all. A Post-it note. Half a Post-it note. Religion scholars have penned volumes and founded entire careers on less original source material than that.

Rachel

October, 2004

In the late fall evenings, the air in the sun porch returns to coolness. Full cycle from spring. I sit wrapped in a blanket on my petrified couch, my breath rising like incense or smoke. The water beyond deepens into the colour of midnight.

The neighbours held a mass this evening, They called it a mass, even though the predominant religion of the island is Buddhist/pagan/stupid/nothing. They called it a mass. They waited till the ice went out once more, till tourists were gone, till the island returned to us again, as Deirdre said.

Gerrard plucked the last of his dusky red flowers. Deirdre hung strips of coloured cloth from branches by the water, where the wind twisted them into rainbow coils. Neighbours wandered down to the pier singing "Be Thou My Vision." It was kind of nice. I think they purposely did it where I could see, to be kind, because they knew I wouldn't come. Carol Blass recited a poem. "Maps Beneath the Skin," one of the poems I wrote for Ruth. They were all for Ruth. When she's not telling her crappy CBC story, I had to admit, Carol does a not bad job at all. Then everyone stood together at the end of the wharf, tossing petals into the waves. Burgundy boats sailing away on black water. I might have wept a bit.

They think we were lovers. I think so too, though I know I'm not forgetting anything.

Later, as it was getting dark, Deirdre came up the path. We sat together on the cold front step. Deirdre said Tibetan Buddhists believe that a soul can stay near the body for forty-nine days after death. A priest sits nearby, reading the "Book of the Dead," instructions designed to assist and encourage the spirit as it prepares to move toward the light. Deirdre said this helps the soul perform a very, very important task, which is either remembering or forgetting this present life, she couldn't remember which. Deirdre wondered if anyone had read the "Book of the Dead" to Ruth. I pointed out that Ruth wasn't a Tibetan Buddhist. And there was no body.

I asked Deirdre if she thought our souls need to be taught to go to the light. She shivered, not quite ready to give up those ridiculous Indian cotton summer smocks of hers. I gave her half the blanket.

"Maybe it's not so much that our souls needed to be taught as that we need to learn to listen."

We sat for a long time in silence.

"What will you do now?" Deirdre asked at last.

"What I've always done. Ruth being gone doesn't change anything, Deirdre."

"It could change everything."

Another silence.

"You could do something with all those boxes of papers that the police officer let you bring back."

"What, burn them and pretend I can forget? Or read them and live through it again? If I want to torture myself, Deirdre, I'll spend more time with you." I felt a little bad about that. "The papers are just here so no one else gets hold of them and turns Ruth's life into something it wasn't."

"You could write about her, Kit. Tell people what the miracle of Ruth was."

"There aren't really miracles, Deirdre."

"Yes, there are. We just don't call them miracles because we're used to them."

"Fine. Then the miracle of Ruth was, that she honestly believed there was something worth searching for."

"I think the miracle of Ruth is that she found it."

In the silence that followed, I reached over for Deirdre's hand. We sat for a long time in the dark, Deirdre and I, on the cold stone, close together, listening to the waves beyond the shore.

December 21, 2002

Dear Kit,

I'm so sorry I haven't written for . . . however long it's been since I haven't written! I realize you don't take the fact that you never answer as any excuse for silence on my part.

I almost don't know what to tell you about what's happening here. On Friday I came out of the manse and today was my first Sunday back in the pulpit. The place was jam-packed. Everyone here to see the crazy minister. I just stood up and announced that from now on there would be no more sermons. In fact, not really any more services. You know what? No one seemed to mind at all. Then I suggested we go downstairs to the gym and do something together, so everyone trooped down and played "Ring Around the Rosie." It was the only game everybody knew. It was wild, Kit. So much fun. Everyone played, even our oldest congregant, although he didn't actually make it to the floor before it was time to start the next go-round, but he was having the time of his life, I can tell you. Then we sang. We sang "Onward Christian Soldiers" and "When the Saints Go Marching In," even though they were struck from the hymn book years ago for promoting war or saints or both. We didn't care about the words, we just wanted to sing. We formed a conga line that went on for well over an hour. It was crazy. I don't remember when I last heard laughing in the church. Or saw people grinning from ear to ear. I know it sounds like madness, but how can you not be a little mad to approach God? I took a whole year's course on "The Fundamentals of Appropriate

Worship," and I pray I'll never have another chance to use any of it. We left behind the expectation of, well, everything, our church, ourselves, the ideas we've had about what God wants, and found a wellspring of joy within. If that requires a leap of sanity, I think everyone here is ready to jump again at any moment. Anyway, having just spent a little less than six weeks alone in a manse, no one expects me, at least, to be sane. There were TV crews here still, of course. But the camera people put down their equipment after a while and joined us for "Ring Around the Rosie." Maybe just indulging the unstable minister. If that's what it takes to get people into a gym, enjoying themselves, I don't much care what they call me. Then everyone went home and came back with food, and we stayed right through until evening, talking and eating and singing. Someone remembered that today is the Winter Solstice, so we trooped outside onto the lawn, standing amidst all these tents, campfires burning dark red swatches onto clean snow, and we held hands and just . . . were. I don't know what happens hereafter. It will unfold as our spirits desire. All I do know is that "God's in his heaven," Kit. All's right with the world.

EPILOGUE

March 2, 2005

Dear Kit,

Thank you for your letter. No, I haven't heard anything. I don't expect to now. More and more, I find myself believing that the police simply didn't realize she'd left her room. Maybe to help someone else. She must have died in the fire. But, perhaps trying to explain it is simply clinging to the past. Wherever Mom is, it has nothing to do with us anymore.

In answer to your other question, I did come here to run away. I thought it was from the cameras and querying, the idea that I owed someone access to my grief. But I think now that I was running from my own failure. I didn't accept. I didn't allow. I fell prey to anger at you, and then to regret. I yelled at police officers. I lied to a few thousand people to get them to do what was acceptable to me. It seemed as if I'd learned nothing in all my years at the retreat centre.

This place will do until I see a path before me again. Margaret has written, asking if I will come and start an order of Buddhist nuns in the manse. Apparently, we will be called the "Ministering Sisters of Saint Teresa of Avila" which, frankly, I see no problem with at all. But for now, I need to stay with this silence, with mountain vistas and steady breezes, until I feel I've returned to myself once more. Maybe then I can come back to the world with something to offer. What I have been reminded of by Mom's death is that this human existence is precious and easily lost. This is the time to practice spirituality with diligence.

Delusions are inexhaustible: I vow to transcend them.
Dharma teachings are boundless: I vow to master them.
The Buddha's enlightened way is unsurpassable: I vow to embody it.
Sentient beings are numberless: I vow to liberate them.

How all that's going to happen will unfold in its own time.

Be well, Kit. Be happy if you can. What you are longing for is still there to be found, when you can let go of calling it Ruth.

May all beings be healed and whole.
May all beings have whatever they want and need.
May all live free from fear.
May all beings enjoy inner peace and ease.
May all be awakened, liberated and free.

I think that's all she wanted, don't you?

With blessings,

Kelly

June, 2005

Someone once told me that we move when it becomes less painful than staying where we are. In the spring, I took the boxes outside onto my newly uncovered verandah, and began laying the pieces out on the table, across the couch, over the floor. Then out the door, onto the stone step, and over the sun warmed ground; a phone message . . . a letter . . . a cry of confusion . . .

Gerrard called over from his garden that my yard appeared to be covered in new snow . . . a letter . . . a list . . . an explanation. . . . Scraps rearranged, as I tried to make shape of it . . . a letter . . . Ruth's sermon . . . a request from Margaret. . . . Soft breezes rustled the papers, curling the line, altering the order. Neighbours passed below, crowing at my paper garden . . . a letter . . . a clipping . . . a poem. . . . The question of why I never called, or came to see her. Building my case, seeing it fall away.

By the end of the day, I worked my way back to the beginning. A letter. Desire. A page from a diary. I gathered them up, carefully, in the last light, took them inside and labelled the package "The truth." Then got up during the night, scratched out the words and wrote "Letting go." Tomorrow, I will send it off on the ferry to Kelly.

And then I will prepare to begin again.